THE PROMISE
A NOVEL

Melody Grace

In memory of Elizabeth, and all those who dare to hope.

CHAPTER ONE

Fall IN CAMBRIDGE, Massachusetts was like nothing I'd ever seen before.

I'd spent my life in a small town outside San Antonio, where the trees let out a vague shrug late in the season, and just like that, it was winter. But here, summer died out in a long, blazing victory dance.

Sunburst gold and persimmon orange, witch's scarlet and deep, bronzed ochre. The colors bragged and jostled loudly under cloudless skies, so bright, it almost hurt to look. I wasn't on the best terms with God those days, but strolling to work under that shimmering canopy, I was almost ready to make peace. It was the kind of day that felt like a fresh start, and made me want to run right out and blow my first paycheck on a basket of new supplies: luscious inks, textured canvas, and thick, rich oil sticks, the kind that stain your fingertips for days.

"What's got you all bright-eyed and bushy-tailed?"

My new co-worker, Kelsey, was unlocking when I arrived at the café. She had sunglasses on, and the hood of her sweatshirt was pulled low over her sleepy glare. "Don't tell me you're a morning person," she added, before I could reply. "Just so you know, I don't even become human until I've had my third coffee. I can't be held accountable if I'm a bitch before ten."

"Noted." I followed her inside. "How about you handle that beast of a machine, and I'll make nice with the customers until you come back to life?"

"I like you already." Kelsey headed for the back, and I started to take down the chairs and set the tables straight, getting ready for the first customers of the day. I'd only been working here a week; a lucky break, I thought, but I know Hope would have called it providence. I could hear her voice when I walked in dragging my duffel bag behind me, the opposite of fresh off that three-day bus ride, and found the sign pinned up by the register. *Help wanted. No hipsters, assholes, or dilettantes.*

"See?" she would have said, giving me that excited nudge of hers. "Everything works out exactly the way it's supposed to."

I wish I could have that kind of faith. It would make life easier, to be able to jump and just believe there'll be something waiting to break my fall. But if she was right, then why is she buried under a bouquet of lilies at the graveyard out past Parson's Ridge, while the rest of the world just keeps spinning, unconcerned?

T HE REST OF the team arrived, toting sweatshirts and backpacks and armfuls of books to study on their breaks. Cambridge was a college town, and we were in the thick of it: from the clusters of startled freshmen slurping down ice-blended mochaccinos, crammed onto the faded blue velvet couches by the windows, to the upperclassmen hiding in the loft space, building forts of their study materials and eking out a black coffee to last all afternoon. I loved the buzz of it already, a crackling shot of caffeine as new customers piled through the doors the minute it turned seven a.m., offering their orders with a pleading note in their voice and sleep still in their eyes.

"Welcome to Wired, what can I get for you this morning?" I must have chirped a hundred times.

"Look at you, Miss Congeniality," Mika drawled, when finally the rush slowed to a trickle. He was on the register with me most days, a tall, rangy guy with a mop of auburn curls and the edge of an accent, Dutch, or German, maybe. "You know they won't tip you either way."

"I don't mind." I shifted, restless in my sneakers. I looked around. "I'll go clear up a little until the next wave hits."

Mika quirked an eyebrow. "By all means, be my guest."

I grabbed a tray and went to bus the tables. I knew the rest of the staff were amused by my eagerness. They'd been working long enough for it to be a chore; they didn't understand. Waking up each morning, I half-expected this new adventure to be a dream that would dissolve with every yawning breath, and when it didn't, I treasured it all over again. My small, shared apartment with the roommate who hogged the bathroom and a shower that always ran cold; the long walk to work along unfamiliar streets; even wiping down the cracked Formica tabletops: this was freedom to me. No rules, no parents hovering over my shoulder, no childhood photos lined up on the mantel in a long procession of guilt. I was anonymous in a city that didn't know my name, a thousand miles from home.

And the people . . . I wanted to draw every last one of them. Mika's cut-glass cheekbones and permanent smirk. The barista JJ's thoughtful stare and smooth-shaven head, midnight black. He was a math whiz, on scholarship at a college nearby, and the rest of them would delight in yelling out the problems whenever the register glitched.

"Two fifty-nine, plus sixty-seven cents, plus three eighty-six, plus tax!" Mika would whip at him. But the kid never faltered, just answered with a steady smile.

"Seven dollars and ninety-seven cents."

The customers loved it, but Mika would just scowl. The two of them bickered all day, a low-level frequency hum of irritation so steady it took me by surprise when I stayed late after closing after my first week and saw them leave together, Mika's arm slung around JJ's shoulder, pausing at the stop-light to tilt his face up for a tender kiss.

"I didn't know they were a couple," I told Kelsey the next day, feeling more like a small-town girl than ever before.

She made a vague back-and-forth motion with her hand. "We'll see," she said with a sigh. "Either that, or the shit will hit the fan real soon."

As for Kelsey, she slouched around the café in lace-up boots and thin flicked eyeliner more precise than any ink drawing I had ever mastered. She played in a punk-rock band and seemed utterly unshakeable. I was a little in awe of her. To be honest, I was in awe of them all. They were the lead characters in their own lives, living out stories of drama and intrigue of which I only saw a glimpse, and meanwhile, I'd barely worked up the courage to tiptoe onto the edge of the stage.

All of this is my way of trying to explain that on the

afternoon in question, that perfect, clean chalkboard of an afternoon, I wasn't looking for a man to walk through the door and change my life. I wasn't that girl at all. My life had already been changed in ways too sharp and devastating to describe, and the idea of another disrupting force—another reckless wild card to send my life spinning off course—would have made me run for cover had I even a moment's warning. I could have called to Kelsey that I was taking my break, ducked out to sit on the back steps in the morning sun, and felt an inexplicable shiver rippling over my skin as the storm passed me by.

But that's not how this story goes.

I WAS REFILLING the sugar canisters when he walked in. I remember because the glass facets were catching the light, reflecting rainbows back against the sun-drenched windows. I twisted them one way and another, painting shards of color over the walls and tables, and squinting faces in their path. I heard the faint *ding* of the door, but was still lost in the kaleidoscope of colors when he rested his elbows on the counter just out of the corner of my eye.

"My heart leaps up when I behold/A rainbow in the sky."

He told me later he felt like a pretentious idiot,

quoting poetry at me out of nowhere. But I'd loved those lines ever since my fifth-grade teacher had pinned them over the art wall.

"Wordsworth." I was already smiling when I glanced up.

There are some faces that burn into your memory, and others that change every time you look in their direction. A new slant of light, a passing shadow; they can either rearrange someone into a stranger every time you meet or etch their features even deeper, carved into stone.

Somehow, his was both at once.

Eyes that dipped from hazel to umber and back again, the dark lashes and faded golden tan, like Midas coming up for air. His features shifted as if they couldn't decide what mood to form, those broad planes stroking out a twist of a smile under a disheveled mop of ash-gold hair. He had his collar half up, that battered navy pea coat crushed around him, and even when I clumsily knocked the sugar canister aside and the rainbows scattered into sunlight, he was still the most vivid thing in the room.

"I'm sorry," he said, grabbing for a napkin. I watched him push the spilling sugar back into a neat square, contained, and felt an overwhelming itch to draw his hands. There was a grace to them, and just like that I realized how da Vinci could have spent a year sketching the same thing over and over.

It wasn't the form; it was who they belonged to.

". . . to go."

I snapped back. He was looking at me expectantly. "Sorry, I missed that," I admitted, my cheeks flushing under the focus of his gaze.

"Coffee, black, to go. Please and thank you." He gave a shy grin that slowly spread wider, unfolding, until it encompassed his whole face and every square inch of the small, bustling café. God, that smile. I managed to inure myself to it eventually, or at least pretend it didn't knock me clear across the room, but back then, I didn't see it coming.

The sugar canister clattered to the floor.

"Get a grip, newbie!" Kelsey swung by. I died a tiny humiliating death, and ducked down behind the counter to scoop it up. *When I stand up again, I'll act like a functioning human who's been in the presence of men before*, I told myself, kneeling a moment to catch my breath.

"Everything OK down there?" He leaned over, his too-long hair hanging down over his eyes as he surveyed me, crouched there on the floor.

"Just . . . taking a time out," I managed to reply.

"A time out?" His lips curled with amusement.

"If I close my eyes, the world goes away. That's how it works, doesn't it?"

"If only. When I was a kid, I was convinced I could use the TV remote to control real life. I spent weeks that summer pointing it at things, trying to make them move in fast forward or pause whenever I wanted." He circled around the counter and offered his hand to help me up, and I had no choice but to take it.

A cool, firm grip; a gentle squeeze as he easily lifted me to my feet again.

"How did that work out for you?" I asked.

"Not great." His smile turned rueful. "My mom said I just needed new batteries, but I tried every last one in the house, and it still didn't work. I was so mad at her, for pretending. I didn't speak to her for days."

"She wanted to keep the magic alive." I could picture him, a little boy, small fists clenched with rage. "She was just protecting you. It's what parents do."

"Some of them."

The words weren't even heavy, a casual ripple in the breeze of our conversation, but I caught a glimpse of something in his eyes that made me want to pull up a seat at the table in the corner and ask exactly what he meant by that; I wanted hours-long conversations that bled into dusk and the night beyond, until we surfaced at two a.m., the layers peeled back, our hearts raw and visible and cradled gently on the table between us. I wanted something I'd never wanted before, with a fierce hunger that took the wind from my lungs.

To know him, every last breath.

That swift longing brought me back to myself. I realized I was still holding his hand and dropped it, stepping away.

"I'll get you that coffee."

I'd never been so glad to face the beast of a coffee machine. It took all my focus to remember the sequence of dials and buttons that set the gleaming chrome engine spluttering and hissing just right. By the time I'd filled a paper cup, and set the sleeve to protect those cool, steady hands of his, he was chatting to Kelsey by the register about an author I'd never heard of, someone doing a reading in town next week.

"You should go," he was telling her. "I've heard he's great live."

"Maybe." Kelsey shrugged. "I just don't want to deal with all the over-pretentious guys jerking off at his feet. God, they drive me fucking crazy. I swear, they take one intro to lit class, and then they camp out in the corner for a month, scribbling meaningful prose into leather-bound notebooks like they're Tolstoy. No offense," she added, breezy.

He shifted, flushing slightly. There was a notebook under his arm, a battered leather satchel slung across his chest. I wanted to tell him this was just Kelsey's regular morning bitch session. Every customer was alike to her, she didn't mean it, I longed to say.

"Here's your coffee," I said quickly. "Did you want a pastry with that?"

"No, thanks." He passed a crumpled five-dollar bill over. "Keep the change." He quickly turned and ducked out of the café, pausing a moment on the sidewalk outside, his hair glinting gold in the midday sun, before he was lost in the surge of pedestrians and tourists beyond.

I felt an odd sense of loss, so sharp it gave me the courage to jab her in the ribs. "Kelsey!"

"What?" She yawned. "Oh, him? Don't worry, he's in here all the time."

The loss eased. "Do you know his name?" I tried to hide my eagerness, but I knew I'd failed by the smirk on her purple-stained lips.

"Teddy, or Theo. One of those dead-president, trust-fund names." Kelsey gave me a knowing look. "To each his own," she said, singsong, and sailed away.

Theo.

I sketched him that night, what I could remember, the glimpses that somehow knit his face into my memory. I spent an hour shading the line of his jaw until it was just right, then ripped it from my sketchpad and tore the page into a confetti of smudged lines. I let them scatter from my window on the knife's edge of the crisp night air, watched them spiral, tiny ghosts in the dark, until he was gone.

The city was humming outside my attic room: sirens in the distance, a trail of neon along the dark riverbank.

He wasn't why I was here. At least, that's what I believed at the time.

We'd both discover I was wrong.

CHAPTER TWO

THE NEXT THING should have been easy.

"Go to a college party and make out with a boy."

I was in a town of a hundred thousand students, all of them ready to celebrate their freedom. I heard the chorus my very first weekend: a clatter of footsteps on the street outside my windows, the victorious whoops of young men discovering their fearlessness, and the slurred shrieks of girls overdosing on excitement and sickly cocktail punch. Hope wouldn't have hesitated. She would have shimmied into her best skintight, boy-bait dress and slicked her lips with a sparkly gloss, fallen in with one of the passing rabbles, and wound up crashing the next destination to dance sweatily under strobe lights until the cops came to shut it down. That was just the way she attacked life. The first day I met her, she marched right up to the free seat beside me and sat herself down with a groan. "These shoes are killing me," she sighed, slipping her feet out of the pink stacked sandals and wriggling her clashing scarlet toes. She offered me a raspberry Popsicle, and by the time our tongues turned blue, we were friends. As if I'd ever had a choice.

But now, without her, I'd lost my biggest crutch, my way to slip behind her into every conversation, the confident coattails I could ride into any social event. I was a week into the adventure I'd set myself, still in a state of disbelief I'd embarked on it at all. I thought that leaving would be the hardest part, but there it was, the next line on my list, and I was stumped.

I THOUGHT ABOUT IT all week. I wondered about asking Kelsey or any of the others at the café if they knew of a party and wouldn't mind me tagging along. I was new in town, it was the perfect excuse, but even so, I held back. Sure, they were warming to me, as I raced to catch up with the banter and in-jokes that drifted around me during our shifts, delicate as powdered sugar in the air, but I knew that the limits of camaraderie were still outlined by our working day. They each clocked off and returned to the rest of their lives, and somehow, inviting myself over that invisible barrier seemed an intrusion, too early to push.

So, I waited. I had enough to occupy my time, more than enough with the dozens of tiny decisions it took to build a life from scratch. I learned the bus schedule and

MBTA routes, opened a bank account, and found a pharmacy and grocery store. I furnished my sparse room with bright thrift-store bedding and books from a sidewalk stall, bought a second-hand bicycle with upright handlebars and a faded mint-green paint. I cycled the city for hours after my shift each afternoon, roaming from Harvard Square to Somerville and back. I learned where to find the best cheap falafel from a food truck, which dollar donuts melted on my tongue, the streets that pulsed with bright echoes of life after ten p.m., and which stayed dark and deserted, to avoid. I hoarded the last of my savings and then spent them all in a single glorious afternoon at the art supply store, setting my brand-new easel in the corner of the living room and inhaling the familiar scent of oil paints as I dented their smooth tubes with those first rebellious fingerprints.

But all the time, I felt Hope's words taunting me. She was the reason I was here, after all: clutching for an elusive freedom that had felt so out of reach back home. I'd made a bargain with myself, yet here I was hanging back on the edge of the cliff, too scared to let go and jump into that sparkling blue.

FRIDAY NIGHT, I was sketching Theo again, feet propped up in front of the TV, when my roommate came clattering up the three flights of stairs and burst, breathless, through the door.

"Oh god, I thought they'd never let us go," she groaned, unloading two book bags, her laptop case, and a brown paper bag of groceries onto the scratched old dining table. "That lab tech acted like we'd never seen a freaking pipette before."

Tessa was a petite, dark-haired whirl of focused energy. A third-year Harvard med student who also rowed crew, she was out of the door before dawn broke, icy on the river, and back each night at six to conjure up a hearty, home-made dinner before striking out again to the library or lab or endless stream of social mixers. I caught her in glimpses, braced against her waterfall of chatter; the neat row of athletic trophies lined up on her bookcase beside academic honors and camp photos were evidence of her limitless spirit. I'm not sure why she picked me out of all the other applicants to share our tiny attic apartment. Perhaps she sensed I would never invite friends over late to interrupt her precious six hours of sleep, or insert myself into that half-person galley kitchen to clash with her routine. She was right, of course. I was content to shape my life around her hours, let her paper the living room with her textbooks and class notes, and leave her neat Tupperware containers untouched in their stacks in the fridge.

"Tough day?" I asked.

"The worst." She hurled herself down in the other

threadbare lounge chair. "My lab partner had some kind of breakdown; he's dropping out to move back to Michigan."

"That's awful," I offered, sympathetic.

"I know, he took half our notes! I'll never get finished on my own." Tessa scowled. "Couldn't he have at least waited until the end of the semester before quitting on his meds?"

I paused, startled, then laughed. I couldn't help it; it was just too surprising to glimpse the cutthroat edge of Tessa's temper after two weeks of perky "Morning!"s and upbeat chatter.

She caught my gaze and then laughed too, looking self-conscious. "I'm such a bitch, I know, but you don't understand the kind of pressure we're under. If I fail this lab, I'm totally screwed."

"I'm sorry." I tried to put myself in her black lace-up Keds, staring down the barrel of midterms and research papers. "Can you find someone else?"

"It's too late for that. But . . ." She paused, looking thoughtful. "Amy and Varun partnered up, and I heard they're on the verge of a major break-up. Maybe if I poke around, I can steal him over to my station."

"Divide and conquer."

"Exactly!" She bounced up again, her usual buoyancy restored by the thought of such Machiavellian dealings. She headed for her room, but then paused by the doorway, looking at me with a fresh gaze. "I'm heading to a party over at Kappa Pi after dinner. You want to come?"

There it was, lying before me. The invitation, all but gift-wrapped with a silver ribbon.

"Thanks," I said, my heartbeat shivering with a new pulse. "I will."

I DON'T REMEMBER what I wore. Everything else about that night is frozen in my mind like a movie I've seen so often I can whisper the words right along with the actors on screen, but when it comes time to picture myself, it's all a vague blur. Theo swears it was my denim skirt and T-shirt, the blue one with an old Coke logo, but the weather had already shifted to a chilly night breeze; I would have been wrapped tight in a parka jacket, a sweater at least. Either way, I remember the nerves more than anything. A sick thump-thump in the pit of my stomach that seemed so stupid, so *young*. It was a party, that's all. I'd been to a few in my time: backwoods ragers that Hope dragged me to, a handful of kids drinking beer in a field; somebody's basement rec room; an underage rave out of town. I shouldn't have felt like it was a big deal, except it was: the simple challenge on that sheet of notebook paper marked tonight as something more than ordinary. I was on a mission, a target firmly in my scope.

It had to be an adventure.

"The gang from my lab will be there," Tessa explained,

as she cut a determined path through the busy streets. Friday night, and it seemed like the whole city was out in search of a good time, just like me. Girls teetering in high heels, and freshman boys with their flushed cheeks and dress shirts; cabs crawling at a snail's pace, and the bright glow of the streetlights strung like jewels through the center of Harvard Square. "The guys act like they've been homeschooled their whole lives, but they're sweet enough, really. I'll see if my crew team are out, they know how to party. Are you seeing anyone? Boyfriend? Girlfriend?" she asked, voice rising with curiosity.

"No. Boyfriend, I mean," I added quickly, but she didn't pause for breath.

"I don't blame you. God, some of the girls drive me crazy, all they do is trail after whatever jock asshole they met during orientation. I mean, hello? Don't you have something better to do, like plan your entire education? I made a rule, no serious relationships until senior year, at least. And even then, I'll probably wait. I'll be applying for med schools then; the last thing I'll want is anyone tying me down."

She came to an abrupt stop on the sidewalk and then flashed me a pixie grin, full of mischief. "But that doesn't mean I can't have any fun first. Come on."

Tessa stepped through an open gate and headed up the path to a vast Victorian-style mansion with brightly lit windows and turrets soaring into the dark. Crowded bodies spilled onto the wide wraparound porch, which was echoing with laughter and the low, steady thunder of bass.

We had arrived.

I trailed up the path and followed her slowly over the threshold, hit right away by a shockwave of heat and bright lights and a dozen loud conversations. The place was packed, seething with young, restless bodies that seemed to swell and ebb like a tide as people jostled between rooms and called to one another. Tessa bounced through the crowd and was immediately swept up by a cluster of similarly tiny loud girls, but I hung back, absorbing every glimpse. It had been months since I'd dived into a scene like this, and now it felt like a jolt of cold water, that first sharp slap breaking through the surface of an early-morning swim. I hardly knew where to look, but suddenly, I was thirsty to drink it all in.

There was a pattern to the chaos, I saw after a few moments. The hosts held court in the main room, a mismatched group of guys united by strong jawlines and broad shoulders. They didn't look like the frat boys back home, there were no backwards baseball caps or sagging denim, but there was still a swagger to them, that universal confidence the world bestows on boys with team colors and a seat up front on the bus. They bumped fists and slapped backs with new arrivals, calling to *B-man* and *Hudders*, *K-berger* and *the Kranz*: each new nickname announced with unbridled delight. Girls orbited around them—not the ones in vintage-print dresses, sharp bangs, hipster glasses; they were tucked away at the top of the stairs sipping beer from glass bottles and comparing pics on their phones—no, these girls were all tight jeans and cute little tops, hair cascading over glossed lips and perfect nude makeup designed to look as if they'd never so much as glanced at a mascara wand. They flirted and posed, leaning casually against the furniture as they laughed at the guys' jokes and twisted hair around peach-lacquered fingertips. A brave few even danced, swaying and grinding to the thundering hip-hop blasting from every corner of the surround-sound room, smiles plastered wide, their eyes flicking back to the boys every few moments, wondering if they were being watched, being seen.

Tessa was out of sight now, so I let the crowd jostle me onwards, through the downstairs rooms towards the hub of a kitchen at the back of the house. Here, bottles teemed on every surface, kegs sitting fat beside buckets of ice and the trail of plastic cups. I took one and hunted down a soda, pouring carefully as the guys beside me fiercely argued about the protests on campus that week.

"It's about free speech!" one insisted, energetic. He

21

had dark hair and black square-rimmed glasses, a rumpled white shirt fitting closely to his lithe body. "You can't go censoring everything just because someone's too sensitive to deal."

"Respect isn't censorship," his friend argued. "Come on, don't throw that bullshit around."

I tried to edge away, but they'd blocked me in against the countertop. "Umm, guys?" I spoke up, but they didn't notice.

"It isn't how we're talking they've got a problem with, it's what we're saying at all." The dark-haired guy smiled, clearly enjoying the argument. He tossed his empty beer bottle towards the trashcan, and it arced in a lazy curl across the counter before it hit the rim, already overflowing, and clattered to the floor. "You want to tell me again that's not censorship?"

"Hello?" I said, louder this time. I finally tapped on his arm.

He turned. "Oh, I didn't see you there. Hey, wait." He stopped me as I tried to slip past. "Aren't you in my poli sci class? Tuesday mornings, Professor Blakemore?"

I shook my head. "Sorry, must be someone else."

"But I know you." He studied my face, taking his time. "Maybe the dorms. Do you live on Radcliffe quad?"

"None of the above." I took another step, but he shifted slightly.

"You can't go now, this is going to bug me all night."
His smile turned teasing. "I'm Jamie."

"Claire."

"So, how do I know you, Claire?" Jamie mused, tilting his head.

"You won't guess," I told him.

"Want to bet?"

There was something in his eyes, inviting. Interested. "OK," I said slowly, feeling a flush in my cheeks under his scrutiny. "What do you want to bet?"

"How about, if I get it right, you give me your number." Jamie leaned back against the counter, all confidence again.

"And if I win?" I countered.

He grinned. "You give me your number."

I laughed. He was unshakeable, and I wondered what it must be like to feel that way, immune to indecision and the fear of rejection, safe on solid ground. "OK." I relaxed. "Then you get three guesses. And you've already used two of them up."

"Hey, that's not fair." Jamie furrowed his brow.

"I thought this was win-win for you."

"True," he said. "But it's the principle of the matter. Come on, let's start fresh."

"Nope." I shrugged. "Your call."

He blinked at me, and I could see his mind ticking

over, trying to figure me out, find a neat little box to put me in. This was genuinely irritating him, I realized. For all the smiles and teasing, he liked to know things for sure. I was a wild card, a challenge, and maybe that's why he was in here arguing rings around his friend instead of flirting with the gloss-lipped girls out front.

"I know!" His friend interrupted us, after loitering in silence, watching our loaded exchange. "The library. You study in the Arabic section on weekends."

"Shh." Jamie actually hushed him. He was still studying me, but then suddenly, his face lightened in recognition. "I knew it." He snapped his fingers, then pointed at me. "That coffee shop on Brattle. You work the register there."

I felt strangely disappointed to lose my trump card of mystery, but Jamie chuckled, all ease again now that he had me figured out. "Told you." He leaned closer and looked in my cup. "What are you drinking? Don't tell me you're sticking to soda."

"Maybe I like soda."

"You should loosen up a little." He reached across me and snagged a bottle of rum from the table. "You only live once."

He poured a long splash into my cup, and I sipped it, the cloying sweetness taking me back in an instant: to that 7-11 parking lot, sitting up on the back of a pick-up truck while Hope danced in the neon lights. *C'mon, Claire-bear*, she would sing, spinning over shattered glass and day-old fast-food wrappers like they were a carpet of rose petals and silk. *You only live once.*

She'd been going out of her mind with boredom all those nights, bitter that all we had of the world was that empty asphalt and a brown paper bag of Bacardi, but I'd loved them, all the same. I hadn't needed anything more, not like she did; I was content to play her favorite station on that crappy AM radio and watch the light fracture like diamonds on the ground under her restless feet.

". . . here anyway?"

"Huh?" I snapped back to find Jamie looking at me, a question between us in the air. "Sorry, I didn't hear you. It's so loud in here," I added.

"Then let's go someplace quieter." Jamie nodded towards the back door, out to the dark porch and the chilled night air. "You can tell me what you're doing here in town—besides serving up coffee and mystery," he added with a wink.

I paused. This was why I was here, wasn't it? *Go to a college party and make out with a boy.* I could hear Hope urge me on, giggling in my ear; feel her nudge me after him with a playful *Don't do anything I wouldn't do!*

I glanced back to the living room, looking for Tessa's

dark hair and bright scarlet shirt. That's when I saw him.

Theo.

He was off to the side of the main scrum, his head bent as he talked to someone, almost unnoticeable—to anyone except me. He was wearing a faded grey T-shirt, and his blonde hair was raked back—except for that tuft on the crown of his head that skewed at a rebellious angle. He laughed suddenly, and the way his face lit up with that smile was enough to make everyone else in the room fade away.

My stomach turned a slow flip, a champagne fizz of awareness shivering through my veins.

"Claire?"

I turned. Jamie was waiting by the door, another couple of beer bottles in his hand. He gave me a charming smile, and maybe ten seconds ago, that would have been enough. Enough to make me follow him out to that dim porch, enough to smile and chat and tilt my head towards him, waiting for the slide of his hand around my waist, the slow descent of his mouth to check another mark off my list. But now? Now I barely recognized him. He was fading into the peeling paint before my eyes, a pale Xerox copy compared to the real thing in the other room.

I slowly shook my head. "I better go find my friend," I said, already backing away. "But it was nice to meet you!"

He frowned. "Wait a sec—"

His voice was lost under the music as I turned and scurried away. My heart thundered with a fierce anticipation, but when I arrived in the hallway again, Theo was nowhere to be seen.

I felt the swift sink of disappointment, hitting solid ground after my brief flight.

"There you are!" Tessa suddenly materialized beside me, and scooped her hand through my arm. "I've been looking all over. Come meet everyone." She steered me over to the corner, where a group of boys and barefaced, athletic girls were collapsed in a tangle over chairs and couches. "This is Claire!" she announced, presenting me like a medal.

"Hey, Claire," they chorused in unison, and then laughed.

Tessa leaned in. "They come off all tough, but they're teddy bears really. Hudders!" she called. "Don't even think about changing this song!"

THE PROMISE

CHAPTER THREE

I STAYED WITH TESSA the rest of the night, letting her group's tapestry of insider jokes and campus gossip weave around me in a comforting blanket. They were an interesting crowd, drawn from a mismatched assortment of college majors and backgrounds, but all united by their early-morning practice sessions on the river and late-night gym sessions, pulling hard on the rowing machines. Tessa was their pint-sized ringleader, chatting loudly with the other girls and teasing all the guys, her bright laughter cutting through the din. She sprawled on the couch, and kicked her legs up into the lap beside her, commanding the space as easily as she dominated our tiny apartment back across town.

"I'm not your furniture," a boy groaned, trying to shove her legs off. He was stocky and sweating through his athletic T-shirt, with a dark buzz cut hugging the lines of his bullet-shaped head.

"You're taking up all the space!" Tessa shoved him

good-naturedly. "See, Claire? This is what I have to put up with all day. These Neanderthals sweating and grunting over everything."

The boy snorted. "Is she like this at home too?" he asked me. "Barking out orders like a little dictator?"

"You love me, really," Tessa beamed prettily. He rolled his eyes, but the affection there was clear. "I should go soon," she added with a sigh.

"It's Friday night!" one of the other girls protested.

"I know, but I signed up for a Saturday lab skills class." Tess shrugged. "And my TA reams you out if you show up even a minute late."

"So don't show, skip the whole thing."

"And have him think I'm a quitter?" Tessa shot back. "No way."

The girl shook her head, lips quirking in an admiring smile. "You're a machine."

"Damn straight." Tessa raised her plastic cup. "What else are we here for?"

The guys laughed. "Beer, women, glory."

"You wish. How is *Jessica*?" And then they were off again, whip-smart, jostling like puppies as the party pressed in around us, dense and packed with bodies and noise.

I'd never been a pack animal like this. Back home, I had my friends, sure, a group of girls I'd known since second grade, and the art kids who hung out every lunchtime in the ramshackle back building that served as a studio—cluttered with ceramics and easels, and the old boom box that Donavan Kline was always trying to commandeer to play his dreary old mixtapes of the Smiths and the Libertines. But I'd never belonged like Tessa clearly belonged here. Cliques always carried too much drama, too many fragile tempers to navigate, shifting loyalties and unspoken slights. I was content to drift between them, watching from a safe distance as the tides of high school shifted with group trips and hashtagged photos, #squadgoals and all. I never quite belonged to anything, anyone, or felt that do-or-die fierce connection when you know you've found your people, your family, your certain place in the world.

Until Hope, of course.

"Where are the snacks in this place?" Tessa finally asked, looking around. "I require care and feeding!"

She was tipsy now, a giggling, happy drunk.

"I saw some chips in the kitchen, I think," I offered.

She groaned, but didn't move. I laughed. "I'll go. Want anything particular?"

"Just bring me carbs. All the carbs!"

I left them and ducked my way through the crowd. It had mellowed a little, a low-key hip-hop soundtrack smoothing the raucous yells to a happy hum. People were three drinks in, dancing more, leaning closer to their dates and slipping off away from the main party, hand-in-hand. I saw Jamie in the corner, gesturing widely as he talked with another girl. He caught my eye and arched his eyebrow, but I just smiled and kept on moving.

You're not looking for Mr. Right, Hope would have scolded me, *just Mr. Right Now,* but I blocked the memory of her voice and headed for the kitchen, finding a bag of chips and some half-eaten jarred dip, and a bag of red licorice sticks, too, the kind I hadn't eaten since I was a kid.

The back door was partly open. A pair of feet were visible, stretched out on the porch: worn brown boots and the fraying cuffs of a pair of navy corduroy pants.

I felt that sick shiver again, a lurch of anticipation.

I don't know how I knew it was him. Looking back, I told myself it was wishful thinking, but when I pushed the door wider and stepped out into the still darkness of the porch and saw Theo sitting there, it felt like a gift. That the universe had taken my wild longings and bundled them up in a neat package, cross-legged on the dusty ground peeling a label from his bottle of untouched beer.

The two of us were alone.

"Hey." My voice caught in my throat.

He looked up, the dim light casting shadows across his

jaw as his face smoothed into a surprised smile. "What are you doing here?" Theo paused. "I mean, you're not a student, are you? Kelsey said . . ."

He stopped, and my heart did too at the thought he'd been talking about me at all.

"No." I managed to speak again. "My roommate is."

I ignored the wild dance in my stomach and took another step towards him, closing the door behind me. The noise of the party receded, replaced by a hum of traffic and the chilled breeze, but I didn't feel the cold. All I felt was the force field around him, those magnetic few feet of electricity ricocheting around his casually folded body.

"Are you?" I asked, trying to sound casual. "A student?"

He nodded. "Graduate school. Poetry."

"The Wordsworth," I realized.

He nodded, with a bashful kind of smile. "That's about all it's useful for. If I could make a living quoting at people, I'd be set."

"Art doesn't need to be useful. It's beautiful, that's all it's supposed to be."

Theo looked at me again, and if I could have paused time right then, I would have: suspended in the reflection of his clear blue eyes, that daybreak light of recognition, like he was seeing me clearly for the first time.

"Tell that to my student loan officer," he finally said with a wry smile.

I joined him on the porch floor, facing him with my back to the wooden railings, twisting my bracelet around my wrist. It was a pale blue band, with 'HOPE' embossed into the rubber; she'd always loved the irony, but even now there was none left for her, I couldn't take it off. "So what are you doing down here?" I asked.

He shrugged. "Just taking a break. It gets kind of . . . chaotic in there."

"I know what you mean. I'm going to be carrying Tessa home at this rate. She's my roommate," I added, but it felt disloyal. "Not like she's wasted, she's just . . . small."

Theo nodded slowly. I cringed. What happened to the girl who was flirting so easily with Jamie earlier? Mysterious and aloof.

Why was it so much easier to talk to a man when he didn't matter at all?

"Are those nacho flavor?" Theo looked to the bag crumpled beside me.

I checked. "Salt and vinegar."

He winced, but reached his hand outstretched all the same and took a handful. "What do they put in these to make them so addictive?"

"Crack, probably."

He laughed, caught by surprise, and sent chip fragments spraying over the both of us. "Shit, I'm sorry. And for swearing too," he added, recovering. "I'm trying to stop."

"It's OK." I watched him brush crumbs off his shirt, a look of faint embarrassment on his gorgeous face, and my nerves eased, just a little. He was human, after all.

"Mika has a swear jar at work," I added, reaching over to take a handful of chips too. "Everyone has to put in a dollar if we catch each other. They're all filthy. Kelsey's out, like, twenty bucks since I arrived."

"You only just moved to town?" Theo looked up at me.

I nodded. "A few weeks ago."

I didn't say anything more, and he didn't ask either. "How do you like Wired?" he asked instead.

I couldn't help but smile. "I love it. Everyone's so . . . so much themselves. We get hundreds of people through every day, and I get to watch them all."

"You're a writer."

"No. Why'd you say that?"

He looked bashful. "Writers like to pay attention, watch people. Eavesdrop."

"Do you?"

"Maybe." Theo's expression relaxed, the trace of a

smile edging on his mouth. "Sometimes," he admitted. "So why do you like to watch?"

I paused. My answer was important, somehow, and I struggled to find the right way to say it, convey the tangled threads that had knotted together in my mind this year. "I guess it feels like I've spent my whole life in a bubble," I said quietly. "My small town, we knew pretty much everyone. I knew every day would be like the last one, but here, there's a . . . possibility. It's unpredictable. This is the real world."

The words felt so familiar in my mouth, because they were the ones I'd hurled at my parents all those times, fighting for them to let me leave. They thought their neat, safe little streets and familiar horizons were real, and I guess they were, but not enough for me. Not anymore.

Theo took a sip of his beer. He was watching me thoughtfully, and even though it made my pulse trip on dizzy footsteps just to look straight at him, I managed to meet his careful gaze.

Oh.

I looked away, I couldn't help it. My skin was hot, my whole body effervescent just beneath the surface. I'd never felt this off-kilter, not in all my nineteen years. I'd wanted unpredictable. I'd craved possibilities. But this? It was too much, and not enough, all at once.

"Do you—?" Theo's next question was drowned out by

the sudden rush of noise from the party again. The door swung open, and just like that, the moment of the two of us was over.

"Theo! What are you doing hiding out here?"

It was a girl, slim and tall in jeans and a cuffed, men's white button-down. Her dark hair was sleek, falling in a smooth waterfall around her inquisitive face; red lips smoothing in a friendly smile as she saw me sitting with him on the floor. "Oh, hi."

"This is Claire." Theo tilted his head up to her, but didn't move.

"Nice to meet you, Claire." The girl stepped closer, then rested her hand on Theo's head, her fingers slipping to stroke through the dark blonde tufts. "They're heading to Becky's now," she added to him. "We could stay, or bail, it's up to you."

Shame pounded, hot in my ears. Of course he belonged to someone. Of course he had a girl like this: sweet and effortlessly stylish.

I scrambled to my feet. Theo looked surprised. "You don't have to—"

"It's OK, I'm heading home anyway." I forced a bright voice. "See you around."

I pushed back inside, found Tessa and my jacket, but all the while, the image stayed burned in my mind: her fingers so casually tousling his hair. The intimacy of it took my breath away.

Imagine, having the right to do that, without a second thought.

"Are you sure?" Tessa's voice was even louder now, when I told her I was leaving. "The party's just getting good!"

"I'm sure." I checked her flushed cheeks and unsteady grin. "What about you? Will you get home OK?"

"Don't worry," one of the other girls answered for her. "We've got a designated driver, and she can crash at my place if she needs."

"Thanks."

"Hey, we look out for each other." She paused. "You're not walking, are you?"

"I can get a cab," I lied. "Have fun!"

I slipped out of the front door, pulling my jacket on against the night air. The street was still well-lit and busy with the trail of weekend revelers; there was no need to spend half a day's wages on a cab ride home, I decided, so I set out retracing our route here, back along fraternity row, past the lumbering houses full of their own bright lights and deep bass notes.

"Claire!"

I was almost at the corner when I heard my name being called. I turned. It was Theo, jogging slightly to catch up with me, bundled in his coat again, with a navy scarf trailing loose around his neck.

I froze, watching him come closer, back to me.

"I thought that was you." He grinned as he drew level. "Are you walking? Which direction? It's pretty late."

"No, I'm fine." I waved away his concern. "It's not far."

"It's no trouble. I'm going anyway." He waited, stubborn on the sidewalk. I took a shivering breath.

"OK. Thanks."

I started walking again, and this time, he fell into step beside me. Our footsteps crunched on the cold concrete, and I tried to think of something more to say. But every thought I had was smothered by the looming presence of the dark-haired girl back at the party, she with her perfect red lipstick and confident smile, touching him like he was hers. Had he left her with their friends? Was she meeting him, later?

"That was Brianna," Theo said at last through our silence. "At the party."

"She seems . . . nice," I managed.

"Uh huh. We're in a seminar together, on Renaissance poetry." Theo took another few steps. "We're not . . . I mean, she isn't . . ."

His words trailed into the city hum, but they were

enough to make my delicate hopes take flight again as I silently filled in the blanks.

We're not together. She's not my girlfriend.

Or maybe this was just more of my wishful thinking. I bit back any response, and instead, looked around, grasping for safer ground.

"It's busy out."

Lame.

"Weekends get that way. Well, any night during the semester," Theo corrected himself. A group of guys hustled past us in a boisterous pack, and we both had to sidestep quickly out of the fray.

Theo placed a steadying hand on my back. The imprint seemed to burn through my fleece-lined jacket, like I could feel his palm on my bare skin beneath.

"Thanks," I muttered, when they were past. His hand dropped.

"Where are you heading?"

I gave him the cross streets, and he nodded. "This way will be quicker," he said, then veered on a pathway leading across the park. Even though it was lit with the glow from old-style iron streetlights, I would never have taken it alone.

"How long have you been here?" I asked, slowing my pace. I wanted this to last, to savor every moment with him alone.

"My whole life."

There was a note in his voice that made me look over.

"Not here," he clarified. "Over the river, in Boston. South End. Have you been?"

I shook my head. "I don't know where that is," I confessed. "I haven't even been over yet, I've been so busy exploring around Cambridge."

"I forgot." He smiled at me. "You're still brand new."

I wished it was true. To be bright-eyed and naïve like the freshman I saw cluttering the coffee shop every afternoon. My heart felt older than all of them, wizened, the bark peeling and hardened from the bitterness I fought so hard to keep at bay.

But Theo saw none of that. I inhaled a crisp breath, and I felt the freedom in that simple act. To him, I was a blank canvas, and he was to me too, in his way. Box-fresh and waiting for the first bright strokes, just like this city, this life I'd managed to conjure out of Hope's scrawled commandments and my own last resolve.

The miracle of it hit me all over again, and I couldn't hold back the laugh that slipped, joyful from my throat.

Theo looked at me. "What?"

"Nothing, just . . ." My smile spread wider, and I spread my arms to take it all in: the distant hum of a strange city, the shadowed moon and the clouded stars. Even the wind felt different to the dry desert breeze back home. "I can't believe I'm really here." I marveled again, flooded with the feeling. "A month ago I was locked in this *ordinary* life, in the same room, going through the same motions, everything all planned out. Every day exactly like the last. God, I could have told you how the rest of my entire life would have played out until the day I died, but now . . . now there's no rulebook anymore."

Theo grinned at me. I didn't care if he thought I was acting crazy right now, he didn't understand.

But Hope had. This was what she wanted for me, and it was a fucking waste she wasn't here to taste it all, too.

"Isn't it amazing?" I grinned. "We're adults. We could stay out all night if we wanted, eat nothing but hot dogs and waffles all day long, and nobody can tell us otherwise."

He smiled, but kept walking. "I hate to burst your bubble, but it doesn't stay fun forever."

"Killjoy," I laughed. "When did you get so jaded?"

Theo shrugged, but he didn't reply. There it was again, the faint shadow drifting over the conversation, the same pause I'd seen back at the café. But he must have sensed it showing, because Theo quickly pointed. "Have you tried Jhandi yet?"

"No, what is it?" Past the park was a brightly lit food truck, with a cluster of students hanging around outside.

"Only the best late-night food around." Theo's smile returned. "You hungry?"

"Hungry is my default setting."

He laughed again, and changed our course, heading over to join the line. "The noodles are best, and the sticky rice." I reached for my wallet as we approached the window, but he waved it away. "No, I've got this."

"You don't have to—"

"Consider it my tip, all those coffees you've been making." He flashed me another smile, and it was enough to silence me into submission as he ordered for us both. Moments later, they passed down two steaming Styrofoam cartons, wafting the scent of ginger and spices into the air. I realized for the first time how hungry I was; I hadn't eaten anything except those chips since lunch, at least.

I took a plastic fork and dug in, a mouthful of exotic flavors hitting me, hot and smoky. "What is this?" I exclaimed.

"I don't even know, I just know it's good," Theo replied, mouth full. We moved off to the side, shoveling food inelegantly into our mouths. "He showed up one day last year; now he's got a cult following. You can track him online," he added, "but you never know where he's going to be next."

"Like a scavenger hunt."

"Exactly."

We ate in silence, leaning against a wall, until I'd demolished the whole carton. I tossed the styrofoam into

a nearby trash can and looked around. There was a group
of students gathered nearby, dressed up to the nines in
formal suits and ties. They looked so out of place in the
brash neon truck lights, the girls all in elegant cocktail
dresses that swished around their bare legs as they
huddled together for warmth.

Theo followed my gaze. "They're from the college,"
he said. "One of the supper clubs, probably. They like to
have formal events, invite-only. It's a whole thing, their
version of a fraternity, only even more secretive."

I didn't need to ask which college. The red-brick
towers of Harvard loomed over Cambridge, and even out
of sight from the manicured campus you could feel its
reach. The country's best and brightest, crammed together
in a few city blocks, ready to shape their minds—and
soon, the nation. Kelsey bitched about it, but there was a
history, an elegance those gingerbread buildings leant to
the town that I loved. Still, there was something
unnerving about seeing so much privilege so casually
strewn around: girls reaching into thousand-dollar leather
bags to pay for their coffees without a blink, and guys
you knew would glide from private school dorms to cushy
corporate jobs never knowing how it felt to come up short
the day rent was due. But I couldn't find it in myself to be
jealous of their soft hands and plump bank accounts. I'd
been sheltered too, I know, my parents over-protective

and anxious to keep a safe layer of cotton-wool between their precious baby girl and the harsh world beyond.

"You must be good," I said out loud without thinking as we began to walk again. Theo looked puzzled. "To get accepted in the graduate program," I explained. "It's competitive, isn't it?"

He looked bashful. "I guess. I did my undergrad at BU, I wasn't even thinking about programs, but my professors recommended me. They offered a great package in the end. I have to work a lot of hours TA-ing, but at least it keeps my tuition costs down."

"TA?" I echoed, confused.

"Teaching Assistant. Basically, I run the lectures and grade papers for undergrads when my professors have better things to do," he explained with a wry smile. "Which is most of the time."

I'd bet his classes are full, the halls lined with adoring freshman girls.

"Is that what you want to be?" I asked. "A professor?"

"Maybe. I like teaching, and let's face it, a master's in poetry isn't good for much else."

I smiled. "I don't know about that. I saw an ad in the newspaper just the other day: wanted, poets. Six-figure salary, full benefits, paid vacation."

Theo laughed out loud, a real belly laugh that warmed me to my bones.

"I wish. I sometimes think they had it right, back in Renaissance Italy. Artists and writers would have patrons," he told me, "Rich aristocrats who would pay them just to create whatever they wanted."

"I bet there were strings, though," I said, thinking of my own parents, and the allowance they used to deposit into my account each month, their wordless bribe to keep me close to home. "Nothing comes for free."

Theo paused. "No, you're right. Nothing does." Then, as if sensing the conversation had taken a darker turn, he added, "They probably had to write poems dedicated to how amazing their patrons were."

"And paint them as the most beautiful people in the world."

Theo smiled. "All those stunning portraits we see in the museums were really butt-ugly in real life."

"Is that the poetic term?" I teased.

He laughed again, then came to a stop on the sidewalk. "This is you, isn't it?"

I was disappointed when I looked up and realized we'd walked all the way back home. My brownstone apartment building stood just a few feet away from the corner, the light left on in my bedroom window.

"This is me."

Looking back, I can't tell you what made me reach

for him. It would be easier to explain if I was tipsy, my inhibitions blurred and drowsy, but I'd barely sipped that red cup, and every instinct was sharp, bright with a crystalline clarity. Maybe it was the streetlights, that fractured glow of neon and headlights casting such a golden light across his face, the planes of skin and jawline and dusted stubble making my fingers itch to touch him. Maybe it was the knowledge of Hope's list, not getting any shorter by the day, and the burden of responsibility she'd left on my small shoulders.

But I know the truth, deep down.

I just wanted him.

Before I could take it back, I went up on my tiptoes against him. My reach was swift and clumsy, my hand against his chest as my mouth lurched towards his. There was barely an inch between us, the heat of his breath whispering on my lips, when Theo stepped away.

"I . . . Claire—"

Oh God.

I recoiled, shame flushing hot through every inch of my body. "Sorry," I blurted, "I didn't . . . I mean—"

"It's fine—"

"I didn't think—"

"No, *I'm* sorry." Theo looked awkward as hell, but

it was nothing compared to the humiliation dragging me back down to earth.

I backed away, and stumbled up the front steps. "Thanks for walking me home," I blurted. "Bye."

I turned and fumbled with my keys, every second out there in the night making me feel more exposed. What was I thinking? How could I have wrecked things in just a single moment?

Finally, my keys fit the lock. I half-fell through the door, but as I closed it behind me, I heard Theo's voice, low and steady on the breeze.

"Goodnight, Claire."

CHAPTER FOUR

SATURDAY, I HAD the morning off. There were errands to run, and a heap of laundry on my bedroom floor ready for the ancient shuddering basement machines, but I couldn't stay home. I'd already relived the humiliation of my clumsy kiss too many times to count, and the city glittered, bright and clear outside the windows. I pulled on my gloves, stuffed my sketchbook in my bag, and thundered down the staircase and out into the world again.

In daylight, the streets seemed brand new. The intimate darkness that had cloaked us during our walk home was replaced with pale, bright sun, and instead of being one of only two people in the world, I was anonymous in a crowd of thousands. The streets were busy, the autumn skies bright and brisk, and the dazzling leaves that had painted the sky only days before now blanketed the ground, crunching under my boots and whirling bright cyclones in the wind.

I found my bearings, then struck out in a new direction: back across the park and into the placid neighborhoods that stretched to the west of the city. I'd never ventured this way before, but walking the wide, serene streets, I felt strangely at home. Here, sturdy oak trees lined the sidewalks, their roots bursting through the concrete, and vast gingerbread houses sat behind thick hedges, surveying the city from their white-trimmed turrets and lazy front-porch swings. It was a long way from the dry Texan streets, stretching in their neat grids as far as you could imagine. The strip malls and suburban tract homes were far behind me now. Every turn in the road felt like an adventure, and I paused to peek through the front gates and up rose-trimmed garden paths, avoiding the curious stares of people out walking their dogs.

Theo probably thought I was crazy, the way I'd been talking last night—even before the cheek-flushing embarrassment of my fumbled kiss. But he'd spent his whole life here, he didn't understand how these cool New England hues could be as fascinating as a foreign street to me. I often wondered if it was threaded into our DNA from the start: who was content to stay, soothed by familiar scenes outside their window every day, and who craved the change of new horizons. The pioneers had struck out West in their dusty wagons, but when it came to choosing my own destination, I'd known the warm shores of California weren't the ones for me.

It had been chance, in the end, like so much else. A rerun of an old TV show, with clapboard houses and winding creeks that caught my eye the day I found Hope's last letter. I discovered later it hadn't even been filmed here at all, but further South, the snow as fake as silicone in the frosted camera frame. But by then, my ticket was booked: hidden in the pages of a sketchbook on my dresser until the day I packed my bag and caught a cab to the Greyhound station, my life savings taped in a brown paper envelope around my stomach, over the tattoo my parents would never know about, and the first stirrings of fearful regret. I shouldn't have been so scared. My doubts faded with every passing mile of cracked highway, until, three days later, the bus spat me out here, stiff and tired, but wide-eyed with new determination.

My life had begun again.

ABOUT A MILE through the neighborhood, I found a quaint stretch of shops and a gold-etched bakery sign. I bought a coffee and a slice of vanilla loaf—the crust cracked with sugar—and settled in at a table by the steamed-up windows, watching the young moms mop up after their playful toddlers in the corner booth, and a pair of old men sitting side by side, quietly passing sections of the newspaper to one another as they sipped their paper cups and read.

I pulled out my sketchbook and my new set of charcoal sticks. There was plenty around me, and I started and stopped my warm-up sketches half a dozen times, but when it came time to settle my hands and still my thoughts, there was only one subject in my mind.

Theo.

Even tinged with shame, my memories wouldn't shift. My hands moved of their own volition, the charcoal cradled lightly between my first two fingers and thumb. I could see him there, on the back porch last night: the shadows casting a sharp line across his jaw, and that lazy, slowly easing smile as he settled back and began to talk.

I'd had crushes before, but this was something different. For years, my fumbling affections were always built more out of fantasy than any truth. I would spend hours daydreaming a random boy into existence, building elaborate scenes like movies in my mind, until the object of my crush became a character, speaking the perfect lines, making just the right romantic moves, so much a figment of my hungry heart that when I saw them in real life again, standing in line at the fast-food window, or walking down a faded linoleum hallway, the disappointment was almost a betrayal. I'd built such heroes in my mind that nothing, not even the real boy right in front of me, could possibly measure up; my crush dissolved in a heartbeat, and my restless imagination skipped on to the next possibility, the next shooting star in the sky.

But with Theo . . . I didn't want to spin those happily-ever-afters, or place the perfect words in his mouth. Every time I felt at the brink of rewriting our brief meetings—*what if, what if?*—I pulled back.

I didn't want him to become a fantasy, like all the others. I was done playing pretend.

The hours slipped away that morning, lost in the thick pages and the delicate smudge of black against the pale. I was better at it now, practiced from a week of portraits, his face and figure adorning every other page, but still, it felt like something was missing. There was a light to him, a soulful solitude that couldn't quite be captured, no matter how long I worked. A photo wouldn't have made a difference either, I knew. Some people were just like that: the true essence of their personality shifting like quicksilver, refusing to be marked down in such a permanent form.

My phone buzzed a bleating reminder, and I finished the picture with a sigh. The burnished light of Theo's eyes stared back at me from the page, and I carefully layered the page with tissue paper, making a note to seal it later, and packed my things away again. I was due for my shift at Wired by one, so I took a brisk pace back, checking my phone for a shortcut through the unfamiliar streets. My phone rang in my hands.

Home.

I stood, frozen there on the sidewalk. A small kid came careening past on a tiny training bike, and I stumbled back, almost losing my footing.

"Sorry!" his mom called breathlessly, chasing behind him down the street.

By the time I had recovered, the phone clicked to voicemail. I tucked my handset away in my coat pocket and forced myself to keep walking, but I felt it, burning through the fleece all the way back.

We hadn't spoken for weeks, not since that last, terrible call as I sat on the Greyhound bus watching my old life ebb away into the sunset through scratched and dusty windows. There had been pleading, and tears, even blackmail in the end, but it was too late for them to change my mind. The calls continued, daily, but I didn't pick them up. I sent texts, instead: checking in every other day. Yes, I'm OK. Yes, I'm still alive. They didn't even know where I was. I knew even a mention of the city name, and they'd be here in a heartbeat, on my doorstep to cajole and guilt me back home again. Hope's list was still tucked in the back of my sketchpad, and until I had worked my way further down that wistful page, I knew I didn't have reasons enough to stay.

But still, the guilt slipped through me, treacherous as I arrived at Wired. It was packed, the line ten-deep at the front counter, with people loitering in every corner for the chance to snatch a precious table.

"Thank God," Mika exclaimed, as he hurried past. "Can you cover the register? We're slammed."

"Just a sec."

I ducked back outside and paused, just by the doorway. I knew I should get straight to work and ignore my mom's latest guilt-laden message, but I couldn't help pressing my phone to my ear just to hear her familiar voice again.

Sweetheart, we're just worried about you. You're being selfish, worrying your dad like this. Talk to us, let us know you're OK. These messages aren't enough, please Claire.

My gut twisted. She was right, I was being selfish, but wasn't it my turn? My whole life, I'd let them decide. It had been no great battle, they'd known best, after all. But I was an adult now, and it was time for me to make my own mistakes, no matter what the consequence.

I turned back to the door just as it pushed open, jostling me back. As I fumbled with my phone, my bag slipped, spilling its contents on the busy sidewalk, and I cursed.

"There's another forfeit." Theo's voice came, and then

he was on his knees beside me, helping collect my things, blonde head bent in the sunlight.

My heart lurched.

My head was still spinning from the voicemail. I felt so off-balance; the world was the wrong side up, and here he was again, to knock me even further off my feet.

I snatched my bag back and shot to my feet. I couldn't face the awkward look I knew would be on his face so I didn't even try to thank him, I just bolted back inside the café without another word.

"Save me from freshman girls and their fucking Frappuccinos," Kelsey greeted me as I slipped behind the counter.

"Swear jar!" JJ called.

"Fuck," Kelsey swore again, and then dragged a couple of crumpled dollar bills from her pocket to lay in JJ's outstretched hand. "You better use that bounty to buy me something pretty!" she called after him, before finally turning back to me. "Are you sick?" She frowned, stepping back. "You look all flushed."

"No, I'm fine. Just, rushed to get here." I quickly stashed my bag under the counter and tied on an apron. "You want me to take over up front?"

"Please, I'm going to poison the next person who asks for pumpkin spiced anything," she announced cheerfully.

I turned, and found a teenage girl looking stricken by the register. "Ignore her," I said. "She's harmless."

"Tell that to my ex-boyfriends," Kelsey muttered, retreating to the relative safety of the espresso machine.

I took the girl's order, and then two dozen more, until the voicemail seemed like just a memory of the life I'd left behind. The rush continued, all through lunch, until at last the flood of caffeine-hungry customers slowed to a trickle, and Mika waved me off the front register to go bus tables and clean up.

Kelsey was on her break, camped out at a booth in the back with a pile of pastries. She pushed the plate over to me as I wiped down the next table. "Take one. They broke in the box," she said, with a wicked grin. "So we can't sell them."

"Broke all on their own?" I asked, laughing.

"Guess the bakery guy was extra-clumsy today." Kelsey stuffed another piece of brownie in her mouth.

I took a piece and glanced at the book she was reading, a dog-eared classic that I couldn't tell was for pleasure or school. She saw me looking. "My study group is meeting later, if you want to come."

"Thanks, but I wouldn't keep up."

She snorted. "More than half the guys in this town. It's like being born with a trust fund and a dick gives them a free pass from actually having a brain." She kicked her combat boots up in the booth, and turned back to her book. "Oh, I forgot," she said, looking up. "Your boyfriend was looking for you."

"My what?" I stopped. "Who?"

"You know who." She gave me a look. "Teddy Roosevelt."

"I don't . . . Oh. Theo." The blood rushed to my cheeks again. "He was asking about me?"

Kelsey nodded, her mouth full. It seemed like an eternity before she swallowed, brushed cookie crumbs from her shirt, and said, "Right before you came in today. He didn't leave a message, didn't even want me to tell you he was here, but I thought you'd want to know."

"Thanks." I went back to wiping down tables, but my heart shivered. I wondered what he'd wanted to say. Now I regretted bolting from him so quickly outside, knowing it was because he'd come to seek me out, and not just another uncomfortable accident.

"Be careful with that one, OK?"

Kelsey's quiet warning made me pause. "What do you mean?"

She gave a little shrug. "Just . . . these guys, they don't mix with townies, not for long. They stay safe in their college bubble, and we're over here, on the outside, bringing their coffee and cleaning up when they leave. That's just how it goes."

I shook my head slowly. "He's not like that. And anyway, why are you talking like this?" I frowned, puzzled. "You're a student, too."

"Not anymore," Kelsey said. She saw my confusion as I took in her books and notes and explained. "I had to take a break last year. I keep up with the reading lists, and still meet my old study groups, I probably work harder than half those idiots, but it doesn't count. At least, not yet." Her eyes narrowed in determination. "At least this way, I can blitz through all the classes and catch up, when I do go back."

I wondered what had made her take that break from school, but I knew better than to ask. There was a bitterness in her expression, and besides, there was an unspoken rule here against straying too far into our personal lives. Too many questions from me might prompt the same curiosity from her, questions I didn't have the answers to just yet: what was I doing here? Why did I come?

How long was I planning to stay?

"Thanks for looking out," I said instead. "But you don't need to worry. Theo and I, we're not . . . I mean, he's just a friend."

Even those vague words sounded false on my lips, but Kelsey could see right through me. "Sure he is," she said. "I'm just saying, have your fun, but don't expect it to last through winter break. Guys like that always have a way of disappearing on you."

She gave me a quiet smile and returned to her reading, and I went back to clean-up, but her words stayed with me—and the regret simmering just beneath the surface. From my very first day, Kelsey had seemed unshakeable, steamrolling past customer complaints and any urging from Mika to *at least try to act like you give a damn* with an attitude I envied. But it turned out she did give a damn, after all.

Was she right about Theo?

It didn't matter anymore, I reminded myself, with a low pang of regret. He had Brianna, with her glossy hair and berry-red lips. And me, I had a different future planned.

IT WAS DARK BY THE TIME I finished my shift, but I lingered, snagging a seat on the worn velvet couch and curling up with a mug of tea and my sketchpad. Tessa had texted to let me know her study group was coming over, and I didn't want to be in the way of their whip-fast flashcard tests. Besides, the café already felt more like home to me than that attic apartment, my bedroom walls still bare, a single inherited box spring and mattress beside the chipped dresser. Here, the lights were warm and cozy against the worn, polished wooden floors, the walls filled with old photographs and new local artists, and the soundtrack that blurred from old Sinatra to the Beastie Boys, James Bay and back again. The comforting hum of conversation lulled me into a sleepy haze as I absently sketched the hurried crowd outside the breath-fogged windows, people pushing through the rush-hour traffic to make it back to their own small corners of the world.

"I didn't know you were an artist."

A surprised voice behind me made me jolt. I knocked the mug beside me as I turned, and it spilled, splashing over my sketchbook page.

"Shit," Theo swore, looking mortified. "I keep doing this today."

He left me for the front counter, and I tried my best to shake the liquid from the pages and steady my nerves, but by the time Theo returned with a handful of paper napkins, my pulse was still skittering, double-time in my chest.

"Here, is it ruined?" He looked on anxiously as I dabbed at the faint stain.

"No, it's fine. It wasn't important," I added, putting the book aside. "I was just messing around."

"But it looks great. You're talented," he added, sitting beside me on the couch. Before I could stop him, he reached for the sketchbook and started leafing through the pages.

"No!" I gasped, snatching it back just as the page settled on one of my late-night portraits of him. I prayed to God he hadn't had time to register his own reflection as I slammed it shut and hugged it protectively to my chest. "Sorry," I added, seeing his startled look at my outburst. "It's personal, that's all. I don't like to show anyone."

"Sorry, I should have asked first. I don't like to share my writing either," Theo added. He paused, then gave me a hesitant smile. "Maybe one day, you'll want to show me."

One day . . .

I took a shaking breath and focused on mopping up the last of the spilled tea. When there was finally nothing else to distract myself with, I looked over at Theo again. He had on a blue sweater, something soft and finely knit, with a shirt collar peeking up from underneath. I'd never liked the preppy look, but on him, it sat well-worn and just right.

"What did you want?" My voice sounded almost accusatory, and I cringed inside. "I mean, Kelsey said you were looking for me before."

"She did?" Theo looked away, and cleared his throat. "I was, but that wasn't . . ." He trailed off, then looked back at me. "I wanted to return this."

He took a small notebook from his inside pocket and carefully laid it on the couch between us. There were faded lines and a torn edge, doodled hearts and boxes fringing one side in smudged blue ink.

Hope's list.

I inhaled in a rush. "When did you find this?" I picked it up, careful, cradling it like tissue paper. How could I have been so careless? I didn't even notice it was gone.

"You dropped it outside," Theo said, but there were a hundred questions in his eyes.

"You read it," I said slowly.

He looked caught. "I didn't know if it was important, something you needed back. So . . . yes. I did."

I didn't know what to say. I felt exposed, even though those weren't my words on the page. "Thank you," I said instead, tucking it safely into the back flap of my sketchpad, where it belonged.

"Are you going to tell me what it's about?" Theo flashed me a smile, boyish and charming. Any other time, and I would have offered him whatever he wanted in exchange for a smile like that: rubies and golden bars and all the treasure of the kingdom, but this time, it wasn't enough.

"It's a long story." I looked down at the paper in my

hands, tongue-tied. *Ask me anything else,* I silently implored him. *I'll talk for hours, I'll tell you everything.*

Just not this, not right now.

The seconds ticked past in silence, and eventually, he got to his feet, and hoisted his bag again. "OK, well, glad you got it back." He looked down at me, as if making his mind up about something. "There is one thing . . . number four, on the list."

I didn't have to look; I knew the list by heart.

Sneak into a show and hang backstage.

"My roommate's in a band," Theo continued. "They're playing Wednesday night at this club in the city. They don't check IDs, and I just thought, if you want . . ."

His voice trailed off but there was a hopeful look in his eyes.

"I don't know," I managed, my mind racing. What was he asking here? Me to go with him, together, a *date*?

"Sure, well, you don't have to decide just yet," Theo said, casual. "I'll put you on the list, and then if you make it . . ." He shrugged, then gave me a smile. "Maybe you can tell me about that list of yours."

"Maybe," I echoed, but he was already gone, back out of the door and into the darkness, his invitation lingering behind him in the cinnamon-scented air.

CHAPTER FIVE

HOPE HAD ALREADY started the list when I met her. Back then, it filled a whole notepad, one of those spiral-bound drugstore books with a battered red cover, and she'd scribble new entries just to cross them off with a triumphant strike.

"That's cheating," I would protest, every time she'd write something down when we'd already done it, or pick things that didn't mean anything at all. *Wear my blue baseball cap. Sing along to the radio. Have a turkey meatball sub.* "These are supposed to be big dreams, the important stuff, not everyday bullshit."

But Hope would just grin, chewing on the end of a cheap ballpoint pen she'd probably stolen from the cafeteria along with the check. "It's not cheating when you make the rules."

This version, the last version, I knew by heart. She gave it to me two weeks before she died, on what I'd always remember as her last good day.

"It's your turn now," she said as I opened the notebook. She still wore that cherry-pink lipstick, had the nurses paint it on every morning without fail, and now it slashed across her sallow face in a grim smile under the harsh hospital lights. "I'm tagging you in to the grand game called life. Don't you fucking dare let me down this time."

Sometimes, I thought it was her parting gift to me, the answer to every last one of the excuses holding me back, but some nights—nights I'm not proud of—it felt more like a curse. I'd look at that page, the commandments unfinished, and feel like she was taunting me, bullying me even from beyond the grave, trying to push me into a life I'd never wanted, using her trademark cocktail of guilt and sly persuasion to rig the game so only she could win. That list taunted me for months, until I was so wrapped up in razor-sharp guilt I could barely look at it, but every time I was ready to tear that damn book up and forget the whole thing, I'd remember her there in that hospital gown: brittle and frail, but so determined. She'd wanted this for me, enough for the both of us, and she wouldn't want anything ever again.

It turns out it's easy to change your life when you have nothing left to lose. That list became my bible, the only thing that gave me any faith or sense of solace in the darkness of last year. I had power over something, at

least: one moment at a time, one new thing she never got
to have, the neat check marks slowly marking that sacred
page. And now that her plan was in motion, gathering
speed in this foreign city so far from home, my world
getting bigger and brighter by the day in the crisp winds
of fall, I knew she'd been right.

Dammit.

Hope had always loved being right.

THE PROMISE

CHAPTER SIX

TESSA WAS BUSY Wednesday night. I thought about not going at all. I went back and forth in my head all day, wondering if people would notice if I showed up to a club alone. What would I do by myself, drifting on the edge of the crowd? I couldn't exactly pull out a sketchbook and draw to pass the time, in some sweaty downtown rock club with the lights dimmed low. But Hope's instructions were clear. Besides, the promise of Theo's invitation lingered, shimmering on the horizon.

He'd asked me. He wanted me there.

Maybe one day . . .

I took the subway after work into Boston, watching the jeweled city lights ripple on the dark water of the River Charles as we sped across the bridge, the skyline beckoning, blazing in the night. I had directions scribbled on a slip of paper in my jacket pocket, and I carefully made my way through the evening crowds, heading away from the glittering avenues filled with shoppers and busy stores until I strayed to the darker part of town. It was quieter here, a stretch of mostly shut galleries and record stores set grimy and graffitied between old warehouses and abandoned buildings. I walked faster, hitching my bag tight as I passed the cardboard blankets and heart-tugging rows of old, worn drunks, but as I approached the club, I realized the street was empty. Nobody was outside.

The door opened, and a burly guy with a greasy beard sat himself heavily on a folding chair.

"Hello?" I asked, looking around. I had the right day, the right venue, didn't I?

The bouncer looked at me, bored.

"I'm here for the Bad Alibi show. It said eight o'clock online."

He gave me a pitying look. "Doors at eight, support nine thirty. BA'll be on around eleven."

"Oh." I flushed. "Thanks."

I hurried away, around the corner and out of sight before anyone could witness my naïve mistake. I should have guessed the show wouldn't start so early, anyone who went to clubs would know, but I'd been so eager to see Theo again, and slip casual into the crowd like I did this all the time. I'd even rehearsed my nonchalant greeting, cool enough to ice over all my previous hot-mouthed fumbling. *Sure, I figured I'd stop by. Why not?* Now I had hours to kill.

I walked another couple of blocks until I found a bright-looking diner, the neon lights winking invitingly in the cold. Inside, a bleached waitress nodded me to a booth, and I ordered coffee and some hot chicken soup. I pulled a handful of paper napkins from the dispenser and began to doodle, idly sketching until the thin paper was covered in a mesh of boxes, neat and contained, as if I could corral my own skittering nerves by sheer force of will. I sipped on my coffee, spooned my soup slow, but still the hours dragged on, and all the while, I kept one anxious eye on my phone, watching for the moment I could stroll back to the club without betraying my own eagerness.

There was a banging on the window, and I looked up with a jolt as the doors swung open, and Kelsey barreled inside. She was dressed up under her leather jacket, in a short black skirt and thick tights, her boots clattering on the linoleum floor as she bounced over and slid into the booth opposite me. "What are you doing out here?" she demanded, looking as surprised as I felt. Her eyes were rimmed thickly in smudged midnight liner and her wrists jangled with a dozen bracelets as she reached across and stole the pack of dry crackers from the edge of my plate.

"I'm here for a show. Bad Alibi," I explained. The

waitress moved closer, waiting for Kelsey's order, but she cheerfully ignored her.

"Me too. Huh." She studied me. "Aren't you just full of surprises? I wouldn't have figured you for a rock fan."

"I contain multitudes," I shot back lightly.

She laughed. "Don't we all. You meeting people?"

I shook my head.

"Great, you can keep me company. My friends bailed on me, so now I'm stuck solo." Kelsey looked unconcerned by the thought of being alone. She got to her feet again, and I saw a flash of a red plaid shirt under her jacket and scarf. "Coming?"

I quickly left ten dollars for the check, and followed her back outside. Her boots strode, quick on the dirty sidewalk, and I hurried to keep up. "How did your book group go?"

"Ugh," Kelsey sighed. "There's this new girl now, she's always trying to run the show."

"Over you?" I asked, teasing.

Kelsey laughed again. "Hey! I'm a benevolent dictator, she's just a bitch."

"What are you going to do to overthrow her?"

"I don't know," she sighed. "I'm sure I'll think of something."

We rounded the corner back to the club, but this time,

the street was busy: a line snaking from the doorway all the way down two buildings back. Kelsey's face fell. "Shit, now I'll never get a ticket."

"That's OK," I said, "I'm on the list."

I felt Kelsey's eyes on me with a new admiration as I walked to the head of the line where the bouncer still lounged, reading a beat-up newspaper. "Claire Fortune," I told him, my pulse suddenly racing with nerves. What if Theo had forgotten to put me down, after all? What if this guy asked for ID? But after a moment of glancing at his clipboard, the bouncer nodded us through, bored.

"Thanks," Kelsey sounded impressed. "I owe you one."

I pushed the door open, and it took a second for my eyes to adjust to the dark. We were in a narrow hallway, the walls papered with fading show bills and lipstick graffiti. A staircase led us down into a small basement room with a stage set up at one end, a bar at the other, and about a hundred bodies in between.

Kelsey surveyed the room with a practiced air. "I need a drink." She struck out for the bar, and I followed, looking around. There were bearded hipsters, and punk guys, and girls with vintage lipstick and cute print dresses, too, all of them slowly shedding their winter jackets and loitering, impatient near the stage.

"Jack and coke," Kelsey instructed the lithe, tattooed

guy behind the bar. She quirked her eyebrow at me.

"Just the coke, thanks."

He slammed our drinks on the pockmarked bar and yawned. "Service with a smile," Kelsey quipped. I reached for my wallet again, but she waved it away. "My treat. It's a good thing you're such a cheap date. Cheers." She clinked her glass to mine, then drank, her dark eyes already searching around the room. She waved to a few people, nodded too, but didn't shift from her position beside me.

"Did you see Mika's bullshit notice about dress code at the café?" she asked. " 'Professional attire,' c'mon, we're serving coffee, not teleconferencing with the New Jersey office. I swear, he wants to turn us into Starbucks."

"I like Starbucks," I replied evenly.

"Of course you do." Kelsey gave me a look. "You probably Instagram pumpkin spice season, floss twice a day, and sing along to Taylor Swift in the car."

I looked at her, puzzled. "Why would those be bad things? You don't know me," I added, feeling strangely defensive. I liked the anonymity I had at Wired, liked the privacy and ease with which I slipped unnoticed through the crew, but still, something in her certain tone made me pause. She was just like Jamie the other night. She thought she had me all figured out. "You don't know anything about me at all."

Kelsey blinked slowly, but she didn't back down. Her lips edged in a smile, still the know-it-all. "So, kitty cat's got claws, after all." She smirked. "Good for you."

I shook my head. I didn't want a fight, not tonight. "I'm going to find a bathroom," I said instead, and left her there surveying the room like it was her own personal domain.

As I slipped my way through the dark crowd, I wondered why she was so defensive; easy to joke, but quick to slam those steel shutters down and keep her distance. Every nice word had a bitter aftertaste, a sugar coating dissolving to leave a tiny razor blade. She judged me, but never asked for more. Either way, it was my own fault, I reminded myself, rinsing my hands over the cracked porcelain tile. I'd learned to hold my cards so close to my chest, I could feel the steady ring of my heartbeat under the ace, secrets hidden so deep even a whisper wouldn't sound. Was it any wonder that Kelsey thought I had nothing to hide?

When I rejoined the crowd, the support act were on stage: a monochrome pair frantically strumming their guitars to an ambivalent crowd. I headed back to the bar and found Kelsey still holding court—with Theo.

My breath caught. Messy hair, dark denim, his bag still slung across his chest. He had on a dark T-shirt with scribbled type I couldn't read, and the pale elegance of his bare arm—the faint curve of bicep, the shadowed forearm stretching down to those steady hands—sent every thought tumbling from my mind. You could have asked me my own name and gotten nothing from me that night, not a goddamn thing.

It wasn't fair.

"Look, I found your friend," Kelsey said meaningfully, once I'd steeled myself enough to approach them.

Theo smiled at me, warm as molasses. "You made it. I didn't know if you were coming."

"I figured it could be fun," I said, trying to stay cool even as my blood ran hotter, my pulse beating in time with the drums rattling through the room.

"I don't know about that." His grin turned playful. "Guy's threatening to play Nirvana covers all night, it might not be pretty. He's my roommate," he explained to us. "The rest of the band, too."

"Sounds . . . peaceful." I grinned back.

"I wish. Except it's not the drums that keep me up, it's Moose playing Xbox with some kid in Omaha at three in the morning." Theo rolled his eyes.

"Moose?"

"You'll see." Theo smiled at me again, so easy, I could almost forget every fumbled apology and halting conversation I'd tried to have. Even the memory of my humiliating kiss couldn't mar this moment in the dark of the club, with the crowd shifting closer and a new heat of possibility, bright in the air.

There wasn't anywhere in the world I'd rather be.

"Finally." Kelsey's bored exclamation broke through the din, and I turned as the next band strolled out on stage. The lead singer was tall, all leather and sienna curls with his guitar holstered like a weapon across his body. There was another guy behind the drums, fierce concentration on his compact face, and a larger guy on bass guitar, face hidden behind a wild thatch of dirty blonde beard and messy too-long hair.

"Moose," I guessed, and heard Theo chuckle beside me.

"That's the one. It started as a bet," he said, casually moving half a step closer and leaning in so I could hear his voice over the bursts of static soundcheck. "Guy offered him a dollar a day he went without shaving. We all pitched in once he hit a month, and he's still going strong. Nearly a year now; he says he won't give it up until we owe him an even grand."

I didn't reply. I could feel his breath, hot against my cheek, and the warmth from his body, a halo just out of reach.

"Time to get a good spot," Kelsey decided. "Come on."

She took off, striking a path through the packed bodies

with all the determination of a battlefield general. I looked to Theo, and he answered with a shrug and a smile, so we fell into Kelsey's wake, following the noises of surprise and annoyance as she pushed them out of the way with a well-placed elbow or a low, pointed kick. Soon, we had the best view in the house, two rows back from the stage, where the lights burned hotly and anticipation shifted, restless all around.

The singer, Guy, gripped the mic and glared at the crowd. "You fuckers ready to make some noise?" he demanded, the words softened by his British accent. The crowd whooped and cheered. "Yeah, you're going to have to do better than that."

He nodded to the other guys, then launched into a fast song, all wild chords and crashing beat, his lyrics howled too quick to hold, something about a girl, and a plan, and a bedroom door; his body flailed across the narrow stage, a man possessed.

They were good. Chaotic and messy, but with the hooks to pull it through. You could feel it in the crowd, that moment when everyone decides it's worth the cover charge and the hours they spent waiting, when they give it up and let the music take them under, and this band? They had us all in the palm of their hands in ten seconds flat. Even I forgot Theo, there beside me, and Kelsey's judgmental stare, and let myself feel it, the deep striking bass and crashing lift of the melody, quicksilver through my tired veins as my synapses sparked alive and I remembered what it was like to lose myself with everyone else, strung out on the same looming waves, a single crest in the ocean, a rallying cry in the dark night.

People never took me for a music girl. Even Hope was surprised the day she scrolled, bored, through my phone for music in the car and found the world I kept hidden between my headphones. I didn't broadcast it like some people, with band stickers and vintage shirts, lyrics scribbled on notepad covers, and playlists shared all day long. To me, music was a private conversation between me and the song playing on the other side of the shivering speaker set. I didn't stay in a straight and narrow lane, from Lucinda Williams to Jamie Cullum, Drake and Beastie Boys and Florence and the Machine, and yes, even Taylor Swift. I would raid my parents' old record collection, feeling a begrudging spark of respect when I found their Fleetwood Mac vinyls, pressed and precious, and the dog-eared Motown jukebox hits my dad always sang along to in the car.

It was all part of the same miracle to me: how brushstrokes on a page, a few printed words, those chords strummed sweetly into the smoky evening air could make you stop in your tracks, hold your breath to feel something so deeply, so profound. Art was like that, it could set you free, or reveal the bars set just outside the window; it could show you a life you'd never dreamed of, and make a heart swell or break. And nights like this, in that small, dirty club, watching the band fall deeper into their songs, and the crowd leave themselves behind—it was a masterpiece, all on its own.

It was three songs later before we all surfaced, as the drummer threw down his sticks with a clatter, and Moose's guitar wailed into static, Guy turning to gulp from the beer bottle waiting set on a speaker amp. I gasped for air, my heart racing in my ears, the crowd blinking awake from our communal dream and remembering themselves again. I caught Kelsey's eye, seeing the flush in her cheeks and the bright fire in her gaze. "They're great!" I yelled to be heard.

"Not bad, I guess." She shrugged, still clinging to her detached cool, but her own quick breaths betrayed her. I looked around for Theo, still soaring, but all I saw was the back of his head as he ducked away through the crowd, the neon glare of his cellphone, gripped tightly in one hand. I didn't have time to wonder: before I could take another ragged breath, there was a war-cry of drums from the stage, and then we were gone again, lost to the sharp endorphins and crash of chords and bass, lifted out of our frail bodies and into something greater, just for a little while.

THEO REAPPEARED JUST AS the band stumbled off stage looking drunk on the crowd's applause and their second encore.

"Everything OK?" I couldn't stop myself asking. The audience was in no hurry to disperse, they lingered, talking in raucous tones and still swaying to the ghost of melodies gone by.

"What? Yeah, fine." He gave me an absent smile, as if part of him was still outside, huddled in the cold with his phone pressed to his ear. "What did you think of the show?"

"They're good. Really good."

"I know." Theo looked rueful. "It would be easier to deal with Guy's rock star routine if they didn't have talent."

"That bad?"

"You'll see." His smile brightened a little, coming back into focus as if from far away. "Come meet everyone."

"Sure. Kelsey?" I asked.

"I guess."

He led us through the crowd to a door back by the stage. It wasn't a big venue, no security here to bar the way for adoring fans, but I still felt a frisson of excitement following Theo into that off-limits hallway. Equipment and boxes were piled haphazardly in the way, and a door was open, a dressing room of sorts with disintegrating furniture, black lights, and a clatter of empty bottles. The band already had company: Moose was collapsed on a threadbare sofa with a couple of icy-looking girls, while the drummer rattled anxiously against a bare dresser, and Guy paced, clearly still pumped.

"Did you see that?" he demanded, when Theo stepped into the room. Guy strode over and clasped him in a hug, pounding him on the back in an amped up rhythm. "Fuckin' aces, man. Fuckin' A."

"You didn't altogether suck," Theo told him, good-natured, and Guy barked with laughter.

"Tell that to the crowd, they couldn't get enough, man." His eyes landed on Kelsey and me. An eyebrow quirked. "And who are these lovely ladies? Come on in, don't mind the sweat and grime. Moose, where are your manners? Get these girls a drink!"

He was all swagger and theatrics, gesturing wildly as he pulled up a couple of chairs and fetched us beers. Up close, I could see he was made for the stage: his broad features almost too large for his head, the kind of face that's always in motion and needs a spotlight, to be seen, all the way to the back. The group around us swelled, more people arriving from the main club, until the room felt packed, with a loose, loud party feel.

"So what did you think, ladies?" Guy asked, when I

was perched on a seat, and Kelsey kicked back in a chair, drinking beer. "Did you like what you saw?"

Kelsey deployed her shrug with devastating accuracy. "You've got potential. A little originality wouldn't hurt, but hey, you guys are just starting out, right?"

A girl beside me inhaled in shock, but there was a teasing smile on Kelsey's lips I'd never seen before, a vivid purpose in her smudged, smoky gaze. I followed her stare all the way to Guy's open mouth. He snorted with laughter. "Tell us how you really feel, why don't you, luv?"

Kelsey smirked. "I'm sorry, were you looking for a fangirl? There's plenty out front, I could go fetch one for you if you want your ego stroked."

Guy grinned. "Nah, let them wait."

He took a beer and collapsed heavily on the chair beside her, leaning in to murmur something only she could hear. The other girls in the room narrowed their eyes, watching his arm drape around her shoulder, their heads bent close. Kelsey shot me a quick glance, smug with victory, and I realized that this had been her plan all along. Indifference as bait, to reel in the most prized catch of all. And Guy couldn't get enough.

I felt a sense of betrayal, swift and hot, and I had to look away. I didn't understand it, the games people played. They were sparring with each other, bitching and teasing, like that was worth anything at all. They could talk around each other all night, as if they had all the time in the world. As if moments like this would last forever.

"So, is this what you wanted?" Theo asked quietly beside me.

I turned.

"*Hang backstage with the band*," he quoted, watching me.

I felt my cheeks heat. "It's not . . . that wasn't my list, the one you found. It belonged to my best friend," I added softly, twisting my bracelet again, a nervous habit. The small room was packed, but still, nobody was listening to us over here in the corner. "She kept it for all kinds of crazy stuff," I told him. "Dreams, ambitions, things she wanted to experience, before it was too late."

The past tense weighed heavy with every word, and I felt a suddenly rush of something like bravery. I didn't want to be like Kelsey, spinning circles in a game that could never be won: revealing nothing, asking for nothing in return.

"She's gone now," I told Theo. "She died before she got to finish it, so now it's my turn. Cancer," I added, before he could ask. "She didn't live to see nineteen."

Theo's clear-eyed gaze didn't waver. "I'm sorry," he

said softly, and unlike the platitudes I'd born that year, I could tell he meant it.

"Me too." I felt the sadness swell, a familiar ache behind my ribcage. "She would have loved this, she was always the life of the party." I looked around, at the clatter of noise and laughter and flirting, hungry smiles. "She would have given Kelsey a run for her money, though," I added. Guy was arguing loudly now, trying to convince her of something while Kelsey just smirked at him and ran her fingertip around the rim of her bottle in a silent invitation.

Theo grinned and shook his head, watching them. "Why do girls always go for the lead singer?"

"Because we want someone to write songs about us." I smiled. Theo arched an eyebrow. "Come on, you have to admit it's pretty tempting, the idea of being immortalized. A public declaration. Our way to live forever. That was another thing on Hope's list," I confided, smiling at the memory. "She wanted a boy to write a song about her."

"And did she get it?"

I nodded. "She seduced this guy who played in coffee shops around the city, she was like a guided missile, he didn't stand a chance." A smile played on the edge of my lips at the memory: Hope's careful lingering after one of his shows, the wide-eyed interest, the coo of her voice, leaning in. "Her plan backfired though." I grinned. "He wrote this terrible song, tried rhyming her name with everything he could think of."

"Rope. Nope," Theo suggested.

"Soap. Dope." I laughed along. "It's not exactly going to set the charts on fire anytime soon, but, she got to tick it off, at least."

"How many do you have left on the list?"

I let out a slow sigh, reality settling back around my neck in a cold, heavy weight. "You saw it. I've barely gotten started."

"Still, you've got tonight, right? Another one down." Theo's smile was encouraging.

"Thanks to you."

I paused, the question itching at me. I knew I should ignore it, should just be like the other girls in the room, so casual and undemanding, but I felt it bubble up, too insistent to ignore. "Did Brianna not want to come tonight?" I tried for casual, but even I could hear the quiet intensity behind my nonchalant tone.

Theo paused. He didn't look over, just sat beside me, watching the room. "We . . . decided to take a break."

His voice was even, but my heart lurched, absorbed his words for a brief moment, then took flight.

"Oh," I exhaled, as a thousand questions sounded like drumbeats in my mind. "I'm sorry."

Theo turned then, tilted his head towards me with a look in his eyes that I'd never forget.

"Are you?" he asked quietly.

Our gaze caught. The drums beat louder, reverberating through my entire body until I was just empty impact and the heart-stopping crash of pure desire. I was on the edge of something, poised to fall into his waiting blue eyes, but for all my scorning Kelsey's cool games, when it came to stepping off that ledge myself, I couldn't take the leap. I was paralyzed from saying the one true thing that sang with every shaking heartbeat, my voice failing me, my glittering hopes binding my lips tightly closed.

No, I wasn't sorry, not at all.

I don't know how long we stayed that way, waiting to spill all my private secrets into the waiting, smoky air, but it felt like an eternity. Then Theo's phone sounded again, flashing bright with a demanding ring.

He looked away, checking the screen, and the shutters crashed hard over his face. In an instant, that golden thread between us was severed, the moment melting away like it had never existed at all.

"I've got to go," he said shortly. "Sorry, I can't stay . . . I'll see you around, OK?"

He was gone from the room before I could even exhale, and although I waited there, in amongst the droll gossip and strummed guitars for another half hour, he didn't return.

IT WAS TOO LATE for the subway, so I walked back alone across the bridge at two a.m., watching barges drift lazily beneath the darkened steel, and the lights of the city beyond wink their promises to the black horizon. I could feel it, even then, the shift in the air like the first pale rays of spring, the day the earth shrugs a little on its axis, turning slowly towards another season. Autumn was still bleeding into winter in that chilled corner of the world, but my heart was already tasting that sweet future. A slow awakening after years of slumber, a gasp of sunshine through the dark, misty clouds.

A thousand headlights sped past on the ribbon of highway, and I saw his eyes in every glimpse of light. Theo. *Theo.* He was a part of my pulse now, a heartbeat sounding, low and steady with every breath. I knew it would end in heartbreak, my own if I was lucky, but that night, I let myself hold his memory close, suspended in that dark corner of that backstage room together, close enough to touch. Even now, I can see us there, feel the wild hope that beat so furiously in my chest. If I'd managed to say something. If I'd told him the truth, from the start . . .

But I can't change it now. And if I'm honest, it was already too late for that, too far down that hurtling one-way track, tumbling headfirst into the sun. So I walked home alone, hugging secrets to my chest that burned like fire.

THE PROMISE

CHAPTER SEVEN

HALLOWEEN ARRIVED WITH the last blue skies of fall. Mika demanded we all adopt the festive spirit for the café, so I spent an afternoon with craft supplies and a row of fat new pumpkins, carving into their flesh and roasting the innards to string in autumn garlands around the room. The jack-o-lanterns sat in a stately line above the coffee machine, keeping watch over the café with their ghoulish smiles.

"If you look at the one on the end just right, it kind of looks like you, Kelsey." JJ peered up at them. "It's got this suspicious sneer. And that one's like Mika—look at all that straw sprouting out of the top of its head. Claire?"

"Must be a coincidence." I turned away, hiding my smile under the dark bangs of my bobbed wig. Mika had insisted on costumes, too, but I didn't need convincing. Halloween had always been my favorite holiday, an excuse to unleash that mischievous inner child for one lone day of mayhem, to don a costume and disappear into the idea of being someone else. Last year, even Hope had insisted on a monster mask and fake bolt through her neck. "Frankenstein's monster, hooked up to his machines," she'd cracked all day long, waving her IV tubes and heart monitor sensors until I laughed along too, so hard it hurt to breathe. This time, I spent a giddy afternoon trawling every thrift store along Mass Ave to assemble my costume. I found the perfect witch's gown, the heavy bodice embroidered in black, with long skirts that swung low around my lace-up boots with every step. The sleeves trailed in wispy black lace down to fingers I adorned with heavy silver costume rings and tipped with black and scarlet polish, but best of all was the wig. I picked it up as an afterthought from the rainbow display at the register, a nondescript little bobbed style in inky black. Somehow, with my hair tucked up tight underneath, and those glossy strands curved sleek around my cheekbones, I looked like a stranger. My eyes seemed larger, their gaze now foreign and elusive, and topped with a crooked pointy hat, my transformation was complete.

Even Kelsey was approving, at least that's what I figured when she dug deep into her bag, then held my chin tight as she smudged a smoky layer of liner around my eyes. She was caked in white makeup and gruesome dark liner herself, her torn nightgown making her a fearsome zombie bride. "Sexy," she drawled, stepping back to admire her handiwork. "Teddy boy won't know what hit him."

"Him, or somebody else . . ." I gave her a mysterious wink. She cackled with laughter and sent me away with a slap on my ass as I spun back to work, my skirts swirling a halo in my path. I felt lighter, freer in my disguise despite the weight of fabric cloaking every step. I whirled through the coffee shop all morning, greeting regulars and passing out candy from a hollowed-out pumpkin to anyone who'd made even a half-hearted shrug towards a costume. I didn't even miss a beat when the door burst open with a boom of ominous laughter—thanks to Mika and his sound effects— and Theo materialized before me in a long tan duster over a khaki shirt; an outback-style hat perched at a jaunty angle over his unmistakable brow like he'd just emerged from the depths of the jungle.

"Indiana Jones!" I laughed.

He did a double take, eyes widening as he recognized me beneath my disguise. "Claire?"

"Who's Claire?" I teased, then swirled away, my heart racing—but not with the sick lurch of nerves that had always haunted me in his presence, no, this was something lighter, delicious. My blood was shimmering with a reckless alchemy, and it buoyed me onwards to casually clear the tables before returning to the register, where Theo waited, watching me anew.

"You look different." He tilted his head slightly, as if trying to align two different pictures of me.

"And you look . . . more you," I decided. I reached for a paper cup and started Theo's coffee. He didn't need to order; I already knew it by heart.

"The kids in school get into it in a big way." He smiled. "It was impossible to teach all morning. You can't move for slutty kittens and superheroes."

I laughed. "How can you even make a kitten slutty?"

"I don't know, but it involves fishnet stockings and whiskers." He took a miniature candy bar from the bowl by the register and looked me up and down. I felt his gaze like warm honey on my skin, before admiring eyes met mine again. "Cast any spells yet today?"

"A couple." I gave another mysterious smile.

"Have they come true?"

I met his gaze dead-on. "I'll let you know."

There was a beat, shimmering with possibility, but even in this new guise, I wasn't bold enough to hold it for long. I busied myself with his coffee again. "I like yours though," I said, from behind the safety of the espresso machine and those wondrous bangs. "Very dashing."

Theo grinned. "I'm recycling. This was my favorite costume as a kid."

"You must have been a big kid to fit in that coat," I joked, and was rewarded with a laugh.

"Not quite," Theo said. "I made some updates. The original had more craft paper and paste."

"Craft paper . . ." I let out a nostalgic sigh. "God, I would get through a truck-load for all my costumes. Halloween was big in my suburb," I explained. "Trick-or-treating was major business; you had to make sure you got the maximum candy, enough to last months."

"Of course." Theo nodded, mock-serious. "We would plan our route for days. You have to hit the right houses, none of that candy apple bullshit."

"My best year, we made this amazing dinosaur costume," I remembered. "I had a cardboard spine, papier-mâché head, the works. I made out like a bandit."

"A sugar-fuelled, hyper-active bandit."

I laughed. "I don't know how my parents handled me; I was probably bouncing off the walls for days." I paused and glanced around the room. "I guess that's why I like this holiday. Everyone gets to act like a kid again, pretend to be whatever they want."

"And you want to be a powerful witch?" His smile was teasing.

"We prefer 'sorceress.' " I set his coffee in front of him. "On the house, magic charms optional."

Theo picked it up. "If I turn into a frog, I'll know who to find for a kiss."

His casual words landed between us with all the impact of a tornado. Suddenly, the room felt charged, electric. My heart spun wildly, and I swear I would have disappeared into the eye of the storm if I hadn't been holding onto the counter for dear life.

"I was thinking," Theo said suddenly. "About that list of yours."

I stopped. "What about it?"

"Just, your friend had the right idea, planning for the extraordinary." He looked thoughtful, toying with the sleeve on his coffee cup. "So many things, experiences, you let them slip away because you don't make the time."

"Time wasn't a friend to her." My reply was cooler than I meant.

"I didn't mean that," Theo said immediately. "I'm sorry. I've just been wondering about it, that's all. What I would put on my list, if I had to make the choice."

I relaxed again. "Well, you got to be Indy again."

"True." Theo smiled. "I can check that off."

"What else?" I asked, and he paused a moment.

"It's stupid."

"No, tell me!"

"I guess, I always wanted to move to California, someday. See the ocean on the other side of the country." Theo looked away, bashful. "What about you? What would be on your list?"

Kiss you, my heart screamed. *Kiss you properly this time, and never come up for air.*

"I don't know . . ." I helped myself to a tiny Reese's cup from the candy bowl and carefully unwrapped it, to buy time as much as keep my hands from reaching for him. "What Hope wanted, too, I guess. To live in the world, really feel it. Leave my mark."

"I used to think that too, that I wanted some kind of legacy." Theo drummed his fingers on that cardboard cup sleeve. "But now, I'm thinking more that the moment matters. What we do right now, not what people will say about us when we're long gone. Taking chances, like it's Halloween every day." His lips crinkled into a self-deprecating smile, but the look in his eyes was something quieter, a hushed intensity.

I was frozen in the beam. "What chance would you take?" I asked carefully, breath suspended in my lungs.

He opened his mouth to answer, but his reply was drowned out by another burst of eerie sound effects from the doorway. "Well, well, what do we have here?" His roommate, Guy, sauntered in, wrapped up in a leather jacket that had seen better days, fingerless gloves curled around an ancient thermos flask. The air shifted, expanding from the heated bubble between us to let the rest of the world in, a rush of sanity again.

Guy intercepted Kelsey on her way to the register and tugged at a loose strip of her gown. "What a charming bride you are."

"Bite me," Kelsey snapped back, but there was a playful edge to her tone.

"You're the zombie." Guy gave Theo and I a smirk, but Kelsey hooked her fingers over the top of his sweater and pulled him halfway over the bar. She kissed him deliberately, until suddenly he winced, and pulled away.

"Ow." Guy touched his lip, looking pained.

Kelsey grinned. "You asked for it."

She swung away into the back without another word. For all her games and manipulations, the girl knew how to make an exit. Guy stared after her for a moment, then caught us watching, and gave a rueful smile. "She's a spitfire, alright."

"So how's tricks with you fine folk?" Guy asked, taking a small model pumpkin and juggling it, one-handed. "I'm surprised to see you here," he added to Theo. Then he looked back and forth between us. "I stand corrected. Not so surprising at all."

Theo rolled his eyes. "I needed a break from grading."

"Of course you did. And what better break than caffeine and good company?" Guy waggled his eyebrows, and I felt my cheeks flush, despite myself.

"I should get back," Theo said, and gave me an apologetic smile. "Thanks for the coffee."

"Anytime."

I watched, disappointed, as he stepped back into the

bustle of the street beyond. Whatever he had been about to say was gone with him now, out into the cold.

When I looked back, Guy was looking at me with an arched eyebrow. "You two seem friendly," he said.

"We're friends," I answered. I began wiping down the counter, as Guy continued his juggling tricks.

"You should call him," he said. "Poor guy deserves a break. He's been grading papers for the last century, has barely been home in days. Either that, or he's reconciled with dear Brianna."

I knocked a stack of glasses, and had to leap to stop them tumbling to the ground.

Brianna—again?

"I jest." Guy tossed the pumpkin to me, and I had to grab to stop it hurtling into a stack of dishes. "Those two are ancient history. And it was never much of an epic love story to start with, in case you were wondering."

"I wasn't," I lied.

"She just showed up one day," he continued, musing. "And never seemed to leave. Don't get me wrong, Bri's a sweet girl, and she would make a mean stir-fry for us lads, but she didn't have that certain *je ne sais quois*. Of course, what do I know?" He shrugged. "Theo keeps his cards close to his chest, that boy. Forever getting mysterious calls and disappearing in the middle of the night. I've often thought him a secret agent, or mercenary assassin."

"Who's an assassin?" Kelsey emerged from the back, this time with her bag hitched on one shoulder.

"Teddy boy," Guy answered. He casually held Kelsey's coat up, helping her into it, then dropped a kiss on the top of her head. "He's a man of mystery. Your Claire should watch out."

"Claire can take care of herself." For once, there was no sarcasm in Kelsey's tone. "She's something of a mystery herself."

"Curiouser and curiouser." Guy winked at me, "Then they're the perfect match."

I WORKED THE REST of the day, dispensing candy prizes and coffees frothed with mountainous peaks of whipped cream, until at last, Mika waved me off duty with a swirl of velvet cape. "Go, leave, before this place traps you here forever," he declared, lisping slightly through his plastic fangs. "I'll be in the coffin in the back."

"But you'll stay young forever." I suddenly leaned up and kissed him on the cheek. "Thanks for all the holiday spirit."

He looked stunned. "Uh, sure. No problem."

I went to grab my things before I could feel embarrassed. But I'd needed to thank him for this gift: without him, I'd never have dressed up alone, or felt the freedom of my brief disguise. Like with Hope's list, I still seemed to need a prompt, that gentle hand pushing me out of my cozy safe corner and into the waiting adventure.

One of these days, I would have to learn to do it all myself.

I walked the long way home through the park that afternoon, still swinging my pumpkin basket of candy as the skies faded to a cool dusk. Our park. It was foolish to think of my brief moments with Theo like pieces of a puzzle strung together, but the city was taking on a new shape through his blue-eyed lens. *There* was the road we'd walked down, *there*, the bench we'd paused to eat. Today, there was some kind of kids' party in progress, over by the play area with its cherry-red climbing bars. Hoards of tiny characters swarmed and laughed and screamed out as they played, a renegade crew of bandits and policemen, fairy princesses and snug plush pets. Their parents lingered on the sidelines, keeping one watchful eye on the crowd as they chatted, hands wrapped around steaming flasks.

My own parents would be a thousand miles away, answering the door to our own parade of trick-or-treaters. Mom always liked to buy the candy in bulk by September. "They'll only jack the prices up," she'd say, hauling enough mini Snickers bars into our cart to feed a small army. She stored them in our garage pantry, but by the time Halloween rolled around, Dad and I had already sneaked half the stash away. Every year like clockwork, she'd be surprised by the diminished stores, and every year, we'd both swear our innocence, wide-eyed. "You must not have bought as much as you thought," my dad would say, sending me a wink behind her back.

Suddenly, I missed them so much it hurt.

I sat on one of the benches and watched the party for a while, trying to resist the hopeful ache in my heart. *If I could just have a real conversation with them . . . If they could only understand . . .* My fingers itched to call them, and I turned my phone over and over in my hands, knowing what awaited me on the end of the line, but still compelled to dial the number nonetheless.

My father picked up this time.

"Daddy?" My voice stuck in my throat. "Happy Halloween."

"Claire." He exhaled in a rush. "Are you OK, sweetie? What's wrong?"

"Nothing's wrong." I tried to swallow back my sadness. "I just wanted to say hi."

"Oh." There was a long pause.

"I want you to know I'm alright." I started babbling, my words a rush of guilt and regret. "I have an apartment and a job, I'm doing fine on my own. My roommate's a student here. She's really nice, everyone's nice." Something twisted, deep in my chest. "I don't want you to think something's wrong all the time. I want to just be able to call and say hi without it being a big deal."

"Honey." Dad's voice sounded thick. "You know you can call anytime."

"But Mom . . . Every time, all she does is talk about how she wants me to come home."

"We both do," he said gently. "We miss you. We worry, it's what parents do. You belong here with us."

"No," I corrected him, feeling that stubborn shard buried deep in my chest. "Not anymore. You know I need to do this. Don't you want me to have a life of my own?"

He gave a weary sigh. "You know I do, sweetie."

"So why can't you be happy for me?" I couldn't keep my voice from cracking, raw in the end. "I'm doing what I always wanted. What Hope wanted."

"Hope's gone now, sweetie, and running away like this won't bring her back. She's not the one who wakes up in the middle of the night and doesn't know where her baby girl is. Your mom, she's going through hell right now."

I closed my eyes, trying not to feel the weight of

their disappointment crushing down on me. "I'm not your baby girl anymore," I said softly. "I'm an adult now. This is what adults do, dad. They go off to college, they get jobs, and move away from home—"

"And if that's what you want, we can make that happen," he interrupted, eager now. "I've been looking at colleges nearby, something in the state. You could take classes, part-time, I'm sure they would work something out. We'd help you with an apartment in town if you want—"

"No, Dad, you're not listening. It's not about that."

"Then what? Please, honey, help me understand. What is it you're looking for out there?"

I opened my eyes again. The sun had sunk just below the tree line, casting long shadows between the glint of the streetlights. Students walked back from the campus, and the kids in their costumes were being hustled, two by two, back towards the parking lot, but still, the city burned with so much life amongst the darkness; a million lives careening past my orbit, a million restless hearts searching just as hard as mine.

"A life of my own," I said quietly. "I'm sorry, I just can't come home. Not yet. Give my love to Mom," I added quickly, and then hung up before he could say another word.

I WALKED THE REST of the way home in a fog, torn between the certainty that I was doing the right thing and that chilled creeping guilt. Then I turned the corner to my apartment building and found Theo waiting on my front steps. He rose to greet me, his smile cutting through the dark, and I knew I was exactly where I was supposed to be.

THE PROMISE

CHAPTER EIGHT

"Hey." HE TOOK a couple of steps towards me. "I realized I don't have your number."

I came to a stop in front of him, my heart beating double-quick time. "What's up?" I asked, so casual, as if finding him there hadn't ruffled me one inch. "Guy and Kelsey taken over the apartment with some kind of screaming match?"

He chuckled. "Don't joke. They kept us all up the other night."

With what, I didn't need to ask. I looked away, and Theo shifted his weight—still dressed in his explorer's coat and ten-gallon hat. "I don't know if you have plans tonight, but I thought, maybe . . ." He paused, then gave me a smile so nakedly hopeful that it took my breath away. "We should go out."

It was a declaration. A statement of intent. And in that moment it folded the world over on itself from a place of shaky *perhaps* and *what if?* to something simple and solid.

"Yes," I answered immediately. "OK."

"Tonight?"

I nodded. His grin widened.

"I just need to go change."

"It's still Halloween," he pointed out. "We'll blend right in."

He was right. And besides, I wanted to keep the bravery of this disguise a little longer, feel the freedom hiding behind my new black bangs. It was a cheat code, perhaps, but I would take it this one time.

"OK then," I said slowly, the moment dawning on me bright as a summer's sky. This was happening, and it was too late to turn back now. "Let's go."

Theo offered his arm to me, like an old-fashioned gentleman, and in my swirling skirts and bodice, it seemed only natural for me to slip my hand into the crook of his elbow and fall into step beside him. It was dark, and the streets around campus were wilder than ever, thick with throngs of spacemen and pirates, and girls teetering in their fishnets and bunny ears. "So, we have some options." Theo cleared his throat. "There's a party at some warehouse, Guy and the rest are going."

I paused. The gift of Theo—alone, a date—seemed too precious to waste on a sweaty mass of noise and bodies. "I don't know if I'm in the party mood . . ." I hedged.

"Me either." He smiled. "OK, next, there's a Rocky Horror screening at the Brattle?"

"I've always wanted to see that," I said, torn. "And we're in costume, but . . . ." I gave him a sideways glance, shy. "Do you want to just see some of the city, walk around, or get some food?" Again, sitting in the dark in silence beside him would have been a cruel joke after how long I'd spent wanting only to see his face, and discover every last secret he was hiding. I wondered if he would think my suggestion boring, but Theo looked relieved.

"That sounds perfect. I actually have some place I think you'd like. It's over the bridge a ways."

"Your side of town."

"The wrong side of the river," he joked along, but there was a rueful edge to his tone.

"Whatever you want," I said, and gently squeezed his arm. "Tonight you can lead me astray."

I'd meant it teasingly, but Theo paused on the sidewalk and looked down at me.

"I promise, you're safe with me," he said, his forehead knit slightly, those blue eyes as sincere as they come.

It struck me, clean through my chest. I laughed and smiled, and started walking again, making some joke about exploring the wilds of the city, protecting me from rolling boulders in true Indiana Jones fashion, but inside, I knew what he'd said, so sweetly, was already a lie.

My heart wasn't safe from him at all.

THE PROMISE

W E TOOK THE MBTA subway across to Boston, crushed together in the sticky car with the rush hour crowds. Every jolt and sway of the shaky journey sent me inches closer to him, until Theo rested a casual hand on the small of my back to steady me; bringing me into the warm circle of his embrace. For once, I was glad the roar of the trains drowned out any hint of conversation; at least then I could be sure my racing heartbeat wouldn't be heard. It was enough to be standing there, feeling the heat of his solid form like the center of the universe, hurling us onward beneath the earth until the doors shuddered open and the crowds pushed up, upwards through the tunnels until we emerged, giddy on the other side of the world.

"Hungry?" Theo asked, when we were clear from the turnstiles. My stomach was tied in knots, but I nodded.

"What is this neighborhood?" I asked, looking around. The streets were quaint, narrow cobblestones in places sloping up the hill, with older brownstone townhouses and tiny corner restaurants. "It looks almost European. Not that I've ever actually been to Europe," I added quickly.

"Me neither," he said with a sigh. "But I'd like to, one day. Rome, Paris, Barcelona . . ."

"Where's that patron when you need him?"

He chuckled. "Probably living right here. This is

Beacon Hill," he explained. "It used to be the wealthy part of the city, but there were publishing houses and literary salons here too. Louisa May Alcott lived here, Thoreau too."

"I love that. The history you get in these cities." I looked around, imagining the streets hundreds of years ago. "It probably didn't look much different to how it does today. Back home, they pretty much tear down any building over twenty years old, but here . . . who knows who walked on these very same streets?"

"So you *are* a romantic at heart."

I turned. "What do you mean?"

"I don't know, you seem so . . . self-contained, sometimes. Like Kelsey." Theo regarded me carefully. "It's hard to tell what's going on beneath the surface with you."

I had to laugh at that. I felt like such an open book to him, all my feelings shining as bright as the neon streetlights lining our path.

"So, food," I said, changing the subject.

"Priorities." He chuckled.

"Always."

"After you." He nodded to a store on the corner. When I stepped inside, I found it was a wine shop with a deli section buried in the back. Cheese wheels jostled with briny bowls of olives, and thick slabs of chocolate were stacked behind the glass, dark and rich. We picked out breads and cheeses and spreads until we had enough to feed a small army, then took our crisp paper bags back out onto the street again. "You'll have to trust me for this next part," Theo warned me with a mischievous grin.

"That sounds dangerous," I laughed.

"Only a little." He led me halfway up the hill, to one of the elegant brownstone buildings. He paused at the top step, and looked cautiously around.

"Why do I get the feeling we're not supposed to be here?" I asked, only teasing a little.

"That depends," he said, reaching for the door. There were buzzers for several apartments, but instead, he entered five digits on the security pad. "If they've changed the code . . ." The final number entered, the panel flashed green, and the door opened with a click.

"Thank you, Professor Martindale." Theo held the door open for me, then quickly led me up the first flight of a polished oak staircase. The building was hushed, our footsteps swallowed by the thick, luxurious rugs on the floors. "He taught a seminar last year, but was too lazy to ever come to campus, so I would have to schlep all the way here at seven on a Saturday morning."

We circled up another flight, higher still. One of the apartment doors suddenly opened. I froze. It was an older woman, dripping with pearls and tweed. She didn't notice us at first, trying to control the tiny yapping dog twisting loops in his leash.

Busted.

I was already trying to think of excuses, but Theo didn't miss a beat. "Let me get that for you." He leapt to hold the door for her, the picture of politeness.

"Oh, thank you," the woman gushed. "Come along now, Colonel Mustard!"

Theo met my eyes over her head, and we both struggled not to laugh. The pair headed downstairs without another glance, then Theo took my hand and pulled me upstairs, faster, muffling our laughter.

"Colonel Mustard!"

I lost track of how many flights we climbed, until finally, Theo opened a door marked "fire escape" on the top landing, and suddenly, Boston lay spread at our feet.

"Wow," I breathed, stepping out onto the roof. We were almost at the top of the hill, rooftops descending below us down along the narrow streets all the way to the inky waters of the river. I could see the bridge, lit up, and the far shores of Cambridge with the neon river of headlights.

"Look behind you."

I turned. Above us, the city kept stretching: old buildings cloaked in a golden haze of lights, with modern office blocks and their sheets of glass looming higher still.

"How did you find this place?"

"I had time to kill marking one afternoon, and it was too hot to go anywhere," Theo explained. "I would camp out here most of the semester. It's completely hidden away. Even the residents in the building don't seem to know it's here."

"Their loss."

Theo dragged a rusting bench to overlook the skyline, and we each sat down on either end, spreading the bounty of our picnic between us. He poured us sparkling grape juice into paper cups, and we used plastic cutlery to construct makeshift sandwiches with the crusty French loaf, gorging ourselves until I couldn't eat another bite. I couldn't tell you what we talked about, all I remember is the laughter and slow easing of my nerves, those tight bands of caution loosening with every passing hour, the world spread before us, but somehow at a remove. On the river, the lights of a cruiser glittered, another train clacked across the bridge, and for the first time in a long while, I felt my worries slip into that distant static hum.

"Tough day?" Theo asked.

I kept my eyes on the distant horizon. "Tough year."

He paused a moment, folding our wrappers into neat squares and tucking them away. "Tell me about Hope," he asked, surprising me.

I felt the ripple of a chill across my skin, and had to steel myself against the sadness that still came, whenever her reluctant smile slipped into view.

"She was trouble," I started. "You know that kid, where your parents always say, 'Stay away from them, they're trouble'? Well, that was Hope. She had a way of saying exactly what she thought, and doing whatever the hell she wanted. And she didn't care whose feathers she ruffled in the process." I grinned. "My parents hated her, they'd never admit it, but she knew. And it didn't bother her at all. She used to say the cancer was her ultimate 'get out of jail free' card."

"That's . . . ballsy." Theo sounded surprised.

"She wasn't always like that. At least, she said she wasn't. Hope used to say there were two versions of her: BC, before cancer, and after. I didn't meet her until she was back in her third round of chemo. She'd been in and out of remission since she was thirteen. They thought they'd got it all this time, but . . . they were wrong."

"You must miss her."

I nodded slowly. "Every day. But it's weird, I see her, I hear her all the time. Something will happen at work, like Kelsey making a crack, or JJ going off on one of his comic-book rants, and I'll know exactly what Hope would say, the look she'd give me, right down to the smile."

I wondered suddenly if I could ever be so indelible, marked so deep on somebody's consciousness that I lasted long after I was gone. What I'd told Theo about wanting to be the subject of someone's song was right: we all wanted immortality. And Hope had hers; with every passing day she haunted me.

I looked up to find Theo watching me. I hugged my knees to my chest, trying to shake off the maudlin thoughts of death and beyond. "Let's not talk about it, not tonight. Anything but this."

"Anything?" Theo's smile took on a teasing edge. "OK, what about your art?"

"Next question."

He laughed. "Come on. You're good, really good. You should be in art school."

I shook my head. "I just play around, it's not real."

"What is real?"

"Now he gets all philosophical." I gave him a look, but Theo wasn't swayed.

"Don't you want to pursue it? Those sketches I saw, they didn't just look like a way to pass the time."

"Maybe, in an alternate universe," I admitted. "But I can't afford it. Even materials add up, and besides, a fine art degree is about as lucrative as a poetry one."

"Ouch," he laughed. "Low blow."

"You know what I mean. Besides," I added softly, looking out at the dark hum of the city. "The timing was all wrong. Going to classes, sitting in a library all day . . . it would have felt like a waste. Hope wanted to see so much of the world, to taste it all."

"And now you're doing it for her," Theo finished for me.

"I'm trying." I gave him a smile. "So thank you, for this. Tonight. I'm glad I got to see this place."

And you.

Theo held my gaze. "I have to admit, my reasons were purely selfish."

I swallowed, my throat dry. We were alone again now, just us, and a distant world that glittered with delicate longing. He was closer now than he'd ever been, his elegant fingers resting on the rusted steel just inches from my skirts; those blue eyes watching me with careful curiosity; his chest rising and falling with steady breath.

The moment swept through me like a wingbeat, a thousand possibilities racing in my blood. It was like an epiphany, dawning through the dark. I could reach out and touch him, to hell with the consequences.

I could do anything at all.

My breath caught in my chest. Staring at the city, I slowly moved my hand, inch by inch, until my fingers overlapped his.

Just as slowly, I felt Theo turned his palm up to graze mine. His fingers closed around me, holding lightly, as if I might crumble to the touch. But I wasn't made from glass, ready to shatter.

In that moment, I was invincible.

He reached across with his other hand and touched the dark strands that lay flat against my cheek. "You look so different like this," he said. I'd forgotten about the costume, the wig.

"It's stupid, I know," I said, flushing, but his touch remained, the gentle graze of his fingertips gently tracing my jaw.

"The Ancient Greeks used to say, give a man a mask and he'll tell you the truth."

"So what truth are you telling today?" I whispered, unable to look away.

Theo smiled at me, a crooked, bashful smile.

"How much I want you."

I inhaled in a rush. His eyes were still on me, dark constellations beckoning me to fall, and oh, how I wanted to. My need for him was so complete it hummed through every cell in my body, vibrating on a frequency beyond mere desire. And I could see it in him too, the way his gaze slipped to my lips, the slow stroke of his thumb against my skin. We were gravity, we were the earth's true orbit, inexorably drawn together under that midnight sky for just one purpose; the simplest thing in the world.

A kiss.

I'd had kisses before him, and plenty since then, but nothing could ever compare to that first miracle of his mouth on mine. His touch was slow, infinite, but as his lips pressed softly, I was already falling. I was already his. I sank against the heat of it, submerged in sensation: his stubble scratching softly against my palm as I pressed it to his cheek; every taste; every last breath.

It was an infinity and a heartbeat all at once, and I came up for air feeling dazzled and raw, like I'd stared too long into the sun.

Theo exhaled in a rush beside me. "Oh."

"Oh," I echoed softly, spinning. It seemed impossible for the world to still exist, but there it was, rooted firmly all around us while I had come apart at the seams. My fingers clutched his hand tighter of their own volition, needing an anchor, and I dared myself to meet his gaze again.

I've never seen desire like the kind I saw burning in his eyes.

He reached for me again, harder, hungrier, but now my mouth demanded just as much more. Our bodies slid together, grasping, reaching. There was no thought process, no logic to weigh; suddenly my entire universe had been reduced to a raw, feral need. More of him. All of him. Anything I could take, and give, anything I could feel. Hands and hot skin and gasping mouths. God, I wanted it all, and who knows how much we would have stolen up there on that empty rooftop if his phone hadn't cut through the gasp of heavy breathing, the shrill blare of a ringtone echoing sharply into the dark.

Theo pulled back, panting. I was under him, somehow, my skirts hiked and in disarray.

"Don't." My hands were still on him, sliding over the wide plains of his shoulders, thin cotton all that was separating me. I tasted his collarbone, felt his heartbeat thundering to escape his chest. "Leave it."

Theo groaned. "I can't."

He clambered inelegantly down from the bench and snatched up his bag. I lay back, staring up at the heavens, and felt the rush of blood sing through my body as he answered.

I was drunk, boneless. I was a star burning brightly in that infinite sky.

"Yes, this is he," Theo was saying, his back turned to me. His voice changed, lower, muttering out of earshot until finally he hung up.

"Who was that?" I asked, tilting my head towards him.

He turned then, but he didn't meet my eyes as he righted his clothing, pulled on one discarded boot. "I'm sorry, I have to go."

"What's wrong?" I slowly sat up, pulling my own clothes back in place.

"Nothing." Theo's tone cut so sharply, I tasted blood.

"Theo—"

"It's nothing." He gritted his jaw, swept our things into a bag. "It's late, anyway. You should be getting home."

He'd flipped the switch again, broken the circuit that had surged between us only seconds before. Something clawed at me from the inside as I got to my feet and slowly followed him to the doorway. The city that had glittered so brightly seemed cold now, and far away. We walked back downstairs in silence, every footstep echoing with questions I couldn't bring myself to ask, not when he wouldn't even look at me. Ten seconds, twenty—how long had passed since we were up there beyond it all? How long had it taken to dissolve into nothing?

Theo held the front door for me. "You know how to get to the subway from here?"

I nodded.

"OK." He swallowed, and for a moment, I saw something crack in his expression. But it must have been my imagination, because when he lifted his head again, there was nothing but a blank resolve on his face, so smooth he could have been talking to a stranger.

"I really have to go."

He left me there on the steps, hurrying fast down the street without a backward glance until the blackness swallowed him whole.

I fought the bitter sting of tears all my way home.

The Promise

CHAPTER NINE

IT WAS DECEMBER before I saw Theo again. He disappeared so thoroughly into the night that Halloween that he left no trace of himself behind, no glimpse of him walking past the coffee shop, no espresso order at the counter in the mornings. It was as if he'd never existed at all.

The weeks passed. I tucked my costume carefully away into a box at the top of my closet and went back to the life I'd been building before: pouring coffee, cycling through the frosted city, and meeting Tessa and her friends sometimes for burgers and beers at the dim pub over on Inman Square, but those simple pleasures that had brought me so much joy seemed flatter now, the cap left untightened long enough for the bubbles to fade away. I told myself it was for the best, that he'd saved us both with his swift escape, but I couldn't forget the way he'd looked at me, up there on the rooftop, the city burning all around us while my heart caught fire.

I had something inside me now, twisting and craving with no way out. I threw myself into my art, spilling over from sketchpads to free-standing frames, to larger-scale works that I pinned on our apartment walls and covered with thick, textured slashes of paint, but still, I couldn't find a way to free the beast caged within. Tessa would come home at night and find me there, fingers dripping, dream-like in my total obsession, a sleepwalker intent on only one thing. The canvas costs were exorbitant, but I didn't care: I worked extra shifts, one eye still on the door, for as much as my mind knew the simple fact of his disappearance should be enough to quell the restless ache in my chest, I couldn't shut it down. Even a glimpse of movement passing outside the foggy windows made my pulse kick, dancing a demanding staccato in my chest. Every blonde head in a crowd, every duffel coat or footstep through the door, and my body would whirl to attention, waiting to see Theo cross over that threshold and give me that quiet, certain smile. But of course, it never came.

THE FIRST DUSTING of snow settled over Harvard Square the morning I arrived at work to find Kelsey had cut her hair short, a blunt exclamation point of a haircut razor-sharp against her jaw.

"Wow," I said, greeting her in the back room amongst

the stacks of delivery boxes and old abandoned sweaters. "It's . . . different."

"I hate it. Whatever. Moving on." She slammed her locker shut and turned, revealing bloodshot eyes and a bare face: no smudged blank ink to disguise the raw, wrecked expression in her gaze.

I inhaled in a rush. "What happened?"

"Nothing."

"Kelsey . . ."

"It's fine." She forced a thin-lipped smile. "If he wants to go fuck every desperate groupie on the Eastern seaboard, that's his prerogative."

Guy. I exhaled. "I'm sorry."

"I'm not." She was blazing and defiant, even with heartbreak written all over her face. "I told you, this is how it always goes. Guy, Theo, they're all the same."

"Don't say that."

"Why not? It's true." Kelsey laughed sharp, rasping. "God, look at you. You're still hoping he'll come back. Like that would ever make up for leaving in the first place."

I tried not to bridle at her disdain. I hadn't mentioned Theo once in all those weeks, and she hadn't asked, but I'd felt the question in her gaze. "It's different," I said softly.

"If you want to spend your life being a total doormat,

sure, go ahead." Kelsey pulled down a black apron and knotted it angrily at her waist. "But for me, one strike and they're done." She pushed through the doors out to the bustle of the café, her boots stomping with determination.

Was that what they all thought of me, waiting for Theo to come back around? The thought needled at me, pricking all day long as I went about my work. Our time together felt so unfinished, barely yet begun. But that was the storybook version of affairs; I was still holding out hope the daydream rules would still apply. The boy would come back, the kiss would be continued. Even when I knew that happily ever after was impossible, I'd still put my stock in all the rest. I should have learned by now that the plotline never worked so simply. Characters could depart your life without a moment's warning, and the resolutions we so desperately wanted stayed lingering, just beyond our reach.

The door jangled that afternoon, and Guy came sweeping in. Theo's Indy outfit had been a costume, but Guy wore his persona like a second skin. Today, it was a button-down shirt and black drainpipe jeans, with a scarf knotted at his neck like an eighteenth-century cravat. I looked anxiously around; Kelsey was wiping down tables in front, with no counter to shield Guy from the scathing slice of her voice.

"No." She stopped him before he'd said a single word.

"But babe—"

"I said, no. Whatever you have to tell me, I couldn't be less interested." She strode back towards the register, and I had to jump out of her determined path, taking refuge behind the pastry cabinet as Guy followed, a hangdog look on his face.

"But nothing happened! You're overreacting, I promise, babe, it's just a misunderstanding."

Kelsey spun, glaring. "I didn't misunderstand the naked photos on your fucking phone!"

Guy blinked, cleared his throat. "I didn't ask her to send them! She's crazy, just looking to stir shit up. Are you going to let her ruin this?"

"Great, turn it all around on me." Kelsey turned to the next unfortunate person in line. "Next," she demanded, hard enough to make the grown man flinch.

"I . . . I can wait," he whispered, looking anxiously back and forth between them.

I quickly edged closer. "Let me take this one." I tried to steer her aside. "Why don't you go talk in private?"

"I'm fine." Kelsey glared at the customer. "What do you want?"

He placed his order in halting tones, and Kelsey set about attacking the coffee machine with enough venom to make all of us shrink back.

Guy rounded the counter. "Baby—"

"Don't you dare baby me."

"Nothing happened," Guy insisted, pushing back his shock of dark fringe. "So she sent me some pics, girls do it all the time. You should see some of the groupies I turn down."

"Oh, lucky me. You want a fucking gold star?" Kelsey set the latte in front of her panicked customer with a clatter, hot liquid sloshing over the edge.

"Baby—"

"I told you, don't call me that. Don't call me at all." Kelsey slammed the register closed, then pushed past me, disappearing into the back room.

Guy stared after her with a mournful expression, then caught me watching. "Nothing happened," he insisted. "It was just a couple of drinks."

I looked around. Their fight had drawn an audience, and I could see the delighted whispers from a group of freshman girls by the window. "You should go," I told him.

"You believe me, don't you?"

I looked away. "It doesn't matter what I believe. She'll calm down," I added gently. "You just need to give her some time."

Guy shook his head, and jammed his hands in the pockets of his coat. "Women," he muttered, but I could tell his heart wasn't in the resigned disdain. I watched him leave—past the table of giggling adoration—and wondered how much of his protesting was genuine, and how much was for show. He'd picked the fight in public, after all, still choosing the spotlight despite Kelsey's fierce privacy. Perhaps he'd imagined it playing out differently: a grand romantic reunion, with us all witnessing, a kiss to charmed applause.

We all grew up believing in fairytales, that the messy chaos of the heart could possibly make sense.

I slipped back on my break and found Kelsey unpacking deliveries. "Can you believe that guy?" she huffed, tearing into another box with an X-acto knife. Guy was lucky he'd come by before she'd armed herself.

"He said nothing happened."

"And I'm just supposed to believe him?" Kelsey looked up, and I saw for the first time the anguish in her naked stare.

"I don't know. But you could give him a chance to explain."

She shook her head stubbornly. "I'm not one of those girls who turns the other way. I'm not going to waste my time on some asshole who doesn't deserve it."

"So you're just giving up?" I asked, feeling a curious twist in my chest.

Kelsey narrowed her eyes. "I can't trust him."

"Or maybe you haven't tried," I shot back.

She got to her feet. "How is this any of your business?"

"You kind of made it our business when you had a shouting match in front of everyone," I pointed out. "Come on, what's the harm in just hearing him out? Just shutting down like this, you're not giving him a chance."

"Whose side are you on?" Kelsey's voice rose. "You're supposed to be my friend, and you're acting like on of his fucking fangirls. Is this about Theo?" she added. "Do you think if I'm still with Guy, you'll have a way of running into him again?"

"No, this is about you, and the relationship you're just throwing away!" I couldn't keep my voice from rising, the heat pounding in my body. "I've seen you with him, you're happier, you actually crack a smile for once in your life. I don't understand why you're ready to just walk away and leave all that for good!"

Didn't she realize how rare that was? Couldn't she see what a privilege she was tossing aside, as if it didn't matter? As if she couldn't care less.

I realized too late how I was overreacting. I stepped back, my heart still racing, a thunder aching in my head. "I'm sorry," I muttered quickly. "You're right, it's none of my business."

Kelsey seemed to soften, to look at me with something like pity in her expression. "It's OK," she told me. "I really am fine. Or, I will be," she corrected herself. "Yes, I cared about him, but it doesn't matter now." She shrugged, reaching to take her jacket down and tug it over her shirt. "There'll be other guys, there always are." She paused on her way out, and touched my arm lightly. "For you, too." Then she was gone.

But I was still wound tightly: my cheeks hot, a vice-like grip clenched around my skull. My head beat with an insistent thunder, so hard it stung to bear.

I was still trying to process my sudden passion when Mika paused in the doorway and looked me up and down. "You don't look so hot. Don't tell me you're getting sick as well."

I shook my head. "I'm fine."

"I'm serious, the last thing I need is another staffer sneezing all over the register. You should go home."

"It's just a headache." I went to my locker and pulled a pill bottle from my bag. I held it up as evidence, quickly swallowing one down. "See? I'll be fine."

He strode forwards and pressed his hand to my forehead. "You're burning up. Get out of here, take tomorrow off too."

"But—"

"I mean it." His usually placid expression turned stern. "You're a walking health hazard like this. Home, bed, hot soup, that's an order."

I reluctantly took my things and wrapped up against the cold. Flu was going around, and people had been calling in sick all week. It had been a boon for me: extra shifts, and tip share too, enough to invest in a new roll of canvas, this one to stretch over ten feet tall, if I could possibly find the space. Now, I reluctantly left the café before my shift was up, counting those lost dollars and resenting Mika for his over-cautious plans.

It was snowing steadily now, but I didn't go home. I found myself cycling a slow loop instead, along the red brick walls that bordered the old Harvard campus. Wrought iron gates invited me in on every block, spilling over with students and dark, thick ivy, but I kept pedaling through the crystalline flakes. To where, I wasn't yet sure.

I was still furious at Kelsey, although I knew she was right. It wasn't my business, and Lord knew, I had no soft spot for Guy's side of the story. But her recklessness stung; it burned with the careless ease with which she discarded him, so sure in the future that would come to take his place.

There will be other guys . . .

Hope had been certain too, once. Sure, she flirted and danced, ticking off men from her list like they were mere playthings along the road, always quick with the sarcastic dismissal, an exasperated roll of her mascara-smudged eyes, but deep down, in the dark of the night, she'd always believed that love, that love with a capital L would be hers by rights before the end. How could it not? Every movie we watched, every song on the radio dial, every poem and story and private confession revolved around the mystery and glory of it all. It was woven so deeply into the fabric of our lives—the one story society told to us in a million different forms from the day we were born, once upon a time, that we never once questioned happily ever after would arrive for us too, one day.

Until those days could be counted off the calendar, measured by pill bottles lined up on her bathroom ledge, and the ever-shortening period outside those hospital hallways. I could see it, the closer the end came: how her studied ease hid a raw, dark desperation as the truth finally dawned. There would be no other guys for her, no "one day," no taste of the sweetness we'd all been sold. Of all the things she wouldn't get to do, this one was the one that tore her up inside, a jagged wound gaping wider by the dwindling day.

"I wanted to feel everything," she told me, her throat raw and rasping as the heart monitors beeped their stuttering song. The failure rang in every word, the razor blade of bitter regret. "Every last fucking thing."

I could only sit beside her and squeeze her grasping hand. We both knew there were no platitudes to save her now, no pretty words to dull the pain of such an empty death. To live and not know love was a slow, quiet cruelty. But to die without that knowledge?

That was the cruelest fate of all.

On my third loop, I veered right through the gates and dismounted, locking my bicycle into a rack with the rest of them and striding up the neat pathway before I could change my mind. I found a campus map etched into a solid statue, and carefully wove my way through the bundled-up crowds until I found Emerson Hall, sitting squarely on the edge of Harvard Yard. The stately red brick looked out over an immaculate quadrangle, the grass covered now with a fresh snowfall, and already, students were attempting to gather the soft flakes into small snowmen; laughter emerging with puffs of steam as they played and jostled in the cold.

I hurried up the front steps and into the echoing warren of hallways and classroom doors. The scent hit me right away, that low musty note of used bookstores, footsteps echoing on the worn linoleum floors. I passed old wooden cubbyholes and peeling notice boards, layered thick with their flyers for class seminars, open-mic nights, and enthusiastic "roommate wanted" ads. A group of girls walked by me, my age I would have guessed; they wore long scarves and jackets, boots and jeans, clutching book bags and binders as they made plans to meet later and study. They didn't give me a second glance.

Were they in Theo's seminar, I wondered? Did they huddle in the back row, watching his every move, seeing the light in his eyes when he got carried away on a subject, or that bashful smile when he said too much, too far? It had been almost six weeks since that night on the rooftop. Christmas was coming, and for all I knew, he could have moved on: found another girl to romance with Wordsworth and that dazzling smile. Another Brianna, older and sophisticated, or maybe a wide-eyed freshman to hang from his every word.

Even the thought of it made my headache grow. I had no rights to him, none at all, but still the sense that he was mine strummed through every cell in my body, despite the silence, the distance, the time. Kelsey would have called me naïve; Hope would have given me a sympathetic smile and braced me for the sting of disappointment, but neither of them knew what I did now. That he'd awakened something I was privileged to even glimpse, and every day that passed made me more certain our story wasn't yet done.

IT TOOK ME SEVERAL wrong turns, up flights of stairs and down echoing corridors before I found the door with his name printed, neat on a card stock slide behind a Plexiglass frame. There were murmurs of voices inside, so I waited, my back to the wall as I tried to corral my now-racing heart.

I could have backed out. I had twenty long minutes there, listening to the voices drift up on a cool breeze through the open window, watching the snowflakes turn thicker, a flurry from the gray glazed skies. Every heartbeat tempted me to turn on my heel and go. I didn't belong there, in this collegiate world, a hum of learning that I'd never even wanted to join. What made me think this wouldn't have ended in disaster? My raw, bruised heart offered up like sacrifice, when by any sound logic I should have been long gone.

I didn't know. I had nothing on my side except blind, restless faith. And Hope, of course, burned deep into my mind, and etched on that rubber band around my wrist. Her last requests, the certainty of her fading stare.

Don't you fucking dare let me down this time.

The voices inside Theo's office grew louder. I caught my breath, straightening as the door swung open, and a teenage boy stepped out, struggling to pull on his coat and juggle half a dozen hardback books.

"Just remember to be concise, and use your footnotes more effectively," Theo's voice came from behind him, steady and reassuring. "It's still early days yet, you'll get the hang of it."

"I'll try." The boy saw me waiting. "Sorry, we ran

long." He turned back. "Thank you again. See you in class."

"Chapters three through twelve! Now, what can I help you . . .?" Theo's question faded as he reached the doorway and saw me standing there. ". . .with," he finished, the word falling to the empty floor between us.

There was no turning back now.

THE PROMISE

CHAPTER TEN

"HI," I WHISPERED, almost lost under the pounding of my heartbeat in my ears. I ignored the headache, the chill of evening breeze, the clatter of students spilling from a classroom just beyond, down the hall. There was nothing in the world but us, just like it was supposed to be.

God, I'd missed him. I'd been apart from him so long it hit me like the first time all over again. The grace of his limbs under that rumpled button-down shirt, the line of his jaw, and that dirty blonde hair falling too long again over steady blue eyes. The way my heart skittered faster in my chest, so wild I could have taken flight from a single word; the word he breathed like a prayer, a benediction.

"Claire."

Theo looked at me, and the shock on his face slowly melted away. He took two steps closer and reached to press his palm softly against my cheek. "I thought I'd never see you again."

I closed my eyes, feeling his touch sink through me,

rolling slowly through every taut wire and shivering string. He was there. He was touching me. "I don't give up so easy."

I forced myself to look at him, so close, so bright, it hurt. "Should I?" I made myself ask, watching his face for the last sign that could send me running, the only way I would have ever walked away. If he didn't want me, not even an ounce of what I felt for him.... I would have taken anything he had to give me; only nothing at all would be too little to bear.

But Theo slowly shook his head. "No," he murmured, leaning to rest his forehead against mine. I could feel his breath on every slow exhale, the shake of tension as his grip tightened on mine. "Don't give up on me, Claire. Please, never give up."

We held each other for a century, not moving there in the fading rays of afternoon light. A heartbeat drummed, mine or his I couldn't tell you; all I knew was the sense of belonging, of rightness that echoed through me, rising stronger until I felt invincible enough to tilt my mouth upwards and seek the answer I needed more than air.

This time, he barely moved, barely breathed as my mouth brushed his. We were suspended on the edge of chaos for one glorious moment, and then we tumbled into the abyss. With a groan, he reached for me: hands tangling in my hair, his body hard against mine. I backed into the wall, wild with the need I'd been controlling for so long. My hands were on him, still half in disbelief he was mine to touch at all. *There. Now. More.*

Theo gripped tight around my waist, and he dragged his mouth from mine to kiss along my jaw, my neck, the delicate hollow of my collarbone—

A clatter came from the far staircase, loud enough to intrude even on our reckless passion. Voices sounded, circling their way down towards us.

"Here," Theo said. He grabbed my hands and tugged me backwards, into his waiting office, shoving the door behind us with a crash. I barely had time to glimpse the small space, crammed with bookcases and a cluttered desk before I was up against the wall again with his mouth on mine.

"You have . . . students . . ." I managed, shivering as his cool hands slid under my jacket, along the bare seam of skin beneath my shirt.

"Study hours are over." He dipped to kiss my neck again, hands sliding higher.

"But . . ." I was dizzy, searching for a strand of logic in the midst of this whirlwind. But there was nothing to cling onto anymore. No distance or cool logic. Nothing but heat, and hands, and that reckless urge spiraling tighter, needing more.

He kissed me again, and this time, I didn't hold back.

With hot mouths, we stumbled back, papers and

folders crashing to the ground as he lifted me onto the desk, pushed my jacket off my body, and held me close to feel him burn. We both were blazing, an inferno beyond control. Hands followed lips followed hard heat and soft breaths. I'd wanted an infinity to explore his body inch by miraculous inch, but those plans were lost to something far more insistent, clawing, dark and deep with every slide of his body. His shirt followed mine to the floor, and then so much more, the metallic ring of his belt buckle lost under my moan as his hands took possession of me. Those steady, sure hands I'd drawn so many nights now, cupped around me, squeezing, roaming further, deeper past my last inhibitions until I was spread to him and gasping for more.

WORDS STILL FAIL me to describe what alchemy passed between us that afternoon, spinning base elements into something golden and pure, but maybe that's the point. Before that sweet December day, I'd always experienced life with an artist's eye. There wasn't a moment I couldn't commit to paper; not a feeling I wouldn't capture in the strokes of brush on canvas, a flare of color and shape. But those moments there with Theo still defy me. They passed not in scenes, frozen tableaus to be recreated, or even emotions I could abstract onto the page. No, it went beyond any language I'd learned to make sense of the world. Even now, I feel it in a rush: my hands closing around him, the hot slide of his tongue on taut, trembling flesh, the imprint of his fingertips clutched deep into my thighs. He paused there, braced above me, breath in ragged pants. There were no words left, only the look in his eyes as he silently asked the final question, and I pressed closer, answering the only way I knew how.

He didn't look away, not even for a moment. And the time that had folded in on itself, gone to the rush, now unraveled again in slow motion—each second strung shimmering with new sensation. It was liquid and sharp, white-hot; it was an infinity coming undone, and still, he didn't look away. I saw the world break open in his eyes, and felt every breath as the gravity shuddered through us both, until we were left gasping and fused together and so brand new.

THE PROMISE

CHAPTER ELEVEN

IT WAS DARK by the time we walked home, the empty streets almost silent with snow. It had only taken hours for pale flakes to blanket the city, muffling the hum of traffic and sending people scurrying for the safe warmth inside. I didn't feel the cold, not with Theo tucked so close beside me, and our footsteps matching, in synch in the snow. We barely spoke, but I didn't need to; I was still trembling from the burning imprint of his touch, my mind tripping over itself to catch up with every breath we'd exchanged, gasping into the silence of the emptying study hall.

"Are you . . .?" Theo finally asked, one hand steadily wheeling my bicycle alongside. "I mean, was that . . . OK?"

Laughter escaped me. "OK?" I echoed, my smile splitting the world in two. "Yeah, I'd say it was OK."

Theo laughed too then, a sharp burst of relief. "I'm sorry, I just . . . I don't want you to feel like I rushed you. We could have . . . waited."

"Waiting is overrated," I said softly. My arm was slipped

around his waist, under the thick drape of his coat, and I squeezed him closer, tighter. Mine. "Besides, we did wait. Months. Too long."

Theo's face clouded. "I'm sorry," he said, the words landing so softly on the snow-powdered street. "I almost called you a hundred times. I just didn't know what to say to you. How I could ever explain."

We'd reached my corner. Three floors up, across the street, the lights from my apartment glowed, an invitation. "So come up," I said to him, taking his hand. "You don't need to tell me everything if you don't want to. But that doesn't mean you can't stay."

Theo looked to the apartment, and back at me. His lips curled in a teasing smile. "How am I supposed to say no to that?"

"You're not." I tugged him onwards. "I'm not letting you go this time."

My words were playful, but beneath their teasing tone, I meant every last one. I'd made my choice, and I could do it again, a hundred times over, but the end result would never change.

It was him, always him.

Inside, I stashed my bike in the hall closet and headed upstairs, Theo chasing behind. "So this is the inner sanctum, huh?"

"It's nothing special," I warned him, my mind tripping

over itself to remember if I'd left dirty laundry lying around. "As long as there's heat, and nobody playing Velvet Underground at two in the morning, you have me beat." His arms were already locked around me, his lips claiming mine again as I fumbled with the lock and backed inside.

"Hey, Claire."

We whirled around. Tessa laughed, over by the table stuffing books into her bag. "Don't worry, I'm on my way out."

I flushed. "Umm, hi. This is Theo. Tessa." I awkwardly gestured back and forth, but Theo snapped into action, polite. He strode over and shook her hand, asking about her course and making small talk about the snow while I fought to act normal. But how could I, when I felt the naked flame of my desire still burning, too bright in our small attic apartment? I busied myself unwrapping my scarf, stripping off my jacket, until Tessa's phone sounded, and she grabbed her coat. "There's my ride now. We're having a snow break study weekend before finals," she added. "So you've got the place to yourselves until Monday."

"Oh, thanks." I swallowed.

"Great meeting you, Theo." She cheerfully hoisted her deadweight book bag and a duffel trailing clothing and a scarf. "See you again, I hope."

As Tessa headed for the door, she paused beside me, and lowered her voice. "Bathroom cabinet, top drawer."

She winked, and then was gone in a whirl of determination before I could find my tongue again.

We were alone again. My stomach turned a slow arabesque, then settled, trembling beneath my ribs. All my earlier recklessness was long gone; now I felt naked in the too-bright lights, wondering what came next.

Theo slowly removed his coat and looked around. "She seems nice."

"She is." I went to the galley kitchen area and filled the kettle to busy my restless hands, setting it on the stove to boil. "She's got so much energy, I wonder if she's on speed sometimes. I wouldn't be surprised if she took over the world one day. I can't keep up."

Hands slid around my waist from behind. "World domination is overrated." Theo's voice rumbled in my ear. I relaxed back against him and he rested his chin on my shoulder, watching as I set out two mugs, and pulled down a pack of cookies and a couple of tea bags.

I wasn't used to it yet, the gift of his body so casually against mine. And to tell the truth, I never learned to take it for granted. From the first time until the last, he made my pulse skip and stutter like fireworks bursting in the night sky.

"It was the police."

Theo's voice was steady, but his body tensed behind me, bracing for impact. "That night, on the roof when I had to leave. It was the police who called me, about my dad."

I turned then, twisting within his embrace so I was facing him, and could see every sleepless night and agonized day reflected back in the planes of his face. I took it in my hands, holding softly, waiting.

"He's a drunk," Theo's words came, bitter. "Has been my whole life. He doesn't stop, doesn't want to." He looked away, but didn't stop, as if this was a speech he'd been rehearsing, lines he knew by heart. "My mom, she put up with it as long as possible, but even she didn't want to stick it out. I've tried to leave. College, and now this. I said, I won't be around to pick him up again, but there's always something. Always one more fucking thing."

For a moment, Theo's resolute expression cracked. In front of me was a boy again: hopeful, vulnerable, trodden down but still believing, the way we all do when it comes to our parents. We want to believe they'll be superhuman. We want to believe they'll put us first.

Theo exhaled, and in that simple motion, I understood the weight he'd been carrying all this time, and what it meant to lay those few precious words between us. I rested my head against his chest, my hand covering the steady beating of his heart. I didn't say anything; there was nothing too say, I only held him until the whistle from the kettle pierced the heavy calm, and I turned back to the flame, knowing so much more than I did before. Guilt pricked me, a splash of boiling water against my skin. He'd given me something, offered a window into his world. I should have responded in kind then, the moment was wide open and waiting for me, but instead, I just poured our tea and passed him a mug.

"Show me your kitties?" he read aloud from the cup.

I smiled, relieved he'd steered the moment on. "It's Tessa's."

"Sure it is." He took a sip, quirking his eyebrow at me over the rim, his old self again.

"I'm more a dog person myself," I told him, leading him out into the living area again. "We had a golden lab growing up, Betsy. She wouldn't fetch to save her life. I would toss a dozen tennis balls around, but she'd just sit there, waiting for a treat."

"Smart girl."

Theo drifted over to the canvases I still had drying by the radiator. I paused, realizing too late the artwork that was out in the open for him to see. It was different with Tessa: she'd barely glanced at the paintings, seeming to understand that although they were draped over chairs and hanging from the easels, they were still private to me. But Theo stood in front of them, his quick gaze absorbing every line and splash of color.

I gripped my mug tighter. "That's Hope," I said, feeling painfully exposed. The canvas was one of the bigger ones, her face stretching almost six feet tall, shaded in an inky purple paint that had stained my hands for days. He turned back to me. "They're beautiful. You can see the anger, she looks so . . ."

"Afraid," I finished for him. "It was the end, or very near it, anyway. I haven't been able to paint her like this until now," I admitted. "After she died, all I wanted to do was remember her in the good days, before."

I stepped into my bedroom and nodded to the pages papering the far wall. It was a constellation of my sketchpad tears, a year's worth of hurried portraits and idle shading. Hope, in her best days, kicked back in the passenger seat or lost to a song on the radio. Customers in the café, passers-by on a busy street. The bridge and Boston skyline, my parents, and yes, Theo too. Over and again, his face, the form, his hands wrapped around their coffee cup. Theo drew closer, reaching to run his fingertips over the patchwork layers, pinned and peeling, a testament of my restless mind. He paused by one sketch, that drawing I'd done so many months ago after our false-start kiss. "October," he read quietly, from the scribbled date in the corner. He turned back to me, quizzical. "Even then?"

I looked at him. "Even always," I said simply. We were

past coy now. Coy lay scattered on his office floor across town, a lifetime ago. "I drew you the first day we met. Tore it all up, but I could never stop."

He looked back at the sketches, transfixed. "This is how you see me?"

I stepped closer, heart full and bright. "This is who you are to me."

OUR TEA SAT cold, abandoned on my bedside table. We had better things to do with our hands, our hungry mouths. We surfaced again late at night, sprawled and lazy in the tangle of blankets and sheets.

"Remind me to thank your roommate for her supplies." Theo traced along my bare arms. I was nestled against his side, listening to the slowing heartbeat drum against his chest.

I smiled into his side. "She's a regular Girl Scout."

"Prepared for anything."

I could feel the smile in every word. The room was dark, but the streetlights outside bathed the room in a pale yellow glow, casting shadows over every corner. I dropped a kiss against his rib cage, slipped my hands across his naked stomach. I was still learning his body by heart, making a note of every flinch and sharp inhale of breath. It still amazed me, then, what power I had over him, after all. The power to bring him to the brink and back, to make that steady pulse race like mine, or send him hurtling over the edge.

Theo brought my face up to his and kissed me, a lazy, breathless kiss. He held my jaw, tracing over my lips with the same wonder I held in my heart. "Who are you?" he whispered, watching me. "Where did you come from?"

I swallowed. "I'm nobody."

He shook his head. "You're somebody."

I tried to play it off cool, to smile and roll my eyes and look away, but Theo didn't let me. His kiss was different then, whisper-soft and deliberate, until I could only melt towards his touch, unfurling in the rays of something certain and sweet.

It was perfect. So fucking perfect.

Sadness swept through me as fast as desire, cold and clawing in my chest. I sat up so fast the room spun.

"Hey, get back here." Theo grinned, reaching for me again. "You need to tell me all about that tattoo."

"Bathroom," I said, tugging my underwear and a sweatshirt on, and flinching as my feet hit the cold bare floorboards. "Be right back!"

I was at the door when my legs gave way. I grabbed for the frame, gasping quick as the lights burst, hard behind my eyes.

"Claire?" Theo was halfway out of bed towards me, but I waved him away.

"I got up too fast." I forced a smile and stood straight again. "Head-rush. Stay."

Those dozen steps were an eternity, every last one a labor beyond words. I walked so carefully through the living room, willing my body not to fail me now. The lights in the bathroom blared brightly, piercing my skull and slicing a blade straight down my spine.

Fuck.

I tugged open the cabinet, my hand shaking. It took half a dozen tries to get past the childproof fastening on my prescription, and as I gulped down two pills with a mouthful of cold water from the faucet, I saw my own reflection in the mirror, the desperate plea in my gaze.

Not now, please, not now.

The pain beat on, a thousand shooting stars roaring through my brain until they drowned everything in red-hot fury. I'd never felt anything like that before, not the supernova, dizzying and wide with an endless shore. I would get used to it soon enough, as used to agony as you could be. It was strange how normal such blunt force trauma could become. I guess if you beat your head against a brick wall long enough, even that can become simple as breathing in the end.

But that night, the pain unmanned me, made an echo of my body, and a shadow of my mind. It was all I could do to cling to that bathroom sink and wait for the end to come, whatever that end would be.

"You want anything to eat?" Theo's voice came from outside the door, mockingly normal. I could hear him open the fridge and rifle through. "Wait, I take it back. What is this stuff? Tofu? Tell me this is all your roommate's doing."

I focused on the tiny crack in the porcelain, winding down to the drain. I was still breathing, wasn't I? I had to remember to breathe.

"Claire? Claire, are you sure you're OK?"

"Fine," I managed to call back through the quicksand. I counted to ten, grasping for each second like handholds on a sheer rock face, all that was keeping me from tumbling into the red. *Please*, I whispered into the neon glare, *pleasenopleasenopleaseno.*

Finally, the chemicals burst to life in my bloodstream. My heartbeat slowed. The knife blade dulled.

OhthankyouLord.

I gulped down air and rinsed my hands, cold under the faucet. I would have stayed there forever, curled down on the floor, but I couldn't wait so long this time. When I opened the door again, Theo was standing in the kitchen with a pan in one hand, bare-chested with an apron around his waist.

"I found eggs," he declared, like a returning warrior. He had a halo, radiant and gold, undulating around his body in the shadows of the night. "And for you, I'll make them any which way. What'll it be: scrambled, poached, fried?"

"Isn't it kind of late for breakfast?" I asked, still gripping the doorframe tight. I squinted, the colors blurring. "Or early. One of those."

Theo wasn't fooled by my jokes. He frowned. "You look pale. Here, come sit down." He abandoned the pan and moved towards me, just as I took my own faltering steps into the room.

"It's just a headache," I insisted, as if those syllables had anything in common with the canon-fire raging behind my skull. "Just a little head—"

The world imploded.

Blood roared, and then suddenly all that existed was the pain, blossoming, blooming, until it devoured me whole. I didn't hear him yell, although he swore later that he did. I didn't hear the water glass go crashing to the ground as I flailed, or the sharp crack of my head against the floor as the room flipped sideways on me. I didn't hear anything at all, just the roar of metal, hot in my mouth as the scarlet sky opened to swallow me up into oblivion.

Then, at last, there was nothing.

CHAPTER TWELVE

I WOKE TO SILENCE. No roar of scarlet, no cannon-fire, nothing but a heavy thick emptiness that seeped through my battered skull like melting snow; a pure, swift relief.

I breathed, unsteady, as the hum of distant conversation and the beep-beep-beep of a machine filtered gently through the sleep-settled daze. White noise, blessed calm rolled over me, and slowly, I remembered how to think again. I was in a hospital bed, somewhere, dressed in a thin paper gown, tubes hooked up to an IV by my bedside, a heart monitor chirping steadily at the end of a tangle of wires. What did I . . .?

"You're going to be OK, sweetie. You need to just relax."

I remembered it then: the fall, the searing pain. An ambulance careening through the streets of Boston, and Theo—*fuck, Theo*—gripping my hand, the steady reassurance of his voice betrayed by the panic in his eyes.

I was already looking around for my sweatshirt when the curtain yanked back and he stepped into the makeshift room. "You're awake." Relief flooded his face. "How do you feel? The doctor gave you something, they said you'd be groggy for a while."

"I'm fine." I tried to sit up, pulling the IV line from my arm. The needle bit into my skin and I flinched at the tear, but I didn't stop. I had to get out of there, the fight-or-flight instinct rearing hard with only one goal.

Theo rushed to my side. "What are you doing? Claire, you need to lie down. They still want to run some more tests—"

"This is all a mistake." I shook my head, then had to gulp as the room spun gently. "I don't need tests, I just got a little dizzy. It happens all the time."

"You hit your head."

"And I'm fine now!" I forced a smile, held a finger in front of my face and moved it from side to side, like an old optometrist trick. "See? Theo, please." My voice dropped, pleading. "I don't want to make a big deal about this. All these tests, the ambulance . . . I don't have insurance. How much is this going to cost?"

"You shouldn't worry about that." Theo stubbornly blocked my path.

"Easy for you to say."

"It's not." He stood his ground. "But you don't cut

corners with this stuff, Claire. Come on, let's wait at least to find out what the doctor says."

"I already know what he's going to say." I shivered in the thin gown. "That I need to stop skipping breakfast, and be more careful when I get up."

"Then you'll get to tell me 'I told you so.' " Theo carefully leaned over and fluffed my pillow, resting his palm against my cheer. "Just do this, please. For me?"

His face was wide open, guileless and true. He'd dressed in a hurry: belt forgotten, his buttons done up wrong, but he was still too golden and perfect in the harsh hospital lights. I didn't want to think of the panic I'd caused him, so I just buried my head against his chest.

"I hate these places," I whispered softly.

"I know. But it won't be long."

I knew better. A late-night emergency room was always one step from chaos. I'd spent hours in my lifetime waiting on hard plastic chairs; Hope loved to calculate it, decrying the time totaled up on the back of a notepad. "Seventeen weeks!" she would curse wildly. "I could have learned to scuba dive, or speak fluent French, or hiked the Himalayas by now."

"You hate the cold."

"It's the principle of the thing."

Sure enough, it was hours before someone came to check on me that night. We passed the time dozing, curled together on the narrow mattress as the nurses outside calmed belligerent drunks, and children cried down the hallway, and my stomach twisted as tight as the rubber bracelet on my wrist until at last, the curtain rattled back again, and a middle-aged man in a rumpled white coat wandered in, flipping through a thick stack of charts.

"Claire Fortune?" he asked, not looking at me. "I'm Doctor Benson, the head of neurology here. I hear you had a fall?" He was doughy and balding, but there was a deftness to his gaze as he finally looked up and stared down the bed at me.

I turned to Theo. "I never did get those eggs," I said softly. "Can you go find me something to eat? Chips, maybe, or some of that pudding."

"You want hospital food?" he smiled, disbelieving.

"I know, I got a taste for it all the time I spent with Hope. Besides," I added. "Doctor Benson here is about to give me a lecture about not skipping breakfast and letting my blood sugar get too low, isn't that right?" I smiled lightly up at him, guilty to the core.

Doctor Benson cleared his throat and looked away.

"Pudding, you've got it." Theo got up. "I'll be right back." He leaned over and smoothed my hair back, dropped a careful kiss on my forehead, so light, it was like I was made of glass. Then he left us, the curtain swinging free behind him as he headed down the fluorescent hall.

Dr. Benson slowly approached the bed. He checked my heart monitor, and made a scribbled notation on my chart. "You were unconscious when the ambulance brought you in, so we ran a CT scan and a full blood-work." He paused, opening his mouth and then closing it again. Another second ticked past, another minuscule rotation of the earth.

Beep beep beep.

"The scans we took," he began slowly, and the hesitation was so heavy I couldn't take it anymore.

"It's OK," I said softly, listening to the hospital shift and whisper, just out of reach. "You don't have to break it to me gently."

I'd swallowed back the words for months now, but they were alive again, fluttering and swarming to escape my mouth.

"I know about the tumor."

THE PROMISE

CHAPTER THIRTEEN

I MET HOPE DURING yet another round of chemo, hooked up to the machines at the shiny new hospital wing in the city, sitting in a room of pale, grim faces as poison dripped into our veins. She marched right up to the free seat beside me and sat herself down with a groan. "These shoes are killing me," she sighed, slipping her feet out of the pink stacked sandals and wriggling her clashing scarlet toes. She offered me a raspberry popsicle, and by the time our tongues turned blue, we were friends. As if I'd ever had a choice.

Her tumor was metastatic: a gift from the cancerous cells she already had lurking in her bones. Mine was primary, the doctors' way of describing the bullseye painted two inches below my cerebral cortex, right there in the back of my skull. A time bomb that had stayed hidden for years, laying in wait, readying for the perfect time to strike.

It had started when I was fourteen: dizziness and a

pounding headache that left me breathless, grasping for solid ground. I lost my balance and fell on the way to homeroom one afternoon, but the school nurse sent me back to class with an aspirin and a juice-box. Low blood sugar. Nothing to worry about. The headache lingered all year. Mom took me to get my eyesight tested, and warned me against sketching late at night under the covers, but I didn't mention my unsteady spells at home, didn't think about it at all until I passed out halfway down the stairs one night, and was taken to the ER with a fractured wrist and quarter-sized bump on the back of my head. This time, the over-eager med student ran up a laundry list of tests and scans, and buried there amongst the blood-work, she found the same aberrant numbers that caused Dr. Benson such pause. Elevated white blood cell count. Shadows on my CT scan. They strapped me into the MRI machine, a space ship of an instrument so echoing and white, it felt like I was passing into the realm of science fiction, a passenger on a voyage heading far away. And there, mapped on my brain, they found it waiting.

Tick, tick, tick.

That first specialist fell in love with my tumor at first sight. He spoke of it in hushed tones, so reverent it was as if the hospital room had become a church in which to worship; he gazed at my scans in awe, describing breathlessly how it had nestled, undetected for so long, slowly creeping to claim more territory until the cancer was gently threaded through my most vital brain functions. Untouchable.

Inoperable.

"It's like it knew exactly how far to grow." He'd sketched the shadows with his fingertip, illuminated up on the lightbox, my mind sliced open in neat segments for the world to see. "Small enough not to threaten your vital functions, but big enough that we can't risk cutting it out. The perfect self-defense mechanism."

It was mutually assured destruction, just the way I would learn about in history class. My tumor and I, locked in a curious battle of the wills, too deeply intertwined to ever be free of each other. Oh, we tried. There were scans and testing, and specialists all over the country; more hours curled waiting in those hard hospital chairs. But all of them agreed, a détente was the best course of treatment. I was stable and young, and could function almost as normal. Better to shrink the cluster of cells as much as possible than risk cutting into my brain and spark some landmine that would irrevocably blow my life apart; losing speech, or movement, or even my memories, too.

So, half-measures it was. A schedule of meds and chemo sessions that poisoned me from the inside out, leaving me weak and wretching in bed all summer while my classmates blithely dated and gossiped and hung out at the Dairy Queen down the block. I learned to live with the panic in Mom's eyes every time I lost my balance; to ignore Dad bent for hours over paperwork in his tiny office, those heavy sighs and days lost to insurance company phone lines, begging for half a chance to let his daughter live. But it was OK. Saying that now, it seems incredible, but those years passed by in a steady equilibrium, at least compared to other patients. Most tumors won their wretched victory within months, but mine seemed content to lay in wait. Fifteen, sixteen, seventeen years old, attending school like normal, studying for tests and worrying about grades, then surrendering myself to a summer of chemo like Persephone in the underworld, my deal with the devil, to secure my place in the world. We believed that the prescriptions were true, that we could box that tumor into no-man's-land, keep it neat and contained, as if it wouldn't define the life I'd yet to lead.

But of course, it was smarter than that. My tumor was worth the praise, outfoxing us all. It grew back, every time, and soon, the chemo was every six months. Every three. By the time my classmates were embarking on their senior years, full of plans for college and beyond, I was too behind to even try. My world shrank, just as theirs was getting bigger, until my life revolved around the thirteen square feet of my childhood bedroom, endless daytime TV, and those hospital rooms, neon and unforgiving. I could feel my life slipping away, leached by the chemo toxins, and worse still, by the endless exhausted days. Is it any wonder that by the time Hope arrived, I'd all but given it up? She was my avenging angel, the one person who could still make me double over with a gasp of laughter, who could drive me into the desert one night to scream into the cold, starry sky, cursing our cancers with every last breath of our poisoned, hopeless souls.

She reminded me what it meant to be alive, after so many years shrinking into the space that my illness allowed. That I was capable of more than just sitting around, pumping poison into my body for the simple privilege of existing one more day. And when her body finally gave up the fight, she made me swear not to slip away the same way: docile in the hospital bed where she'd spent too many years, like that was any way to greet the end. She didn't go gently into the good night by any measure, she raged long and hard, clinging to this world for months by her bare and bloody fingertips.

And still, it made no difference.

It was too late by then; her chance to make it matter. All the big ambitions in the world are out of reach when you need a machine to breathe, morphine on a steady drip just to make it through an aching hour. Waiting for the moments to slip past, waiting around to die. The final insult to a sick joke from a world that had once shone, full of vivid possibility.

"You have to do it all now," she would insist, every time I sat by her bedside. "Why are you even wasting your time here with me? There is no fucking tomorrow."

"You should put that on a greeting card."

"I mean it." Her hand shot out, her cheeks flushed and fervent. "Think of all that time we spent sitting around in chemo, the years I believed this bullshit treatment was going to save me. I can't get it back, Claire. It's too late, I can't get it back."

Neither would I.

CHAPTER FOURTEEN

DR. BENSON FROWNED at me, our corner of the hospital suddenly hushed. Blood was pounding in my ears, and I prayed that Theo took his time, that the warren of hospital hallways swallowed him up in a dozen wrong turns. Anything to keep him away from this pathetic bedside. Anything to keep my secret locked tight.

"When was your last MRI?" Benson demanded, his sleepiness gone now, that stare alert. "I'll need records from your regular physician, and to run more tests." He started scribbling notes. "You should be in treatment, aggressive treatment, we can—"

"No." I cut him off, final. "More tests won't tell you anything I don't already know. It's inoperable."

"But surely—"

"I've seen every specialist in the country, tried every new drug. I'll be dead in three months, six if I'm lucky and it doesn't spread to my spine." My voice cracked. "One more round of chemo isn't changing that."

There was silence.

There's one thing I'd learned about doctors, after all that time on the other side of the consulting chair: that for all their noble goals and sworn do-good determination, nobody likes a losing battle. Sure, they would wade in with treatment plans, as if they alone could face down the beast lurking in my skull, but once they grasped the true nature of the demon—once they surveyed the battlefield of scans and test readings, and realized just how outflanked and outmaneuvered they were—the fight simply faded away. I used to take it personally, but in the end, I couldn't blame them. The number of bodies they saw in my chair—it must have been exhausting to care, to hurt, to grieve. So they marshaled their resources for a fight they could win, kept their gunpowder dry until there was someone on the table who could be saved. And we all knew by then that body wasn't mine.

But this one surprised me. He gave me a measured look, unconvinced. "I'd like to talk to your primary physician, all the same."

I shrugged, the sleepless night catching up with me. "Knock yourself out."

Before he could push any more, the curtain rattled back. It was Theo, bearing a pudding cup in one hand, coffee in the other. Sleepy-eyed and messy-haired, and the only thing worth a damn in this entire building.

"Perfect timing," I said, slipping out of the bed before anyone could say a word. "Doctor Benson said I can go. Nothing to worry about."

"That's great." Theo's whole body exhaled in relief. He paused. "But what about the headache, and the fainting?"

"Low blood sugar, like I said." I met the doctor's gaze. "I've got some pills, everything will be fine. Once I get some sleep, that is."

Doctor Benson stood, blocking my path for a moment. I pleaded with him silently, my world poised on the knife-edge of his indecision. Then, at last, he stood aside. "This is my direct number," he said, passing me a card. "Call me if you show any more symptoms. If you change your mind at all."

I tucked the card away and grabbed my clothing from their plastic bag on the chair. "I'll change," I told Theo. "Don't go anywhere."

I was about to step into the hallway, when he caught me against him, holding me close. "You scared me," he said softly, pushing my hair back from my face. "Don't do that again."

His smile was gentle, but the look in his eyes made me cringe, unsettled deep in my chest. He kissed me then, and when I looked up, the doctor's eyes were still on me.

I held Theo tightly all the way home.

THE PROMISE

CHAPTER FIFTEEN

I WOKE AT DAWN after only a few hours sleep. Theo was sprawled beside me, his face so clear and innocent in the pale morning light. The guilt in my chest shuddered awake. I tugged a blanket around my shoulders and padded softly out to the kitchen. Two pills swallowed down with a glass of icy-cold water, and the dull ache in my head began to ease.

This was my life now, the end of it, at least. I'd ignored the slow creep of symptoms as long as possible, pushed those familiar headaches and dizzy spells aside for weeks, but now they were finally catching up with me, nipping at my heels so eagerly as they saw their victory in sight.

How much longer could I play pretend?

Theo was waiting when I slipped back between the sheets. His arms closed around me, his warm mouth pressing a good morning kiss onto the back of my bare neck.

"How do you feel?" he murmured, tucking me into the

waiting curve of his body as if I belonged there.

"Fine," I lied softly. "Embarrassed I caused all that trouble."

"It was no trouble at all."

Now he was the liar. I twisted around, facing him, side by side on my narrow bed.

"I'm sorry."

"What for?" Theo frowned, gently stroking the outline of my jaw. "I'm just glad you're OK." He smiled then, a dawning light on the dark horizon. "And that your roommate is out of town."

He grinned as his hands skimmed lower, lazy and exploring, and even through the dull pain still echoing in my head, through the shadow of nausea and twisting betrayal of guilt, I still felt it. I felt every whisper of touch like a blaze of sensation, strong and sweet enough to blot out the dark. And as Theo leaned in to kiss me, rolling us until I was pinned beneath him, reveling in the weight of his body, I let that sweetness spread; I surrendered to that bright gasp of hope, those restless hands, our hours together exploring each new plane of his body. I clung to the heat until it suffused every last cell, chased away all my bleak and lonely shadows and made me feel, just for a moment, like I was more than flesh and fallible bone.

Like I was infinite, and the world had only just begun.

The next time I woke, sunlight was bright and insistent outside my windows and the bed was empty beside me. I could hear the shower running in the next room, and when I rolled over and checked my phone, I saw to my shock that it was already past noon. I felt a lurch of panic, thinking of the lines of customers at the café, then I remembered: Mika had ordered me to stay home. As if a day in bed with hot soup and the TV would cure me, have me back good as new come Monday morning.

But then, at least, I was glad for the stolen moments away from coffee orders and cleanup duty. The shower turned off, and a moment later Theo was framed in my doorway, a threadbare towel barely wrapped around his golden torso, hair wet from the shower, dripping sunshine to the honeyed floors. I inhaled in a shiver, seeing the light dance off those taut, muscular planes.

"Morning, sleepy." He smiled, slow-boned and lazy.

"It's late."

"You were knocked out like the dead."

I sat up and pulled a blanket around me, suddenly self-conscious. "I didn't snore, did I?"

"Only a little." Theo grinned. I covered my face, flushing. "Aw, don't worry. It was cute."

"Because honking like a freight train is really adorable."

"On you? Yes, it is." Theo took three casual steps to

where his clothes were discarded on the floor, then let his towel drop as he reached to pull his pants back on. "Breakfast?" Theo turned, and caught me staring. He smirked at me, so familiar and at ease, it took my breath away. He suddenly launched himself onto the bed, tackling me with a full-body, half-naked hug until our laughter echoed through the empty apartment.

"Hey," he whispered, inches from my face.

"Hey," I echoed, because real words were still beyond me, and that simple syllable was all I had.

He kissed me quickly, then got up again. "I'll make us some food." I made moves to pull myself upright, but he stopped me. "Where are you going?"

"I have to get up."

"Says who?"

"But—"

"It's the weekend." Theo grinned. "I don't have classes, and you don't have work. We can stay in bed the whole day, if we want. In fact, you're going to. Doctor's orders."

I paused, those two small words rushing me back to fluorescent lights and that cold, narrow bed. "He didn't say—"

"That you needed to take it easy? He didn't have to." Theo's face softened, and I saw for a moment the worry still lurking behind that golden smile. "You're staying in that bed even if I have to tie you down myself."

"Promises, promises." I joked to cover the guilt, wide awake now and slicing at me in a dozen small paper-cuts. Theo lifted one eyebrow and gave me a look that curled my stomach. "See? It has its perks, I promise. Now relax, that's an order."

I flopped back into the mismatched pillows, hating myself for the joyful song that sang in my bloodstream. I shouldn't be happy, lying through my clenched teeth like this, but I couldn't help it.

This was what I'd wanted, wasn't it? What had propelled me onto that east-bound bus, not even imagining what lay ahead. To know this joy, this desire that hummed so vivid in my weary veins. It was the Hail Mary pass Hope had wanted for me, a last shot at a life I'd hidden from, but now that I had it, now that I knew exactly what I'd been missing, I was faced with the cruelest irony of all.

How long could I keep it? How long until this blissful moment shattered in my palm?

WE SPENT THE DAY in a lazy cocoon of each other, talking our way softly through the slow glide of afternoon sun outside the windows. I made Theo sit for me, properly this time, and committed his face to the page with a hundred careful strokes. He watched me from the chair I'd stationed in front of the window, examining me as carefully as I studied him, with the look of someone committing a sight to memory, safe in the treasure chest of our minds.

"Let me see."

I shook my head. "It's not done yet."

"But you're too far away over there." Theo drummed his restless fingertips on the ledge. "I haven't kissed you in, oh, ten minutes, at least."

My smile split my face apart. "Patience."

"Is not a virtue of mine."

"All things come to those who wait," I teased, smudging the line shadowing his jaw.

"You said it yourself last night, we've waited long enough."

"You just want to make sure I'm not drawing you with horns, or three heads."

"I don't know." He grinned. "I think I'd look pretty good with horns."

I laughed and gave a final shade to the page. "OK, you can look now." Theo moved over towards the couch, and I felt another pause of nerves as I slowly turned my sketchpad to face him. "See? No horns."

He took it in silently, then turned his gaze to me. "Can I keep it?"

"Sure." I ripped the page out, and he winced at the sound. "It's just a sketch," I reassured him, but he placed the page on the table like it was solid gold.

"One day, they'll display all these sketches in a gallery," he said, bending to kiss me softly. "Claire Fortune, the early works. People will offer me millions for my original."

I laughed and shook my head. "Or you can use it for scrap paper."

I turned away to tidy my pencils, but Theo caught my hand. "Don't do that. Pretend you're less than you are."

I looked up, seeing nothing but fevered truth in his eyes.

"Trust me, people will know your name, one day."

One day . . .

I ignored the terrible lie of his words. "And you'll be a famous writer," I said brightly, changing the subject. "With a bestselling volume of poetry to your name."

Theo laughed, loud and true. "Because there's nothing that gets fame and riches like poetry."

"Just you wait." I grinned. "You'll see."

He shrugged. "I'd be happy teaching, to be honest."

"Really?" I intertwined our fingers, still marveling at the easiness of our touch.

"I've been thinking about it, and it's one path to go," he said, but I could see he wasn't convinced. "I like teaching the seminars well enough, but . . ."

"But?" I echoed, prompting him.

"Academia isn't such a safe option anymore. There's so much competition for good gigs, even professors find it hard to make tenure. They have to travel all over, take jobs wherever they can find the positions free."

"That's not so bad, you'd get to see the country."

"Still, it's tough to live like that, uprooting every few years. Hard to build a life with anyone." Theo's gaze skipped up to meet mine, and then away. I didn't have time to weigh the meaning of that comment—if there was any meaning to be had—before he pulled me into his lap. "Enough about the future," he said, when my head was resting against his chest, my body curled safe in his arms. "It can wait."

"A thousand years," I agreed, feeling his heartbeat, faint inside his chest.

"Besides," he added, voice rumbling. "We could all be abducted by aliens next week."

I smiled. "What would aliens want with us?" Theo chuckled. I lifted my head. "I mean it, they're an advanced species, travelling millions of miles with technology we can only dream about, and they look around, and think, 'Sure, these are the ones we want'?"

"They must have seen you."

It was so cheesy I groaned. Theo smiled at me. "Too much?"

"Way too much."

180

"Get used to it." He dropped a light kiss on my forehead. "From now on, you're getting at least one lavish compliment a day."

"The price of dating a poet," I laughed.

"Just be glad I'm not composing you sonnets." Theo settled back into the couch cushions, and I lay against him a moment, feeling the world slow its rotation, and the sun sink lower, over the horizon. We were suspended in our own private world, so sweet, time seemed to pause for us, leaving us alone in the hallowed space of our own steady breathing, stretching those moments into a golden infinity.

At last, Theo stretched and yawned, his fingertips circling vague soft circles on my back. "I'm hungry."

I laughed. "We just ate."

"That was hours ago," he protested. "Besides, you need to keep your strength up."

"I'm fine."

"I wasn't talking about that." Theo kissed me, hard and hot, until I saw the glittering night rush behind my eyelids, bright with stars. When he finally pulled away, I couldn't have argued with him if I'd tried. "I'll order takeout," he said, unfolding his long limbs. "What do you feel like? Mexican? Italian?" I moved to get up too, but he shook his head. "No, you stay there."

I sighed. "I'm not an invalid. Come on, let's go out."

Theo paused. "Are you sure?"

"Yes." I ignored the head-rush that swooped through me as I got to my feet. "I've been taking it easy all day. Let's go do something fun."

WE STALKED THE THAI food truck across the city and found it almost hidden in an alleyway by a movie theatre across town. They were showing *Die Hard* movies, booming through the old brick walls, and we spirited our food in like contraband, hidden under sweaters in my purse; sneaking triumphant past the bored ticket clerk to set up camp in the back row of those dusty velvet seats: cross-legged in the half-empty theatre, gorging ourselves on the food and each other as the fiery explosions burned in the corners of our eyes. We emerged, giddy and breathless after the final credits rolled, his arm slung tight around my shoulders, and every step full of a gleeful freedom. The streets disappeared beneath our eager feet, darkness cut through with the shimmering neon of the city as the hours sped past, magic, and wholly our own.

We couldn't keep our hands off each other, spinning with the pent-up longing that had fuelled me so many lonely nights. Now, Theo kissed me a dozen times over, in doorways, and shadowed hollows, secret as the city sped past; his hands anchored me to the earth, and his lips made me his own. If I could have made myself liquid, I would have: dissolved into air and slipped into his lungs, trickled soft through his bloodstream, made ourselves one, but this was a fine consolation. We laughed and teased, raced breathless through the dark, and when at last we tangled back in my bed, peeling shadows from each other with every touch, there was a new fervor in his eyes, a new fierce freedom to every slow thrust. I cried out for him without shame, spiraling deeper into the glittering rush, so that when the world shattered around us, his was the only heartbeat I could use to mark the time.

THE PROMISE

CHAPTER SIXTEEN

Do you blame me?

I often wonder now, thinking back to those first reckless nights, if what I did was unforgiveable. To take that man's heart, the most precious thing of all, and lose myself in him knowing full well the price. Because it wasn't just mine to pay, not then. Once I'd felt his body move inside me, seen the depths of those blue eyes filled with wonder and brief, biting panic, I was ruining the both of us, and it was only a matter of time.

But still, he was all I wanted.

They don't warn you how lonely cancer becomes. That part, I never saw coming. The fight is a team sport: your family, specialists, church, and friends, all united to cheer you on from the sidelines and push you through chemo and treatment and hard, backbreaking work to that cancer-free finish line. But dying . . .?

Dying you do alone.

Hope understood. Maybe that's what brought us

together, bonded more tightly than sisters ever could be. She knew how it felt to see the world with a slow, dreadful countdown ticking in the back of your mind, to be consumed with jealousy and rage for every person you ever knew, waltzing oblivious through their precious days as your bitter mantra demanded the truth. Why me? Why not them? *Why, why, why?* It's a chasm that opens between you and everyone else, and no matter how much they love you or how hard they try, they're still trapped, suspended safely on their side of the canyon, while the ground beneath your feet keeps crumbling, closer to the brink.

From the day of my diagnosis, until the day I met Hope, I was alone. Every moment, every breath, I felt it in my bones. Some days, I thought the loneliness would kill me long before my tumor ever did, that's how deep it sliced through me, the steel-hot sadness that felt like a cancer all of its own. I was apart from the world, facing down demons they could never dream. Until her.

Until Theo.

That night, I crawled out of bed and sat curled in the window, wrapped in the smell of his sweater, watching the lights of the city wind their way through a million strangers' lives; a hundred thousand restless, dozing couples, five hundred figures at the window, just like mine. I felt it then more than ever before: how vast the world was, and how small and insignificant my own frail heart.

Tick, tick, tick.

The tears stung wet on my cheeks, and I had to clench my fists, digging half-moon nail-prints into my palm to keep from weeping out loud.

This was supposed to be the beginning.

Girl meets boy, girl dreams and hopes, relentless, to bring their bond to life. They overcome all obstacles and find each other. Happily ever after. Everyone knows how the story is supposed to go; sitting old and grey on a porch swing somewhere, watching the sunset they earned with every slow-passing day. Except that sunset was beyond me now, my *ever* was dwindling by the hour: a cruel countdown speeding ever closer to impact.

All I had was this. Every second, every last breath of present tense. It was all I would ever have of him. God, looking back now, I can feel the slicing ache all over again, fresh as those tears staining my silent cheeks. It had started with such small, measured desire: a last few months alone in the world, a chance to taste the life that would soon be out of reach. No chemo drips, no hospital rooms, no parents hovering anxiously in the back of every hallway. I would lose myself in the world, witness everything Hope would never get to see, everything I hadn't realized I was missing until she dragged me, laughing, into the sun.

It wasn't asking much; that's what I told myself, at least. Surely the world owed me a few months of freedom after my years tethered to those IV tubes. But even so, would it have been easier to face the end without Theo, or would I still have felt that same futile rage claw desperately behind my ribcage? The café, Kelsey, cycling those leafy streets alone; that much was something to lose, something to mourn. And now I had so much more. That man's heart, sound asleep in my bed, and my own resting beside him, open and bruised and reveling in every last measure of love.

Don't scare me like that again.

I watched the night bleed into daylight, and felt the time slip away. Then, like now, I was helpless to stop it coming. And then, like now, I would have moved mountains to get it back.

One more night with him. One more laughing, reckless day. An hour tumbling into his steady stare, one more minute of his mouth on mine.

All I could do was vow to make the moments count.

CHAPTER SEVENTEEN

AFTER SUCH A miraculous weekend, I felt as if nothing should ever be the same, but come Monday morning, there I was: behind the register at Wired again, serving up too-sweet coffees and flakey croissants that showered the countertop with buttery crumbs, as light as the snow falling once more outside the windows.

"You look better," Mika noted, as I settled into my swift ballet of order and pour, feeling so weightless I was just about ready to turn pirouettes there on the scratched and polished floors.

"Much." I beamed. "You were right, I needed the break."

"Good." Mika was already distracted, flipping through delivery forms. "They're still dropping like flies from this flu thing. The last thing we need is to infect every customer that comes through the door."

"You make it sound like a pandemic," JJ teased as he

passed by, arms laden with a teetering tower of paper cups.

"Influenza's killed over fifty million people," he answered grimly.

"Yes, in 1918." JJ grinned. "Before they had a little something called antibiotics, and bleach."

"You can never be too careful."

JJ winked at me, brushing his hand across Mika's back as he passed, a tiny gesture that rang truer for me now that I knew exactly what it was to feel that magnetic draw, wanting to reach out and touch any chance I got. Theo was in classes all morning, but my heart still swooped at every ring through the front doors, a heady drum of expectation. By the time midday rolled around, spilling another wave of patrons wrapped snugly in their thick parkas and scarves, I felt the caffeine withdrawal written on their faces, craving just another fix.

And then there he was, stepping over the threshold with his navy duffel coat dusted in a powdered sugar snow. It felt like the first time, that bright September day when just a glimpse of him had thrown my whole world off kilter.

"Coffee, please, ma'am. Black." Theo sauntered up and leaned his elbows on the countertop with an irrepressible grin on his face.

"Like your heart?"

He laughed, and leaned even further, to drop a kiss on my waiting lips. "Don't you know it?"

I poured him one fresh, and slipped a pastry onto a plate, too, my blood singing with every step. "How was your morning?"

He shrugged, still smiling. "I can't remember. I spent it missing you."

There was a snort behind me. I turned and found Kelsey rolling her eyes so hard she could have blinded herself. "Spare us the schmaltz," she sighed, her new haircut slicing sharp across her jaw. "I mean, not that you two aren't poster children for young love, but some of us need to make it through the day without losing our lunch."

"Sorry." Theo didn't sound at all apologetic. "But you're just going to have to learn to live with it."

He leaned over and kissed me, longer this time, and I followed, slipping one hand around his neck as the stars burst again behind my eyes. I surfaced to a slow clap, and Kelsey's irrepressible scowl.

"Five points for technical proficiency," she drawled. "But the Russian judges docked a few for public nuisance."

I flushed, realizing there was a line behind him now, café patrons not so impressed with our affection when it blocked their path to hot coffee and snacks. I stepped aside and let her take the first orders, but Theo lingered, toying with my hand. "When do you get off?"

Kelsey smirked before I could reply. "Soon, if you keep that up."

My cheeks burned hotter. "I'm done at four."

"OK." Theo smiled at me, warm enough to heat my blood from the inside out. "I'll come pick you up. I've got a surprise for you."

"What kind of surprise?"

"Not telling." He glanced around, then leaned in again. "Quick, while Elvira is distracted."

"I heard that!" Kelsey's voice echoed through another kiss, and then he finally left me, hitching his bag and blowing on the coffee cup, ducking back out into the crowd.

I turned back to work, still smiling giddily to myself. Kelsey was watching me, eyes narrowed. "What?" I asked, already defensive. I quickly moved behind the coffee machine and reached for the first slip of paper order stuck along the rim. "And don't give me another lecture about college boys, and town girls, and how it'll all end in tears."

"I wasn't going to," she replied.

"So?" I prompted, impatient.

"You're hands are shaking," she said, softly. "Do you want a minute, to get your pills?"

I froze. Blood rushed, pounding in my ears, and I set the

rattling mug down, suddenly naked and exposed under the old-fashioned iron sconces. My mind tripped over itself to process the words. What did she know? How much had she seen? I thought I'd been so careful, that nobody had noticed my momentary lapses, but now, the sick realization dawned: my secret was slipping out, one glimpse at a time.

Kelsey was still waiting for me, silent by the register. "Too much coffee," I covered at last, with a nervous laugh. "I guess that fourth espresso was a mistake."

"This place should post a warning," she agreed, but somehow, her even tone only made it worse. I wished I could ignore her, pretend like she'd never said a word, but even when I squeezed two tight fists and willed my hands to steady, the tremor still remained. My bag was under the counter, the pill bottle in the back zipped pouch. I swallowed them down with a gulp of water from the tap, but it felt like a failure.

"I guess this means you and Teddy made things official." Kelsey didn't skip a beat, her voice bright now as she swiftly dispensed coffee cups and rang up the correct change. "What did you do, show up at his doorstep and seduce him?"

"Something like that." My voice caught, still reeling.

"Well, I never. Didn't think you had it in you." Kelsey shot me a smile and a playful wink. "It's always the quiet ones."

JJ bustled through. "Always the quiet ones who what?"

"Have the most delicious secrets." Kelsey nudged him. "Case in point."

"Me?" he laughed. "Wouldn't you like to know . . ."

"Mika's the real dark horse though," Kelsey continued. "I bet he's hiding all kinds of deep, dark confessions. Five cats at home with matching knit sweaters. A secret love of Abba."

They continued to tease as I worked silently at the espresso machine. To any outsider, Kelsey's banter was effortless, but I knew she was covering for me. A dazzle of jazz hands here, a snort of scathing laughter there; nobody gave a second glance at the girl hiding behind chrome and steel, her trembling hands clattering the countertop until at last, *God, at last*, the chemicals did their dirty work and my limbs followed orders again.

It was the first time that had happened in public, but I knew it wouldn't be the last.

Later, in the back staff room, I pulled my snow boots on and readied myself for the cold outside, but Kelsey lingered in the doorway, watching me again with that all-seeing stare.

"I'm fine," I said shortly, before she could even open her mouth.

There was a long pause. I braced myself for more questions I couldn't answer, but instead, Kelsey just nodded. "Call me if you need someone to cover a shift sometime. I could use the extra cash."

I nodded, fumbling with my knit cap. "OK."

That was it, all she'd ever say on the matter. Even later, when I couldn't hide it anymore, she never asked, never said a word. She found me curled over in the café bathroom once, flailing desperately as pain split my skull in two, but even then, all she did was grip my hand tightly and wait with me there on the cracked tile floor for it to pass. No judgment, no demands to know the score. She was a true friend, in her way, beneath all that balled up sharpness, and I only wish I could have known her better in what brief time I had then to make it count.

But on that snowy December day, I couldn't get away from her fast enough. I took my chances on the bustling sidewalk outside, waiting on the frozen concrete, sheltering from the flurries still lazily drifting from the somber skies. People rushed past, trying to escape the cold, but I was still enchanted by the snow. There was something so fresh and clean about a snowfall, pristine before the world had a chance to drag its muddy tracks through the powder and turn it to a grimy slush. I'd spent my whole life in the desert, where winter came brittle and blazing from the same clear skies that spread above us year-round. Snowfall was an adventure, magical on my TV screen for Christmastime. I would snip diamonds into white craft paper every year, string them around our windows to filter the bright sunshine outside. Once, when I was fifteen, we travelled to see a specialist in Chicago when the sidewalks were still thick and powdered, the river a frozen block snaking through the city. I remember watching the snow fall for hours, hypnotized as we waited in offices and testing labs. I ignored the hushed voices and grave discussion of my new scans, and imagined myself far away from those sad little rooms instead, sledding through a great forest, perhaps, or tumbling snowmen with a group of friends.

"Think fast!"

I turned just as a tiny snowball burst against my chest, spraying icy droplets into the air. Theo laughed, bundled behind a thick plaid scarf, and just like that, the clouds seemed to part to let a little sunlight filter through.

He pulled me into a slow embrace, kissing me like we had all the time in the world. "Hey." He cradled my cheeks with icy hands, his expression a mirror of what I felt inside. That gleeful smile, as if our bodies couldn't contain this kind of happiness alone.

"Hey." I grinned back, all sadness forgotten. I know it was fickle, to let the guilt and fear melt away so easily, but it would have been a crime to waste one single moment with him on such a heavy heart. "How is the youth of America today?"

"Staring at their cellphones." Theo tucked one arm around me, steering us into the flow of afternoon pedestrians. "The only time I can get a rise out of them is when I assign rap lyrics to study."

"You do that?" I laughed.

"Anything to get their attention. Jay-Z and Keats have more in common than you'd think."

We crossed the square, then Theo turned right, down a narrow, winding street. I looked around at the old townhouses, crammed narrow with their gingerbread trim. "So what's this surprise?" I asked, my curiosity growing.

"You'll see." He was grinning, excited about whatever lay in store.

"You got me a pony?"

He laughed. "Almost."

"Give me a hint," I pleaded, playful. "Is it animal, vegetable, or mineral?"

"Hmmm." Theo pretended to think. "None of the above."

I didn't mind about the surprise, all I wanted was another night with him. All day long, I'd slipped back into memories of our nights together, hidden in the fort of sheets with my door closed against the world; the restless shiver of his fingertips on my skin. What I'd discovered with him was nothing new, there were millions of people on this planet craving somebody the way I hungered for

Theo, but still, I marveled at the secret of this desire. How did anyone function, carrying such a wild fever in their hearts? How did the world spin on, through morning commutes and midday snack breaks, laundry sessions and grocery runs, when there were better ways to spend the time, tangled up in each other, paying tribute to the curve of flesh and bone?

"Nearly there . . ." After leading me down another maze of winding streets behind the college, Theo came to a stop outside a non-descript building. The ground-floor tenant was a boarded-up restaurant, and the labels by the buzzer listing were peeling and illegible. I gave him a dubious look.

"Is this like your professor's rooftop, where we're hoping nobody calls the police?"

Theo laughed. "It's all above-board, I promise. See, I even have a key." He produced it with a virtuous look, unlocking the peeling blue-painted door and heaving it open so I could duck under his arm inside. The lobby didn't inspire any more confidence, if you could even call it that: stained carpet in a narrow hallway, with flyers and discarded mail littering the floor, and a dimly lit staircase circling up into the dark.

Still, Theo's smile didn't fade. "Third floor," he said, buoyant. "Apartment B."

So up we climbed, my hand trailing the bannister for

steadiness despite the unseen grime. My thighs ached and my head spun by the time we reached the landing, but Theo's excitement was infectious, and I couldn't wait to see what he had in store. "Admit it, you got me a pony," I said, breathing hard but hiding it. He laughed, and ceremoniously threw open the dusty blue door.

"Even better."

I stepped inside. It was dark, heavy drapes pulled across the windows, but then Theo flipped a switch, and the ancient light bulbs flickered to life.

"It belongs to a friend of mine, but he's out of town, studying in London for a couple of months. He's happy to let you use it while he's gone, just as long as we keep the pipes from freezing, and call the super in if something leaks."

Theo kept talking, almost nervous, as I took it all in. We were standing in an artist's studio, a tiny space barely thirty feet square, but with double-height ceilings marked with steel beams and industrial girders. Canvases leaned against every wall, the concrete floors stained with a dozen layers of paint and graffiti splatters, an easel abandoned in one corner, and old stubby brushes lined up, congealing in empty mason jars along one ledge.

"It used to be a factory, before they split it into apartments," Theo continued. He crossed to the windows, and started yanking the blackout drapes aside. Light spilled in, falling softly through the dust to graze the stacked bookcases and haphazard rows of old, cracked paints.

Theo looked to me, his expression hopeful. "Is this OK? I know you didn't say anything, but I saw those big canvases all crammed together at your place. I thought . . . well, I figured it would be good to have the space."

I was lost for words. A knot bubbled in my throat, and I had to blink back a sudden rush of tears. I nodded, turning away a moment to collect myself. Everywhere I looked, there were half-scratched canvases and peeling layers of forgotten paint, but I'd never seen anything more beautiful. It was a palace, a place of dreams, and for now, at least, it was mine.

"You got me a studio," I said, my voice still soft with wonder. "I can't believe you got me this." When I looked back at him, Theo's smile spread with relief.

"You like it?"

I laughed. "I love it!" I flung my arms around him, holding tight as emotion sliced me clean apart.

"Good." Theo pulled back, looking so proud. "Like I said, he's gone for a few months, but even when he's back, maybe you guys could figure something out. Store your stuff here, at least."

A few months from now . . . I kept my smile bright and caught his hand. "How are you so sweet?" I kissed his knuckles, the perfect curve between thumb and index finger.

Theo looked bashful. "I'm not."

"Yes, you are."

I tugged him closer, traded that perfect hand for the belt loops that could bring him flush against me. Theo's hands came to me then, a soft skim over my arms, sliding my jacket away. "It's only what you deserve," he whispered, finding the shivering hollow of my neck, and I sank against him, wanting so much for it to be true. If I deserved this, then it couldn't be so wrong. Not wrong to take his mouth, and his body, and his pure, pure heart, right there amongst a decade of spilled paint and crumbling canvas, bare flesh on a cool concrete floor. Not wrong to lose myself in him until I forgot the reasons I was there at all, as if the fact of our existence had made it providence, part of that plan they had told me to believe in all along.

Well, I was a believer, for those few endless hours at least, watching the pale winter light fade into the starburst dark, feeling oceans rise and empires fall, until I ceased to exist. Like before, at the concert, a crowd strung twisting on heavy bass and shivering snare drums; those hours with Theo made me more than myself, somehow.

More than my body, flesh and poisoned bones. More than the time bomb *tick, tick, ticking* down towards zero in the back of my brain. We both took flight, until there was nothing left of the both of us except the breath that passed between us in whispers and echoes and deep, wild gasps.

For just a little while, I was free.

HAVE YOU EVER BEEN in love like that before? Maybe not for a lifetime, or even a year of endless pleasure, but a single moment: those pure, perfect hours. Feeling that devotion, your heart peeled wide open, made something more than flesh and wet, surging blood. If you haven't, then I can only hope for you an afternoon like that, one day. A chance to live forever in the pure, sweet rush.

And maybe I do.

I read once that for every moment, each split-second event, there exists a different world, an infinite number of universes spinning on in parallel, separated by that single heartbeat of change. Hope and I would talk about it all the time. A world where we're still sharing popsicles together in those chemo chairs, holding on fast, fighting the good fight. Or maybe I woke up one morning to a scribbled note and a postcard from California, her smile shining bright in the dazzling waves. A world where cell clusters knit themselves a different pattern in the grey matter of my brain, and I slipped effortlessly through high school, flipping that tassel on a graduation stage, unloading boxes with my dad in a lemon-fresh dorm room on some campus far away.

A world where Theo and I had more than those few, precious weeks together, where our paths slipped and skirted past the dark, looming storm—delivered safely somehow beyond the end to a new horizon, crammed together in a tiny faculty apartment as the letters accumulated after his name. A white dress. A long walk on my father's arm. A whisper-soft baby's blanket. A row of penciled notches rising on the wall beside the staircase. A half-century of his fingers threaded through mine, learning every constellation in his soft, endless gaze.

Somewhere out there, it's a truth. I loved him for months, years to come, more than this too-short lifetime, at least.

Somewhere, Hope is still raging brightly, cherry-stained lips full of song.

But not this world, not today. The concrete floor became too cold, and we bundled up again, hands still slipping to find hands, backs, any touch we could. Theo presented me with the key like a medal, and I held the curves tight in my palm as he walked me all the way home.

"You think Tessa's still away?" he asked with a teasing

grin as we approached my front steps, the cold biting against the heat that blazed from my body.

"Let's hope."

I pulled him after me up the stairs, praying for an empty apartment and another endless night. "Even if she's home . . ." Theo started, suggestion in his voice.

"You're staying," I decided, and he laughed at the fierce note in my voice.

"Yes, ma'am."

The door was unlocked, but I didn't think anything of it until we were inside, propelled into the warm lights and muggy attic air, and Tessa was giving me an anxious look, caught in her sweatpants and college tank top with a table of study notes.

"I tried calling," she said, reluctant, standing aside.

"Claire, thank God."

My mom jolted up from a chair. My dad stood, silently waiting.

They had found me, and there was no hiding anymore.

CHAPTER EIGHTEEN

Panic FROZE ME, the rush of guilt and heart-stop discovery, but as usual, Theo didn't miss a beat.

"Mr. and Mrs. Fortune." He strode forward to greet them like a true gentleman, with a strong handshake and welcoming smile, while I gripped tight to the nearest chair-back, watching my life unravel in a heartbeat. My naïveté hit hard. God, how stupid could I have been? Did I really think I could just disappear? All my careful planning and those past months of freedom turned bitter in my mouth, imagining that they wouldn't find me, that I wouldn't wind up standing in a room just like this, against the onslaught of demands and frantic concern. The inevitability sank through me, but I could do was stand and watch my worlds collide as I braced for impact.

"I'm Theo. It's a pleasure to meet you. Claire didn't say you were in town."

"Theo," my mother repeated faintly. Her dark eyes were on me, and I felt the wing-beats of her anxiety pounding, clear from across the room. My dad was watching too, but his was a more assessing look, moving measured from me to Theo and back again, as if he could see every shirt button done up wrong.

"It's great you're here," Theo continued, oblivious to the stampede of terror thundering in my chest. "Are you visiting for the holidays?"

Christmas. I'd forgotten. By the look on their faces, they had, too.

"Yes," my dad finally spoke up. "We thought we'd surprise Claire and drop in. It's a time for family, after all."

The words sat, heavy. I cringed to hear them. I'd been gone only four months but it could have been years from the panic-aged faces staring back at me, worn lines around my mother's eyes, and that weary look of my father, so defeated.

I'd been so selfish, I could see it now, but still, I wanted more from them.

Don't say a word. Please, don't say a single word.

The silence stretched, and even Theo sensed the tension. "Well . . . I'll let you guys catch up. It was good to meet you, sir." Theo shook my father's hand again, then turned back to me, questioning. He wanted a sign, some permission to stay, but for the first, and only time in my life, I needed him gone.

"I'll call you tomorrow," I told him, still desperate, still so guilty.

Theo moved towards the door, but paused beside me, touched his hand to my arm, brushed a kiss to my forehead. It took everything I had not to flinch, or back away from the golden touches that had been so pure. "Goodnight." He gave me a smile, that same reassuring crinkle in his eyes, and then he was gone. The door closed behind him, and the terror in my chest eased, just a little.

"Theo." My mom repeated his name, louder now. There was a bitterness to her voice, a sharp-edged scorn. "*Theo*. Is this the reason you disappeared halfway around the country, and scared us half to death? So you could stay out all hours with some boy, and shack up in this garret doing God knows what?"

Dad placed a calming hand on her shoulder. "Your mother's just worried. We both are. We got a call from some doctor, he said you'd collapsed, refused treatment, and just walked out. God, Claire what were you thinking?"

Somebody cleared their throat. Tessa was still stranded just on the outskirts of our world, looking mortified. "I'm going to the library," she said, carefully avoiding our gazes.

"No, Tessa, you don't have to—"I tried to protest, but she gave me a look.

"You take your time. Nice to meet you, Mr. and Mrs. Fortune."

It was all so formal. Mr. and Mrs., handshakes and polite farewells as Tessa packed up her things and struggled into snow boots, and finally left us in the silent wreckage of our family.

Where could I even begin?

"I'm fine." I said the words slowly, still holding my chair-back tight. It was a life raft, my only tether in this storm. "You didn't need to come. I've been texting you. I'm doing fine." But my mother only snorted, her cheeks flushed like a high fever.

"That's not what the doctor said. Claire, you need to be back in treatment. He sent us the CT scans, the tumor's growing. We need an aggressive plan, right away—"

"No," my voice whispered.

"You're coming home," she continued, determined. "We can pack up your things and have you booked in with Doctor Mortimer back home first thing Thursday morning. We've already talked and had the scans sent. He agrees it's late, but if we get you back into chemo as soon as possible, we could stand a chance. I'm sure your roommate won't mind, we can pay for the notice on your lease." She was pacing, restless, as if she was about to go start pulling sweaters from my dresser drawer to hurl in a suitcase. "I'll call the airline, we can have a delivery company pick up the rest. It's not too late, we can still buy some more time."

"Mom!" My voice echoed sharply. "Mom, stop, please. You have to stop."

"What am I supposed to do?" she shot back, her face cracking open to reveal something desperate and raw. "Just sit around back home waiting for a goddamn phone call to say it's all over? Waiting around for my baby to die?"

I felt her grief like a slap, shocking the last of my afternoon reverie from my body, and wrapping me instead with a smothering expanse of guilt. This I knew by heart, the cotton-wool concern, pressing gently, dry and scratching, making me gasp for air. She'd wrapped me tight for years, locked in the soft anxiety of her embrace until I couldn't breathe, crushed under so many delicate layers of fear and desperate hope.

She loved me. She loved me, and it still wasn't enough to save my life.

"I'm sorry," I muttered, looking down. "I didn't mean for you to worry. I told you I was doing fine."

"This doctor said you were brought in unconscious in an ambulance." Mom's voice was still wretched, every word an accusation. "That's not *fine*."

"I would have collapsed back home, just the same." I lifted my eyes, pleading with them both. "Don't you see?

It doesn't make a difference where I am, or what we do. This thing is going to kill me, and it's just a matter of time."

Mom clenched her jaw and looked away, as if death was standing right in front of her, and she was just plain refusing to acknowledge its existence. My dad stepped up, instead. "If it doesn't make a difference, then why can't you just come back home?"

"Because I need to be here."

"For this Theo?" he asked, those watchful eyes on me again. It felt like he could see every sweet, reckless hour we'd spent tangled in each other's embrace, but I refused to feel ashamed of anything we'd shared.

"For everything." I held on tighter. "I have a job here, friends. Don't you see?" I asked, begging them, "This is my last chance. My only chance to have a *life*."

"You have a life with us," my mom insisted.

"It's not enough."

"We're not enough?" She threw my words back at me, and my heart broke all over again. For their grief, for the years of anguish I'd brought them, and this, the last simple truth.

"No."

I saw the betrayal in her eyes, but there was no taking it back. I'd made my choice the day I boarded that Greyhound bus and set off into the unknown horizon, and now, with Theo's lips sill burning their imprint on my body, I wouldn't change it even if I could. Maybe that made me selfish, but she was too, to want me back where she thought I belonged. Safe at home in my childhood bed, swaddled in her hand-stitched comforter, just down the hall. Cuddled on the couch together watching daytime soaps, my pills lined up neatly on the counter to follow a grilled cheese sandwich and tea. The hours slipping past, same as they'd ever been, as the cancer grew and my body failed and my heart ached, restless in my chest. I had so little time left, God, so little fucking time. I couldn't sacrifice another day to stay there, safe, in my mother's embrace, even if it broke her, even if it broke both of our selfish hearts.

"It's too late," I whispered, begging. "You know it's too late. There's nothing you can do anymore."

She pressed her lips together in a thin, frantic line. "No. I refuse to believe it."

"So don't. But this is my life, what's left of it, and it's my choice now what that means. I'm staying, mom. I'm not going back there."

She turned away, and my father cleared his throat. "Let's talk about this in the morning."

He was always the reasonable one, steady with plans and charts while my mother barreled ahead, full-steam with determination. "We've been travelling all day, I think we could all use a little rest." He took my mother's hand, a reassuring squeeze. "We're staying at a hotel over the river. Why don't you come meet us for breakfast?"

"I have work."

"Then we could come to you. I'd like to see this café of yours," he added, hopeful, and I felt the guilt again, moving my head for me in a nod.

"Fine. But, you can't say anything. Nobody knows I'm sick, I can't . . ." It was too much to even put into words, the great aching fear trapped just below the surface. "Please, don't tell them. You're just in town for the holidays, there's nothing wrong."

My mother pressed her lips again, furious, but my dad nodded. "OK. We won't mention it."

"I mean it." My desperation was clear. "Not one word about hospitals, or treatment, nothing around them. Promise."

"I promise, sweetheart."

I let out a shaking breath, and gave them the address for Wired. I told them to come after the first morning rush, and please, not make a fuss. They moved to the door and reclaimed the suitcases I saw propped there for the first time. They really had come straight here, fleeing headlong through airport check-ins and taxi ranks, driven on by the panic of that unexpected phone call. Doctor Benson. I should have known.

"Tomorrow?" Dad gave me a stern look, as if he half-expected me to pack my cases and run again before they could make me stay.

But there was nowhere to run to, not anymore. I nodded. "I'll see you then."

I closed the door behind them and rested my head there against the scratched wood, listening to their footsteps drift away down the stairs. It was aching again, that dull, desperate throb that seemed to be in the background of every thought, waiting to rear up and break through. Soon, the pain would be as much a part of my life as breathing, but then, it still came and went in waves, pushed back to shore by the line of neat prescription pills until another swell could rise. I let myself feel it for a moment instead of racing for those white tabs. The roar, the sharp rush. This was my tumor screaming its victory, the only way I would ever feel its presence, that taunting, vicious pain.

God, I hated it. Some therapists try to make you personify it—give it a name, a presence to fight against. I would see it in the hospital wards, those childish scribbled pictures, like a twisted version of a family portrait. There was one girl who drew it as a piranha, sneaky and sharp. I shared a room with her, during a week-long battery of tests for an experimental program out of state. Lucy, she was called, a sprite of a ten-year-old with a fuzz of copper red hair. She was already shorn from her last surgery, sitting patiently hooked up to her IV and the monitors in the middle of her row of plush teddy bears. She was too old for them, she told me, with all the weary wisdom of a battle-scarred warrior, but her mom liked to bring them to keep her company at nights, while she worked double shifts at a call center downtown. It was the two of us in the room, and Lucy and I would play gin rummy on her tray table, late into the night when the wards slipped into that otherworldly neon silence, nothing but the yawning night-shift nurses and an occasional intern on the rounds. That was her fourth surgery in three years, she informed me, matter-of-fact, as we traded out vital stats: cancer, location, stage of decline. She'd already had her Make-A-Wish trip to swim with the dolphins in Orlando, and now it was nothing but Hail Mary shots in the surgical dark. She hoped to make it past Christmas, for her mom's sake. She didn't want to ruin Christmas for them by dying too soon.

I didn't tell her that Christmas would be ruined, regardless. That every year they would weep for her, whether she lived those extra few weeks or not. I never found out if she made it that far; my tests were finished, my cancer deemed all wrong for the program, and I went back home to a brittle, dry Texas December. I didn't try to track her down; by then, we all knew it was a useless task. The guy from chemo, that girl waiting on an MRI. We were passengers on the same trip but after the first few funerals, we learned not to get too close. Hope was the only one who broke that golden rule, but then, I still hadn't met her yet. So my mom made eggnog, and my dad put up a tree, and I thought of Lucy as the clock ticked over into dawn on Christmas morning, and some other family, miles away, faced the day with her death looming large.

And now it was my turn. My family, my last Christmas, one way or another.

The fear gripped me again, and suddenly, the attic was too small to contain it.

This was the end.

I'd been running from it for months, carefully ignoring all the symptoms and warning signs as if the words strung together didn't make a death sentence, but it finally crashed through me then, unavoidable, the realization as cold and unforgiving as frigid steel.

This was the end I'd been hiding from.

You'd have thought that after living years with the inevitability hanging over me, I would be used to it by now. Calm and resolute. But it was still the thickest black panic I'd ever know, an abyss I couldn't bring myself to gaze into, despite all the warnings. I'd seen it play out in a dozen other tumor patients, one excruciating heartbeat at a time. I wouldn't be like Hope, wheezing and stuttering as the domino effect of decay tumbled through her vital organs. No, my cancer would hit my brain hard and just keep hitting. First, the blackouts would become more frequent, the headaches blossoming into an electric storm that the painkillers wouldn't touch. My shaking hands would get worse, my motor functions confused. Speech would slur, my eyesight fail, even my memories would snag and unravel. And the pain, that pain would consume me, devour every waking moment and breath— unless I picked the half-life relief of a drugged-up, woozy end, trapped in bed and clinging to a plastic cord delivering opiates to my poor, weak system. Maybe I would slip away easy, or maybe it would be me begging by the end, but one day soon, that tumor would consume some last, desperate function and I would be gone.

Just like that, a flat-line on a flickering monitor. There, then not.

I gasped for air. The unfairness ripped me apart, and I sank onto my heels, biting down on my shirtsleeve so I wouldn't weep aloud. Alone on that floor, I felt the loss that would soon become so familiar—not of what I wouldn't have, but the things I'd only just begun to glimpse. Theo. God, *Theo*. He was mine now. This was what I'd wanted, wasn't it? This was all I'd craved. And now, having it, having it to lose, it felt like the cruelest punishment of all. Maybe I couldn't run from this again, but I could run *to* something this time. To the only thing that mattered now, the one spark of life bright enough to burn the pain away.

I swallowed my pills like a promise, grabbed my bag, and set out into the night again. I'd never made this trip before, but I had the address printed in a text on my phone. Six blocks to the subway, four stops, and another three streets to his door, but when I rang the ancient buzzer, it was Kelsey's smudged kohl stare that greeted me through the crack in the door.

"Claire?"

She unhitched the chain and stood aside, dressed in a pair of men's boxers and a threadbare tank. I didn't ask about Guy; I didn't have the words in me to keep from crying. Her eyes swept over me, at the hands I had clenched into two bitter fists at my side. "Down the hall, last door on the right."

I nodded a thanks and followed her directions to his door. Theo answered on the first knock, and I kissed the surprise from his lips before he could even say a word. We tumbled back, the door barely closing, and then there was nothing but a soft mattress, and ink-blue sheets, and his hands, God, those glorious hands pulling me under, someplace safe and golden, and far from the future I was fighting so hard to ignore.

If anything could have healed me, Theo's hands would have been it. His hands and mouth and the sweet press of his body. That distant look of wonder in his eyes, unraveling above me. He wasn't even trying, but it was everything to me, a pleasure wild enough to blot out the sun, to wrestle even my head-splitting pain into submission as it carried me past the darkness into a fresh, pale dawn.

CHAPTER NINETEEN

ONE MORE DAY GONE. One more night I was never getting back.

I would tell him, I promised myself, watching the sun rise across his body the next morning, his breath so steady, that sleeping face so unaware.

Next year.

It wasn't far now, a week until the clocks turned over, and that fresh calendar page sat waiting, full of resolution and promise.

A week to savor him, enough to last my lifetime. A week of half-truths I couldn't admit were lies. Didn't the universe owe us that much, however desperate it may be?

I would tell him, soon.

Just not today.

"You're awake." His eyelashes fluttered, then his mouth spread in that sleepy smile. He crushed me closer and let out a yawn. "Did you sleep OK?"

"Enough." I smiled, sitting up. In the light, I could see

his room for the first time, the teetering bookcases and simple lines of his furniture and desk. A laptop, light winking, a lamp beside the desk. There were no photographs, I realized, no souvenirs. It was as blank a slate as my own attic room, before the sketches and canvas frames expanded to claim every last wall. I twisted my head to look at him, still splayed there, half-dreaming. "My parents are coming to the café today," I said slowly. It was the first time I'd ever mentioned them to him; it felt like breaking a secret, and worse still, breaking it far too late.

Theo played with my left hand, tracing gently in the crevice between my fingers, and twisting his thumb around mine. "Is that OK?" he asked, measured.

No.

"I guess."

I hated lying to him, hated every sharp guilty word. But still, he didn't ask, that wasn't his style. Instead, he just watched me, waiting for me to want to share enough that I opened my mouth and offered up my half-truths, carefully weighing every almost-word.

"I ran away," I admitted. "Not, really. I mean, I was nineteen. An adult. I left a note . . . God, how pathetic does that sound?" I caught myself right away. "A note. But I couldn't tell them I was going. They would only have found some way to make me stay."

Theo kept tracing my hand, the fine fortune-teller lines of my palm. I closed my eyes. "I needed to get away, make my own life, but they don't understand. They want to keep me safe."

"And they're worried about you? I know it's a big city, and you're far away, but . . . you can take care of yourself." Theo's grin spread. "You can be pretty bad-ass."

I smiled. "It's not so simple. After Hope . . ." I paused, my voice fading to a whisper to remember it, the months stretching in a haze of black and grey and slashes of vivid red. "I was in a bad place. So, I understand why they worry."

"But you're doing better now?" His voice lifted, a careful question.

I nodded and squeezed his hand with a smile. "The best I've ever been."

It was true. Sure, my tumor was twisting and writhing through my brain, spreading one cancerous cell at a time. But my heart? It had never beat so wildly, or sang out such a breathless song.

It was the best of times, it was the worst of times. That long-forgotten high-school English paper flooded back to me, and I felt it, suspended there in Theo's bedroom between the two poles of my fate. "C'mon." I scrambled to my feet, wincing as my bare soles hit the cold polished floor. "I'm going to be late, and you have classes."

He groaned, catching my wrist before I could dance out of reach. "Don't make me."

I laughed, falling back into the warm covers. "We can't play hooky," I warned him, even as my body sank against his. "Not today."

"What if it's a snow day?" Theo grinned up at me, his eyes bright. "We could look outside that window and find the whole city shut down. Drifts ten feet deep."

"Ten feet!" I leaned in to kiss the tip of his nose, his forehead, his earlobe. "If that was true, we'd be snowed in. We'd have to stay home."

"Exactly." Theo rolled, crushing me beneath him. He settled his head against my chest and let out another lazy yawn. "So, bed it is."

"But it might not be. You haven't looked yet," I pointed out, stroking those tufts of sleep-messy hair.

"Maybe it can be both. Schrodinger's snow day." His arms circled me tight, pinning me happily in his embrace.

"Schroding—who?"

"He was a physicist." Theo propped his head up on my ribs, his smile still so dazzling, it took my breath away. "He posed an argument that something can be and not be, at the same time. Only he made it with a dead cat locked in a box."

"Poor cat!" I protested, and Theo laughed.

"It wasn't really there. But it was the idea, that the cat could be both alive and dead at the same time, and it wasn't until someone looks, that it's either."

I shook my head slowly. "This is why I didn't take physics."

Theo laughed. "Me either. I nearly failed it twice. But I had a great professor, this really eccentric guy. He made me think about things in a whole new way, you know, what's real: how everything we take for granted in the world is really just our senses sending signals to our brain, there's nothing really more than that." He paused, self-conscious. "Don't let Kelsey hear me talk like this, she'll go off on some rant about freshman guys getting a hard-on for *the Matrix*."

I laughed. "Promise."

As I stretched, his words echoed. "Hope said something like that, too. She got all kinds of hallucinations, near the end. Seeing things that weren't there. Feeling cold when it was boiling inside, or even tasting her food wrong. She would insist it wasn't her body playing tricks on her, it was just the world going by a new set of rules, just for her."

"Maybe it was."

Why do I have to be the crazy one? she would demand, so contrary. *Maybe you're the ones who are getting it wrong. You'll see,* she added, warning, and I knew she was right. The doctors always asked me, any auras, any weird scents or tastes? That was the next phase, still to come. I wondered how it would feel, the world shifting off its axis away from the reality I'd known, to something entirely new.

"There are people who have religious experiences," I found myself saying. "You know, the really intense ones, where they feel God's presence—God, or whoever," I corrected myself. "Scientists have done tests, and they can see the part of the brain that lights up when someone's having that kind of epiphany. Rapture. Sometimes it's all chemical, a serotonin rush, but sometimes it's a tumor. But that doesn't change what they felt, that experience, it's still real to them."

Theo looked interested, but I realized too late I was on dangerous territory. Tumors, cancer, this conversation was a minefield even without trying to dance lightly through the bombs.

"Come on," I said again, rolling out from under him. "Let's see which reality we're in."

I went to the window. The streets were clear, the skies a frozen, crisp cerulean, my breath fogging the cold glass. "No snow," I announced, and Theo sighed, swinging his legs out of bed.

"Next time," he said, like a promise.

"Next time," I echoed, and prayed I could keep it.

224

CHAPTER TWENTY

MY PARENTS ARRIVED at Wired halfway through my shift, stepping over the threshold and looking anxiously around the café like it was foreign soil. I was stationed behind the counter, and I beckoned them over, already determined to be bright and shiny and about as brand new as I could manage on three hours sleep and too much caffeine.

"What can I get you?" I asked. "Espresso, right, Dad? And Mom, we've got a great herbal tea."

She nodded, looking slightly stunned. But there I was, dressed in a festive red sweater dress and thick ribbed tights, concealer under my eyes to hide the shadows, and my shower-damp hair caught up in a braid. I poured their drinks and added buttery croissants too, whirling between the register and coffee machines like I was back in third grade, trying my hardest to point my toes in the holiday dance recital.

Despite everything, I wanted them to be proud. To see

what I'd done here, building a life from scratch.

"On the house," I told them, delivering their heavy porcelain mugs with a smile. "Why don't you grab the couches? I can take a quick break, just let me finish up with the people in line."

Kelsey emerged then from the back, yawning. "How are you so perky?" she demanded, not noticing my parents—or rather, noticing, but not caring about them at all. "Don't tell me you managed to sleep, with Moose on the Xbox and the guys having that fucking midnight jam session right down the hall."

"The guys?" my mom echoed, blinking.

Kelsey turned and lifted one eyebrow in a challenge.

"These are my parents," I announced brightly. "Dave and Susan."

My dad cleared his throat. "It's great to meet some of Claire's friends. Are you a student here?"

"Nope," Kelsey answered shortly, and walked away.

"She's . . . prickly," I covered. "But she's great, really. And that's Mika and JJ." I nodded, pointing them out. "It's a really nice group."

My mother nodded faintly, still looking dubiously around as if she'd ventured into some dark, remote corner of the dangerous city, not a coffee shop crammed with study-break students and tourists snapping pictures of their perfect latte foam. A line was forming behind them, and my dad glanced around. "We won't keep you," he said. "We'll just be over there, when you get a moment." He steered them over to the couches, and I caught my breath, just for a moment, before the next demand for low-fat, no-foam, triple shot came hard and fast, and I was back to the rush again.

I worked with one eye on the corner. They sat, talking softly over their untouched drinks, and I could only imagine what they were saying. Plans to drag me back to Texas, or strong-arm me straight to a hospital bed. I wished they would look up, just for a moment, to see how I handled the long, impatient lines with ease: remembering orders, giving my regulars a special smile or greeting, keeping the tide of demands moving on. It wasn't much, certainly not the dreams most parents have for their kids: no college graduation gowns, or law-school diplomas, but this was all mine. I'd done this myself, and it still ached the way I so desperately wanted them to recognize my life here as a blessing, not a curse.

Kelsey bustled beside me, taking over duty on the espresso machine. "So, the Brady Bunch comes to town."

"Yup," I answered, deadpan, refusing to rise to her bait. "We're going to sing Christmas carols and make pie later, if you want to come with."

She snorted with laughter, clattering another bag of coffee grounds into place.

227

"Are you heading home for the holidays?" I asked, cautious. I half-expected her to give me an eye-roll and flounce away, but Kelsey just sighed.

"I go tonight. Connecticut. Five days of my mom's obsessive cooking, and my annoying brat of a half-brother, and my creepy Uncle Nate walking into the bathroom without knocking. Joy to the world," she quipped. "Mika said you were covering shifts?"

I nodded. "I didn't think I was celebrating. I guess they had other plans." I looked to my parents again. Last year, they'd tried so hard to drench the season in holiday cheer. Hope was spiraling towards the grave, and I barely had the spirit to lift my head out of the covers in the morning, but they didn't relent: shopping trips and tree-lighting, the radio tuned to Christmas classics from the moment Thanksgiving dinner was cleared away to the morning the scent of cinnamon cookies wafted upstairs and I awoke to a room packed with presents in their shiny paper. Now, I wondered if they were doing all of that for me, or if it was their own fierce bargain with the universe, playing pretend hard enough to make it true.

This year would be different. I didn't want rituals and traditions, going through the motions of celebration for one last time. All that mattered to me was on a scribbled notebook page, Hope's last requests. I'd let my scare and Theo distract me, but I hadn't forgotten that slim

228

scribbled list, and with winter now blanketing the streets around us, I could make some progress with the next demands: snowball fights, snow angels, and sledding. Like me, she'd loved the snow, spent a last, glorious winter with her grandparents in Colorado, and came back breathless, the sparkle of a fresh snowfall still in her eyes. *It's perfect,* she told me. *Perfect and pure, good enough to taste.*

A LULL CAME BEFORE noon, so I poured myself a mug of cocoa and pulled off my apron. But when I finally turned to the corner, I saw that my parents weren't alone. Theo had joined them.

My heart lurched. I hurried over, skittering with a guilty beat. "Hey," I greeted him, interrupting. "I didn't know you were here."

How long? I looked quickly between them, searching for any sign of the revelations, but Theo just slipped a hand around my waist and squeezed. "I had a free period between classes."

"Theo was just telling us about his teaching job," my father added with a tiny nod, as if to reassure me. "It's a very prestigious program, I understand."

"Not really," Theo answered, modest, at the same time as I replied, "It is."

Theo laughed.

"And is that what you'd like to do when you graduate?" my mom asked, her voice still a little strained, so polite. "Teach?"

"Maybe." Theo's voice was relaxed, but his shoulders felt tense under my hand. He was trying, too. "It's still a ways off. I have my thesis ahead to worry about first."

"Your parents must be proud."

Theo nodded, but didn't reply. I quickly spoke up. "How long do you have?" I asked him. "Do you want some coffee, or food?"

"I'm fine. You're on a break!" Theo tugged my hand, pulling me into a seat. "What about you?" he asked, frowning. "Have you eaten yet? You need to be careful about your blood sugar, remember what the doctor said."

I caught my mom's pinched stare, and felt trapped all over again: walking that careful tightrope wire between my separate lives. "Theo was with me when I had that little fall," I said carefully. "Anyway! What have you guys been up to? Did you have a chance to see any of the city yet? Any sightseeing while you're here?"

My mom gave me a look, as if she knew exactly what I was doing. Then she smiled. "I thought we could plan it together, sweetheart. Maybe going shopping this afternoon, the two of us? You need some proper winter boots, I can see. We can make it a girls day, doesn't that sound nice?"

I was trapped by my own distraction, and she knew it. "Fine," I agreed, reluctant.

"And then dinner, tonight," she continued. "Theo, why don't you join us?"

"I . . . sure." He glanced at me, questioning. "I'd love to. If that's OK with Claire?"

I didn't have a choice. I nodded.

"Perfect." My mom beamed. "It'll give us a chance to get to know you. I'll make reservations somewhere nice."

"Well, I better get back." Theo rose and reached for his satchel. "It was nice to meet you both again. I'll see you tonight."

I walked him to the door. "You don't have to do this," I said, shooting a look back across the room. "It'll be boring and tense, and—"

"Hey, it's fine." Theo interrupted me with a soft kiss, a split-second ray of sunshine. "I want to get to know them. And don't worry, they're just looking out for their baby." He smiled at me, like these were any other protective parents. Like this was any other trip from out of town. "We'll have dinner, and they can see I'm not leading you into a life of debauchery.

Everything will be fine. They'll love me." He winked, so confident, but that wasn't the problem.

Of course they'd love him. How could anyone not? I was already too far gone to catch myself, a free-fall into thin air.

"OK," I murmured, choosing to believe in his golden certainty. One dinner, two hours at the most. I'd kept my secret locked safe for months now, I could make it one more night. "I'll see you later."

He left, back onto the brisk, ice-chilled street, and I made my way through the café slowly back to my parents. "You promised," I warned them quietly, but my mom was energized now, full of the promises I'd had to make.

"We didn't say anything, did we, hon?" She nudged my father. "And it'll be good to get to know him. If he's the reason you're doing all of this, it's the least you can give us, don't you think?"

As usual, I had no answer for that. I never did when it came to what I owed them, how I could possibly repay the debts and sacrifices they'd made. She stood, looking brighter and determined. "When do you finish here? We can take a walk around until you're done." She sized me up, assessing. "I saw a couple of stores with winter coats. And I noticed your teakettle is cracked back at the apartment, and you don't have a matching towel set. We'll need to pick some things up."

This was my mother. Ten minutes in my home, wracked with worry and tired from an eight-hour trip, and she still managed to clock the dollar-store hand towel in the bathroom and the lack of matching plates. But behind her words, I realized, there was a surrender of sorts. I wouldn't need snow boots back in Texas, or a kettle for our gleaming range back home. She wasn't talking about packing me up and whisking me away anymore, and that had to be a good thing, so I gifted her with a smile. "My shift ends in an hour," I agreed. "I can meet you back here, and then shop."

My father disappeared off somewhere, "to see the sights," my mom said vaguely, but she was waiting outside on the stroke of one. "Boots first," she said, already powering through the festive crowds. "Then maybe we can find a salon and do something about your hair."

I let her propel me through store displays and dressing rooms, standing obediently as she dressed me in boots and sweaters and thick winter jackets, fleece-trimmed and scratching with wool-lined warmth. My nails were a disaster, my split ends crying out for mercy, but I soon gave up my protests. She was determined to cram months' worth of mothering into a few short hours, and it was all I could do to simply keep pace, our footsteps sharp on the parade of gleaming department store floors, the bright lights catching silver in her crop of ash blonde hair. She navigated us across the city with determined ease, not hesitating for a second despite the unfamiliar streets. Taxi cabs arrived the moment she beckoned, and surly store clerks melted into acquiescence with a single measured request. Her years of steering me, unrelenting, through the tangled paperwork and red tape of a dozen hospital wards had made her an army major, battle-ready, and unwilling to ever back down.

She hadn't always been like this. Before my diagnosis, she'd been gentler, free. She'd worked as a graphic artist at an ad agency in the city, wearing brightly colored print dresses and trailing armfuls of jade bangles that clattered with every touch. She loved her job, and when I was still a toddler, she'd bring me by the office sometimes when she needed to stay late on a project for a big client. I would sit under her desk with a crumpled stack of craft paper and colored pens, happily scribbling the lurid designs she'd proudly pin to the refrigerator door back home. I inherited her artistic streak, she'd always say, and I, in turn, watched proudly as she rose through the ranks until the day that first specialist pinned up my scans and introduced us to the shadow lurking on my MRI. She quit that afternoon, and wouldn't hear a word of argument. One of them had to handle this, and she'd decided it would be her.

I didn't understand it at the time; their talks were all kept in hushed whispers in the next room, but as the years passed, it began to press on me just how much she'd had to sacrifice. I was a teenager, I should have been becoming more self-sufficient, not less—getting my driver's license, fixing my own snacks after school, and amusing myself without a babysitter or constant supervision—but instead, we'd plunged back in time. I was completely dependent on her, a newborn at fourteen, fifteen. She ferried me to appointments, scheduled specialists and travel the way some moms organized play-dates, and carefully fed me all my prescription pills. When the chemo sessions poisoned my body and made me a hollow, aching shell, she was there: fixing me a tray, wrapping me in that soft baby's quilt, and sitting up with me those long afternoons as I wretched, sobbing to feel the toxins clawing in my veins. Her life became my tumor, just as much as mine, and although I was grateful, it weighed on me, too, a debt I could never hope to repay, especially once those last results came in and we knew the years had been in vain, and there was no winning this fight.

After watching the way Hope slipped away, I knew I couldn't go the same, but still, my mom wouldn't quit. There was always another trial to submit for, always another round of tests. She would have hooked me up for

an infinite round of chemo if she'd had her way, eking out
another precious day through sheer force of will. Maybe
she thought that if she fought hard enough for the both of
us, she could magic a cure into being, that if I could hang
on another month, another year, it would make a
difference. Those were the fights that crushed me, trying
to work up the courage to leave. I couldn't make her see
that existence wasn't enough for me, not when I was
running out of time. I needed a life, however short, but
she could only see the cruel trade-off: four good months,
or eight bad ones, to her, more was the only chance we
would get.

But today, there was no mention of the bitter
equations, or the time I was wasting here with every
passing day away from the hospital bed. She steered me
briskly through the city, our arms laden with crisp paper
bags, until we could barely make it back up the stairs to
the attic, we were so weighed down.

"I like you in the blue," Mom announced as I unlocked
the door and unloaded our bounty on the table. "And that
green sweater brings out your eyes. You should wear it
for dinner tonight."

I nodded and sank wearily into a chair. I was getting
tired more easily, and my autumn of late-night bicycle
rides seemed like a distant memory now, the way my
lungs burned after a single staircase and my head

pounded, that background of static pain. Mom's eyes flickered with concern, but she didn't say anything, just found the package with my new teakettle and bustled for the kitchen, setting it on to boil. She looked around. "It's a cute place. Reminds me of my first apartment, out of college. Me and three girls in a fourth-floor walk-up." Her face softened in a nostalgic smile. "There was never enough hot water, but we would throw pizza parties every Friday night, and the whole building would stop by."

"Tessa's really nice," I offered. Every morsel of my life here felt like a test, as if I was displaying for her each new item in the palm of my hands, wanting to reassure her, but craving her approval all the same. "I hang out with her and her friends sometimes; we go to the college bars, or just grab a meal together. They're all in college, but it's not like I'm an outsider or anything."

"Does she know?"

I shook my head slowly.

"Don't you think she should?" Mom pressed. "In case something happens again?"

"What could she do?" I countered. "You know, there's nothing."

"She could keep an eye on your meds," Mom said, looking anxious again. "Tell the paramedics what you're on, and how they can—"

"Mom!" I stopped her, sighing. "I can't ask that. It's not her responsibility to take care of me. Nobody can do that."

"I can."

There it was again. My heart twisted, seeing the sorrow on her face. Nineteen years she'd kept careful watch, and it still wasn't enough to protect me. If this had been a predator on the city street she would have stared him down, thrown her body in the path of a moving vehicle to protect me from impact. But this was a poison snaking in my skull, and she couldn't take the pain away if she tried.

"I'm sorry."

I don't know how many times I'd said it, but I meant it, every time. Sorry for my broken, wretched brain, for her wrecked dreams, for the sleepless, tearful nights and the endless, angry days, sorry that the child she'd wanted so badly had brought nothing but grief in the end. I loved her with all my heart, I wanted her to be happy, but I knew that because of me, she never would be. Every moment I lived, she waited for the end, and when one day it would come, she would never be happy again.

She would have to bury me, soon, and nothing I could do would ever make that OK.

The kettle whistled. She made our drinks, then walked

over to my bedroom doorway. "You're painting again."

There was a note of wistful pride in her voice.

"I can't stop," I replied, wrapping my hands around the heavy porcelain mug.

"You care about him a lot, don't you."

It wasn't a question. I knew she was seeing the sketches of Theo, all my sleepless nights consumed with the line of his body.

I swallowed. "I love him."

The words were a whisper, but still, I was proud I even had the courage to say them aloud. It felt like a rebellion, to even stake a claim to love at all, in the face of everything. Love was a luxury, but at the same time, it felt as necessary as air. "It's my last chance." I tried to make her see. "I know it's not much, but it's all I want. Please, Mom. Can't you let me have this?"

Mom looked across the room at me. "This shouldn't be all you get," she said, and I could see the heartbreak in her eyes. "Can't we sit down with this doctor, at least? Look at the scans. Boston has some of the best cancer treatment programs in the country. Maybe there's something new, we haven't tried just yet. A drug trial, something experimental—"

"Mom!" I cut her off. "Please. We've tried everything. Can't you just let me be, so I can make peace with this?"

She shook her head, abrupt. "No. There's always

something. Can't you just try, a little longer, for me?"

"I don't have much longer," I whispered.

"But a few months, hiding it like a secret . . . I wanted so much more for you—"

Her voice cracked, split wide with grief, and then all that determination in the world couldn't keep her tears at bay. I watched her unravel right there in front of me, and I realized to my horror, it was the first time.

The only time she'd ever let me see her cry.

"Mom." I went to her, and wrapped my arms around her tightly, but it wasn't enough to keep her grief inside. She sobbed against me, those ragged hiccupping cries of someone fighting a losing battle to swallow it back, hold it down, keep it together just once more, just this time. "Mom, it's OK."

My words were useless, of course they were. There was nothing OK about this, the torn-up remnants of a future we both clung to with both hands; a sheer rock face with only one way down. So we held each other tight there by the windows, as the city kept up a stream of neon flowing into the night; a thousand tiny charges of electricity racing out through the distant grid. My mother wept, and I did too, not for myself, but for everything I was taking from her.

It wasn't right. It wasn't fair. But it was all we had together, the raw sobs binding us as much as blood. What we wouldn't have given to take the other's weight away. How are you supposed to make sense of this world when death cuts through it, uncaring?

"OK," I murmured into her hair, my cheeks wet. "We can meet with Doctor Benson. It won't make a difference, but . . ."

It was the least I could do for her. Parting gifts to ripple in the endless sea of her grief. To me, it felt like screaming into a hurricane, but her sobs eased. "Thank you." She pulled away, dabbing at red eyes. "I'm sorry, sweetheart. I shouldn't be laying all this on you."

I gave a hollow smile. "What, so we should still be talking about my split ends?"

She wiped my tears away with her thumbs, cradling my face between her hands. "I'm so proud of you."

I looked away, flushing. "I haven't done anything."

"You have. This. Being here. We were wrong to try and keep you. I just . . ." Her face slipped again. "I just wanted to keep you safe."

Isn't that all a parent wants for their child? I guess I would never know.

So I leaned forward instead and kissed her forehead, as if she were the baby for a moment, needing comfort the way I did, those long dark stretches with the nightlight on and a pillow fort built to ward of evil spirits.

"You did, Mom," I whispered. "You got me this far."

THE PROMISE

Neither of us said what we both were thinking.
This far, but no further. No further.

CHAPTER TWENTY-ONE

W E MET MY DAD at the hospital that same evening. When it came to grenades like my tumor, they don't like to wait around. I lay in the MRI chamber in my new green sweater, my hair brushed out and mascara on my lashes, ready for us to dash across the city in time to make dinner with Theo back at their hotel.

"OK, Claire," Benson's voice came through the loudspeaker from where he was stationed in the observation room. "I'll need you to stay completely still."

I knew the drill. I'd made this voyage a hundred times, sliding smooth into the belly of the spaceship as the lights danced around me.

"We're starting now, it won't be long."

The whir came, and it began: the magnetic pulses gripping through my body, assembling a map to the constellations hidden behind my skull. When I was younger, it was easy to panic, trapped there like a coffin, but now, it felt like a dream. I drifted, trying hard not to think what this was costing, the endless tally of expenses that blossomed and bloomed with every new hospital trip. Cancer didn't just eat into our bodies, it ravaged our family's bank accounts, too. Insurance fought every last charge and test, like they were bitter exes splitting an unwanted restaurant bill. I was lucky, I know; my father had a bulletproof policy, and my mom made it her full-time job to hold them to account, but Hope's parents went bankrupt long before her final decline. Her bills were paid through the end by a haphazard assortment of charities and loans, and it kills me to think of them now, still making monthly payments on their only daughter's death.

"Good job, Claire. We're all set."

They were finished before I knew it, sliding me out of the chamber and back into the yellow fluorescent lights of the hospital room. I sat up too fast, and had to grip the platform as my head spun and the lights burst, stardust behind my eyes.

"Sweetheart?" My mom opened the door and was beside me in an instant, but I didn't take her hand. I slid down and stood on my own two feet, waiting until the lurch slipped away before I gave her a smile.

"I'm fine," I said, and it stuck me just how feeble those words could be, in this room, in this place, with the evidence forming on a screen in the next room.

She smoothed my hair down. "You look lovely. I told you the green was your color."

"We can't be late," I said, pleading.

"I know. Plenty of time."

W E MET DOCTOR BENSON in a spare office I knew could never belong to him. He was all neat caution and a pressed white shirt, looking smart and spotless even at this late hour. He glanced around, disgruntled, as we picked our way around stacks of files and books, finding a place to perch.

"Apologies, the conference room is closed. Flooding."

"That's fine. We've seen worse." My father was upbeat, gamely shifting a box of supplies off a chair for my mother to sit. I found a spot in the corner, between a half-dead ficus plant and a pile of files three-foot deep. Dust lay in a thin film over the top, dented with fingerprints, and I wondered about the lives bound up between the covers.

"So, I was able to visualize the full mass." Doctor Benson didn't even try to sit behind the desk; he leaned against it instead, holding the familiar rubber-banded files that my parents must have shipped in from Texas. "The good news is, Claire's motor functions and vision are still relatively unaffected," he began. "Which is no small thing, considering the late stage and extent of the growth."

Yay me, not yet blind.

"However, I'm concerned about her pain levels, and I'd like to start her on a targeted pain relief program as those symptoms escalate. We are seeing growth in the mass compared to her last scans, but I understand, that was to be expected."

My father cleared his throat. "And the speed of the growth . . .?"

"Is still what your last doctor discussed," Benson finished, with a resigned nod. "There's definite acceleration,." He showed us the overlay of the films, how the dark traces of my tumor were snaking on through the pale matter of my brain. Shadows looming, storm clouds racing closer.

I turned away, watching the snow fall lightly outside the windows. My parents kept quizzing him, but I already knew the answers. I'd heard them a dozen times over; there would be no changing them now. Still, my mom reached to squeeze my hand and ask, "Now that you've been able see it up close, do you have any other ideas for treatment? Anything at all?"

Doctor Benson paused to glance at me. "I thought the decision had been made to focus on end-of-life care."

"It has," I answered for them, but Mom couldn't stay

silent. She pulled a crumpled sheaf of printouts from her purse.

"I've been researching, and an experimental trial was just approved at Johns Hopkins. And there's a new treatment, a surgical protocol that you've been testing here—"

"Mom," I tried to interrupt, but she pressed on.

"I was talking with a woman whose kid is in the first test group, she says this is specifically for tumors like Claire's."

Benson looked reluctant. "The FDA approved human trials last month, and we have begun a limited test group, it's true. But this is very early in the process," he added. "We're still refining the process, and I'm not sure, given that Claire has already decided to end treatment—"

"What he means is, it hasn't worked yet." I cut him off bluntly. "I'm right, aren't I?" I was being harsh, but I'd spent years listening to men just like him extolling the possibilities of their new, different trial. I could read between the lines, see the truth lingering, resigned in his dark eyes. "Has anyone even made it through the surgery alive?"

A pause.

"We've had limited success," he admitted. "But we have learned some valuable data to refine the approach."

"How limited?" I challenged him.

"Of our initial test cohort of ten, we've seen positive outcomes in two patients."

"And the others?"

"They didn't make it through the surgery."

Two out of ten. Eight trips to the morgue. That should have been enough for my parents. Even in all their wild longing, they couldn't argue with odds like that. But instead of accepting the math, Mom just squeezed my hand again. "Would Claire be candidate?" she asked, and the naked hope in her voice made me ache.

"Please, don't," I begged quietly. "You heard him. It doesn't work."

"It did for two of them," she corrected me. "And this is how it goes. They fail, and try again. If they've learned from the first round of surgeries . . . the chances for the next round are better."

Her voice quavered; she wanted so desperately to believe, but I was numb to it now. We heard this all the time. Experimental drugs, new radical treatments. Those were the watchwords of the cancer wards, the prayer every broken parent and pleading wife and weeping child offered up to the gods of science. And sometimes, those prayers were answered. Spliced gene therapies, targeted auto-immune programs—they made new advances every year. The brightest minds in the country were waging war on cancers like mine, pouring billions of dollars and every ounce of their limitless imaginations to the campaign. It sounded so determined: we would win the fight, one day. But they weren't the foot soldiers, gasping in the trenches; they weren't the ones bruised and bloody in the firing line.

We were the body bags returning home from war.

"Claire does fit our profile," Doctor Benson admitted. "But it's an aggressive treatment, and given the risks involved and her preferences . . ."

"I'm not interested." I said it loudly and got to my feet. "Thank you for taking the time," I told him. "Mom, Dad? We have dinner, remember?"

Slowly, they followed, shaking the doctor's hand, offering thanks, wishing him a happy holidays.

"I'm here if you need anything," he told me. "If you have another incident, have the intern on call page me. And like I said, you'll need regular check-ins to manage the pain as things become more advanced."

I nodded. "I've still got some time, though."

"Yes." He gave me a faint smile. "Yes, you do."

MY MOTHER DIDN'T SPEAK until we were in the cab, the lights of Boston blurring bright outside the windows as the snow fell thickly, and I sank deeper into the folds of my new winter coat.

"If you'll just think about it," she started, but this time it was my father who cut her off.

"Susan, we agreed."

"But this is something new," she protested. "And all the research says it could be the next frontier of treatment."

"In ten years, maybe," I told her, trying to stay calm. "But this is the first real trial. It'll be five, ten rounds before they even start to get it right. You know how this works," I added, pleading. Just when I thought I'd gotten through to her. Just when I thought we could possibly find peace. "Don't do this, not now. I have a few months left, good months. Would you rather I died on the operating table tomorrow instead?"

"But if the surgery worked," my mom protested again, not hearing my stark words. "You heard him, two of them saw positive results."

"Two!" I exclaimed. "Two people, that's what you want me to risk everything for? Some long-shot, last-ditch fantasy drug they've barely begun to test? You'd really have me walk in there next week and have the surgery, with odds like that?"

She couldn't reply. The cab driver kept his eyes fixed forward, focused on the wet road.

"I've made my choice," I said, determined.

"To give up."

"No," I said quietly, as the city sped by, neon glittering in a shattered snowdrift, great brownstones and office blocks standing watch over us all. "To live. The way Hope never got to do."

I felt her tense beside me, felt the venom in her words even before they made it out of her lips. "Sometimes I wish you'd never met that girl. All this trouble, over one damn list."

I set my jaw and gazed out of the window. I didn't expect her to understand, but it wasn't just about the list anymore. Back in September, it had seemed like a statement of promise: me going out into the world to taste those precious moments she'd left unfulfilled. But now, with those new shadows looming on my scans, I thought of the last few entries with a new chill.

Would I have enough time left for them? And what happened when that last entry was struck off and her final wishes were complete?

LOOKING BACK NOW, it's easy to see why I clung to that list for as long as I did. It gave me a focus, a simple fixed point when everything around it was storming with self-doubt. For a few months, at least, I had clarity, some purpose to keep my own despair at bay. And God, I needed it. Depression was lurking, every bit as deadly as the tumor: that darkness clawing at me, that endless, empty night. Hope's death was done, but mine still loomed ahead of me. You could call it denial, or even self-preservation, my way to get out of bed each morning even with a death sentence marked in red on the page, but the ending—*my* ending—was still too much for me to deal with.

If you stop a moment to think about it, you'll understand. Go on, imagine. What you would be leaving, who you would be leaving behind. It's too much for the heart to take, that kind of inevitable grief, the vast expanse of it: every heart you'll be breaking, every drop of love you'll never get to keep again. It was all-consuming, a bright terror that blotted out everything else in my heart, like staring too long into the sun will leave you blind and wretched. All I could do was take sideways glances to glimpse the wreckage, and then avert my eyes.

Maybe I should have done it differently, but I honestly don't know how. Because there's nothing simple about death. It is a maze of contradictions, of raw emotions that cannot be contained. They tried to counsel us through it, but the truth was you never found peace. I'd wasted months to anger, years to fear, and still, it changed by the hour, by the second: emotions fleeting across the water, a tempest storm quickening from the calmest pond. I used to pray for it to come suddenly, just steal me swiftly in the night with a sudden hemorrhage. Wouldn't it just be easier that way? No deathbed gasps at goodbye, no watching my parents falter and the world slip out of my desperate grasp. It may have been selfish, but I dreaded their pain just as much as my own. Then, sometimes, it felt like I could almost touch the grace they talked about, accepting of the end. I held onto that blessing with both hands tight, even as the rest of my faith ran dry. I had time to prepare; that was something. I knew exactly what my future held. Some people went suddenly, not ever knowing that their last casual kiss as they headed out the door would really be the last one, that they would never have the chance to do everything they'd promised, "one day."

I heard a country song playing once, how you should live like you were dying. Hope flew into a fury when I shared it with her; she almost smashed a vase on my dresser as she whirled and fumed.

How could he know? she cursed. *How the fuck would he know?*

There was no grace with her. No reckoning with the inevitable. No calm accepting of her fate. Death and Hope were locked in constant battle right up until the end, and even as I watched her fight, watched her pour every one of her last, rasping breaths into staying alive, a treacherous part of me wished she would just give up. Wouldn't it have been easier? Couldn't she have found some peace?

But Hope was dying the only way she'd ever known how to live. Bright and bloody, her middle finger raised to the skies. Back then, I couldn't understand. I didn't realize what it felt like to want to claw every last moment of life from the precipice, clinging tight when you can't bear to let it go.

At least, not until Theo.

He was my last contradiction. Because during those final weeks with him, I finally understood Hope's last stand. I was more alive than I'd ever felt before, even as my cancer ate away inside my brain, and my breath came, sluggish and burning raw at the edges. I was more alive, and more painfully aware of everything death was snatching from me. Perhaps that made it sweeter, knowing I'd never have days like that again. Every first time became the last; every moment of pleasure would never be repeated. Every second was a glimpse of life I would never get back, already ashes, scattering in the winter wind.

CHAPTER TWENTY-TWO

THE NEXT MORNING I woke to find the city blanketed in a snow, the skies clear, pale sunlight gleaming off icy diamond boughs. It was Christmas Eve, and Hope had gotten her wish. Snow, as far as I could see, pure enough to taste. Theo was still dozing beside me, but my blood was jittery with a restless itch, like if I stayed still too long, I would have to admit this feeling for what it truly was.

Guilt.

Dinner had passed the night before in a blur. We made polite conversation, about the holidays, Theo's coursework, my art, but I couldn't relax, couldn't focus at all. Every word was a tiny grenade lobbed into the middle of the finely set table, sitting there so innocent among the festive streamers and starched white napkins—ready to explode at any moment. Theo could tell I was tense; he held my hand beneath the tablecloth, out of sight, giving me a reassuring squeeze whenever my mom's questioning took on a desperate tone or my father made a pointed comment about family, and security, and home. We were in this together, Theo was trying to tell me, but he didn't know the real reason for the tension laced thickly through mulled wine toasts and all the trimmings. My secret sat, as much a guest at that table as the rest of us, and although there was no place laid for it, or sweet holly wreath beside the plate, I could feel it, watching, waiting for just the right moment to reveal itself and blow my brief happiness to ashes.

Now I wanted to forget the past few days, and wipe my slate as clean as the spotless powder outside the steam-fogged windows. My parents had made vague claims about their plans, so the day was all our own. I slipped out from under Theo's arm and silently tiptoed through the apartment to the bathroom; on my return trip, I found Tessa pouring hot coffee in a bright red thermos flask, dressed in ski pants and a warm, padded vest.

"Hey," she greeted me with a wide-awake smile, despite the fact it was barely seven. "A group of us is going sledding. You want to come with? Theo's welcome to join, too," she added.

My heart lifted. "Sure, that sounds fun." I paused. "Listen, I'm sorry, about my parents just showing up . . ."

Tessa shrugged. "It's fine." Her gaze caught mine for a moment, and I wondered if she was about to say something else. Then she looked away.

"I hope they didn't give you the third degree," I added, trying to sound casual. "They're pretty over-protective."

A smile played on her lips. "You think this is bad? My dad insisted on touring apartments with me when I was moving out of the dorms. He went and knocked on all the neighbor's doors and wouldn't let me pick a place with a single man for two floors in either direction."

I relaxed, relieved. "OK, so maybe mine aren't the worst."

"It's what they do," Tessa agreed. "They worry."

Her phone buzzed, and she checked it. "That's Henry, they're on their way now." She looked to my pajamas, and I backed away.

"Give us five minutes!"

I hurried back to my room. Theo was awake, propped up on the pillows and smiling at me, sleepy-eyed. "We got our snow day," he said, reaching his arms to invite me back into their snug embrace. Any other minute of my life, I wouldn't have hesitated to dive headlong back against his body, but today was different, the world outside crisp and so brand new.

I launched myself onto the mattress, bouncing heavily

beside him. "Tessa and the group are going sledding. They're leaving now."

He laughed, my childish excitement clear to see. "Sounds like fun. But I'm not exactly equipped for snow." His clothes from last night were still discarded on the floor where I'd left them: best-behavior dress shoes and a button-down shirt.

"We can stop by your place on the way." I bounced off the bed again, and started rummaging in my mom's shopping bags for those store-fresh lined boots and waterproof winter jacket. Then I paused. "But only if you want to go." I looked up, checking that I wasn't steamrolling him, but Theo only smiled and swung his legs out of bed.

"It's on the list, right? Of course I want to go."

He remembered every line of Hope's list.

I didn't have time to kiss him for that, or even for scrambling into his clothes in double-quick time. By the time we were dressed and thundering after Tessa down the stairs, they were waiting out front in a mud-splattered Jeep: Henry and Katie, Lexa, and Steve, and Roy, armed with scarves and more thermoses and bags of bakery-fresh bagels.

"Hey guys. This is Theo," I announced, as we scrambled into the crammed backseat over ski blades and blankets.

"Hi Theo!" the chorus came. Roy thrust a map straight into Theo's hands. "Can you navigate?"

"There's a little something called GPS," Katie called, as Tessa leaned forward between the front seats to commandeer the stereo jack.

"Or Siri."

"Siri hates me," our driver, Henry replied, through a mouthful of bagel. "She's trying to kill me, I swear. She keeps sending me the wrong way up one-way streets."

"What did you do to piss her off?"

"Nothing." Henry looked woeful.

"It's all that porn you make her find." Lexa kicked the back of his seat.

Theo shot me a smile, squished tightly beside me in the middle seat. They were a colorful cast, and the bright sounds of their gossip and laughter flooded me with warmth as we made our way down silent, snowy streets. "Where is everyone?" I asked, looking out at the deserted avenues that only yesterday had been teeming with festive crowds. There was a hush over the city, the usual traffic and roar muffled by white.

"Everyone clears out for the holidays," Tessa answered, crushed on my other side. "All the students disappear back home."

"Except for the smart ones, like us," Katie announced, up front. "No lines at the library, all the labs still open.

You can actually get some work done, instead of stress-eating leftovers in front of bad TV."

"All work, no play . . ." Roy teased behind us, and Katie reached back to swat his hat.

"What do you think I'm doing today?"

W E MADE IT TO THEO'S for his quick change, and then set out again, crossing the salted, slush-drenched bridge behind a slow procession of traffic and winding our way through the busier streets of Boston, downtown.

"Take a right, up ahead," Theo directed from the map, as we inched our way deeper into the tangle of streets. "It's just another few blocks."

"We could have just taken the T," Steve told me, passing the bag of bagels. "But *some people* didn't want to carry their gear."

There was a chorus of protest from Tessa and the other girls. "Liar!"

"You're the one who wanted to bring like, a hundred pounds of camera equipment."

"You try hauling a sled down three flights of stairs."

But they all fell silent when we turned the corner past the last row of brownstones and saw Boston Common spread before us: pristine and white, the hills rose and fell in perfect valleys, already dotted with splashes of color from the early-morning sledding crowds. It was beautiful, sparse and secret, and even though I'd walked these park pathways a dozen times, it looked like a foreign landscape, lunar wild.

We parked and tumbled out of the Jeep. I expected a lazy shuffle through the snow, but Katie let out an excited, "Last one to the top of the hill buys the beers!" and suddenly, they were off, grabbing sleds and skis from the trunk and staggering fast through the snow. Theo claimed a plastic dime-store sled, cherry-red, and we raced after them, air crisp in my lungs. Snow crunched under my boots, and laughter echoed, all under the watchful eye of the snow-tipped monuments that stood guard along the path, guiding us up to the crest of the first hill. I was panting and out of breath by the time I reached the summit, but there was no time to wait, not with this group, jostling for victory.

"Ready, set—" Tessa called the orders, and we all piled into position: two to a sled, me clinging on tight to the cord with Theo braced behind. The slope before us was steep, and my gut lurched, but I was too caught up in the rush to ever think about stepping back from the ledge.

"Go!"

Theo pushed us off and leapt on behind me, his weight sending us surging down the first stretch as his legs came tight around my waist. We hurtled down, airborne, in a flurry of noise and action, the wind biting into my bare cheeks.

The others whooped and jostled, sliding on past us. "Left, left!" Theo's shout was laughing in my ear, as I yanked the strings and tried helplessly to steer.

"I can't!"

"Pull harder!"

It didn't matter; gravity was running the show now. I laughed and let it pull us on, wild and fast, Theo's arms around me, and our bodies leaning in a single blade. The other sleds swirled by, cheers echoing as we plummeted through the snow. It was dazzling, the powder slicing by in a white rush, and for a moment, it felt like I could even take flight. Soar up from this hilltop into the wide blue beyond and—

"Watch out!"

Theo's call came fast, but I was too late. There was a sudden hump, a wide swerve as I lost control, and then the ride came to a jolting end as we tumbled out, dumped unceremoniously into the wet snow.

My heart raced. I caught my breath and rolled onto my back, icy crystals biting at my cheeks. God, it was glorious. The sky was powder blue above me, stretching cloudless as far as I could see, laughter echoing across the sweep of the hills.

Theo's face appeared overhead with an upside-down grin. "We nearly had them there." He offered his hand to help me up.

I laughed. "Next time."

I took his hand but yanked hard, tumbling him down into the snow with me. He let out a noise of surprise, then rolled, pinning me with his weight. His lips were as cold as mine as he kissed me, cushioned there in the snow. We were suspended, alone with our pounding hearts. My blood was on fire, but my skin was shivering, cold and burning up all at once.

I've never felt so alive.

I never wanted it to end.

W E STAYED ON the hilltops all morning, hurtling ourselves down the icy slopes as the park filled with a cacophony of clumsy kids and bundled-up teens, and parents toting a rainbow of woolen hats and mittens. We built crooked snowmen and swiped wide angels in the snow and hurled snowballs in a dizzying battle to the last. I'd never seen anything like it. For a few bright hours, we were all united, ten years old again, playing hard like no other world existed. I forgot myself that morning; Tessa's know-it-all smirk was lost under a hail of snowballs, and even Theo's careful, watchful stare was filled with a gleeful lightness as he ducked across the warzone and dove us time and time again down the bumpy hills. I wished it could have lasted forever, but too soon, I felt the burn in my chest, and that dizzy cloak slip over my vision. My legs gave way suddenly, so I sat in the snow and watched them, the last attack of our snowball war in progress as Tessa and Lexa drove the others into a wooded, spindly copse at the bottom of the hill.

"You OK?" Theo was beside me in an instant. All it took was the concern in his eyes to bring me crashing back to reality again.

"I'm fine." I gave him a smile, as bright as I could manage. "This is what I get from sitting around with a sketchpad while these guys are out training in the gym every day."

Theo laughed and helped me to my feet. "From one lazy bookworm to another, I'm with you. I say we make a strategic retreat and let them fight it out."

We crunched through the snow to a park bench, then sat. Exhaustion had ripped through me in an instant, and I was glad to take the rest. I'd pushed too hard, and I shivered again, not from the cold, but realizing that my body's limits were closing in on me.

Not today.

I pulled off a mitten and found Theo's bare hand. I slipped my fingers between his and squeezed. He looked over and smiled, perfectly content. "OK," he said, with a wry twist to his beautiful mouth. "I admit this is better than spending the day in bed. Just."

I laughed.

"And now you get to tick off another part of your list," he added, sounding happy. "You're closer to the end now, right? What's left?"

I took a breath, remembering. "A few things. Wild dance parties, and sunrise skinny-dipping. Hope wanted everything to be a big dramatic adventure," I explained. "She didn't get to see sometimes the adventure is just . . . this." I looked around. "Every day."

The scene washed over me, so clean and bright. The city was muffled, every echo of laughter crisp over such a soft, powdered base. I longed to paint it, the flash of brightness cutting through the hills, the dozen tumbling figures halfway up the far ridge.

"We got the best of it," Theo said, sounding content. He squeezed my hand. "This place will be packed by the afternoon. Then it all melts into rivers of slush, you can't cross the park for days without some serious boots."

"Then I'm all set." I stuck my legs straight out, swathed with ski pants and knitted leggings beneath, topped with my new navy boots, thick-gripped and snug.

"You're ready to scale Everest," he laughed.

"Maybe after lunch."

Theo looked around. "I would come here every winter

when I was a kid. I would beg my dad to take me," he confided, "but he never would, so I took the T, hauled one of those little plastic sleds all across town. I got all kinds of looks, can you imagine it? This seven-year-old kid with a bright-green sled bigger than he was, right there in the middle of the subway car on a Sunday morning." Theo's lips were curled in something sadder than a smile, a bittersweet memory that still cut somewhere, deep inside.

"Didn't anyone notice you were gone?" I asked, not believing anyone could let him wander like that, so careless with his trusting excitement.

He shrugged. "Dad was permanently hung over, even then, and Mom wasn't about to ruffle any feathers. She figured I could look after myself." Theo looked out at the snow again, innocent and clean. "But when I got here, it didn't matter. There were plenty of other neighborhood kids out, you couldn't tell who was all alone. We just threw ourselves down the hills, had snowball fights for hours. I used to pretend I belonged to one of the other families here," he added. "One of the fathers who built snowmen, and was always tugging their kids' scarves and mittens back into place. There was one family, I saw them every year. Three kids, two boys and a girl. The dad would bring these old-fashioned wooden sleds, and they'd play all day long. Once, I took a bad spill, and the mom patched me up with a Band-Aid and gave me hot chocolate from the thermos she had in her purse." Even now, decades later, I can hear the wistfulness in his voice, the affection for that one tender gesture, twenty years ago. "I used to imagine that when it was time to go, I'd leave with them instead, and we'd go home, and nobody would ever notice. I would just belong to them instead."

I could see him, just a kid, sitting on this same hill, watching the worlds he would never be a part of. But before I could say anything, Theo took a breath, and the past seemed to melt from his face, parting to reveal that warm smile. He leaned over and kissed me lightly. "Sorry, I shouldn't ramble. Ancient history."

"You don't need to apologize," I said simply. "I want to know. All this stuff, who you were, what you went through. Everything."

Theo looked bashful, his nose tipped pink in the cold. "I try not to think of it. Being here just brought it all back. I haven't come out here in years."

I paused. "How is your dad?" I asked, not knowing if I was crossing a line, but unable to stop myself from edging over the boundary all the same.

Theo let out a long breath, steam shivering in the crisp air. "I don't know. I haven't heard from him since the fall. That could be good or bad."

"I'm sorry."

He shrugged. "I'll find out tomorrow, I guess. I go for Christmas lunch every year," he explained. "It's our depressing version of tradition. We go eat dry turkey and stringy casserole at a café around the corner, and he gets drunk, and I get mad, and every time it's done, I swear it's the last year."

"Sounds delightful," I quip, bringing a smile to his mouth.

"The best. I'd ask you to join us, but . . ."

"I'd love to." This time, I wasn't joking, and Theo looked over, confused. "I mean it. I'll come with you. But only if you want," I added, wondering if I was trampling that boundary again, but Theo just shook his head.

"I can't ask that. I wouldn't wish it on my worst enemy, let alone . . . you."

"You aren't asking, I'm offering," I said, and I cradled his hand between both of mine, twisting our fingers together so you couldn't tell where one of us ended and the other began.

"What about your parents, don't you have plans?"

"They're not staying," I replied. "So we'll go see your dad, and eat dry turkey, and maybe he won't get so drunk, and maybe you won't have to get so mad. And even if he does, then I'll be there, and we'll blow it off and go ice-skating afterwards, and make

268

out on every street corner, and everything will be OK."

I made it sound simple, even though I wasn't naïve enough to believe it could be true. Still, I meant every word. I thought of Theo, all those years ago, sitting on this hilltop, alone—going back, every holiday, biting his tongue and holding back the disappointment, alone. Had anyone ever been there for him? Had anyone made him feel like they were on his side?

"You don't have to do this on your own anymore," I said, determined. "You've got me now."

Theo didn't speak for a long moment, he just looked out at the snow, and for a terrible moment, I wondered if I'd gone too far. This was his story, these were his scars, and I had no business meddling, not when secrets of my own burned deep beneath these layers of cotton and wool.

Then he leaned over and kissed me, his mouth hot and sweet, his hands pressed warm to my frozen cheeks. He kissed me, and I felt the ache in him, felt the tenderness of his confession, something fragile spun like sugar on our tongues. It hit me then, what I'd never realized before, echoing out across the sunlit valley.

He needed me, too.

"OK." Theo sounded raw when he finally pulled away. "Dysfunctional family Christmas ahead."

Make that two of them, I silently added, thinking of my own parents, waiting in their hotel room.

"Come on," I said instead, getting up. "Let's go find the others, before our toes freeze right off. I'm starving."

CHAPTER TWENTY-THREE

W E MET THE OTHERS and trudged back to the Jeep, worn out and wet through, but glowing in the pale sunlight. Lunch was steaming hot soup and sweet cherry pie; we crammed into a booth at a college haunt on Boylston as the gang chattered and flirted and Theo's fingertips drew blazing circles on my knee. And when the last mug of coffee was drained and we had split the bill with worn dollar bills, I was so buoyant that I decided to have them drop me at my parent's hotel.

"See you later?" Theo asked, dropping a kiss on my lips as I squeezed out between them, climbing down to the curb.

"I'll call, see if I can come over," I agreed. "I might be working."

"No holiday break for the caffeine junkies." He grinned. "Get home safe."

I headed into the lobby, trailing wet snow from my boots across that spotless floor. My parents were on the third floor, down a worn, carpeted hallway that led me past cheery tourists and bored-looking staff. I knocked, not sure if I should have called first, but when my dad opened the door and his face spread into a delighted smile, I knew I'd made the right call.

"Claire, what are you doing here? Come in, you're soaked through."

"I'm fine." I followed him into the room: a small, navy-appointed space with heavy drapes and a view to the buildings beyond. "We went sledding in the park, a whole group of us, Tessa and all her friends." I looked around. "Where's Mom?"

"She just went to take a walk," he said, the smile slipping, just a little, and I knew my good mood couldn't last for long.

I sat on the chair by the desk and made a slow swivel, bracing myself again. "What did you guys do today?"

He cleared his throat. The past months hadn't worn him the way they did Mom; his hair was a little more salt than pepper now, but he was still sturdy, dressed in his cable knit sweater, as comforting as ever.

"We met with Doctor Benson," he said slowly, and I was pulled back to reality again. No snow-swept hilltops, no warm friendship. My sickness lived in sparse hospital wards, and just the mention of it brought a sting of antiseptic scent to the air.

"Why?" I was immediately on edge. "We did the tests. You saw the new scans. It's all going the way we knew it would."

My father sat on the edge of the bed nearest to me, resting his elbows on his knees as he leaned closer, beseeching. "Your mother wanted to find out more, about this trial."

"Daddy." I deflated. "No, please. You know she's clutching at straws."

"Maybe not. He took us through the science, all the progress they've been making. Those two patients who made it through the surgery, the results really are remarkable." His face was brighter now, animated. "They use new genome technology. They map your DNA and come up with a targeted delivery system, so they can use a much stronger cocktail, and it only attacks the cancerous cells. See, I have the reports here." He reached for an envelope on the bed, sheaves of paper. "The ones who made it through surgery, they saw a dramatic shrinkage of the mass, one was even downgraded from Stage Four to a Stage Two."

He offered them to me, but I refused to take them. "Your mother thinks there's a real shot," he added. "At least read the material."

"Why?" I countered. "You can't let her do this again. You know it only gets her hopes up."

273

"But if there's a chance . . ."

"Like with Stanford?" I countered, and he stopped. His hand lowered, pain skittering across his face, and I felt it too, after all this time. That ache of what if, almost, not quite, what might have been.

Stanford. The last surgical trial. The last big experimental drug. I was sixteen then, and we'd heard about it everywhere; news like that never stays hidden for long. Whispers on the hospital wards, phone numbers scribbled and passed between every parent support group. They were using a new cocktail, radiation, and targeted surgery, and to everyone's shock and wild, distant hope, it seemed to be working. Shrinking tumors, extending prognosis. Even failure wasn't a death sentence, the cancer simply continuing its crawl. In our world, thirty-, forty-percent success rate was a lottery win, an embarrassment of riches, and even I let myself hope that this, finally, was the answer we all were praying for.

My mother set about hunting me down that winning ticket, with a fervor I'd never seen before. We flew in half a dozen times for tests and assessments: physical exams, psych evaluations, essays, and more, like a college application where the stakes were life and death. The competition was fierce, can you imagine? Every dream-starved parent in the nation laying siege to that research hospital, but only a dozen of us would even make the grade. Even Hope got in on the act; her cancer was all wrong, but that didn't stop her poring over my materials right along with me, approvingly noting my white blood cell count, the growth on my latest scans. "They'd be a fool not to take you," she'd say with authority. "Your tumor is perfect for this."

The day I was accepted into the next round of trials, we celebrated with dinner at my favorite local Italian restaurant. My mom was laughing, bright-eyed; my dad choked up over the sparkling cider toast. And I was swept up right along with it. The dreams I'd been blocking for so long began to unfold, right there in the cramped vinyl booth, laid out on that wax-paper tablecloth. Maybe I could go to art school. Maybe I could move to the East Coast.

Maybe I'd live to see twenty-five, after all.

Those sweet daydreams propelled us across the country to a new city, another short-term rental for my parents, a bright new hospital room. The California skies were clear that spring, and the cab from the airport took us past palm trees and stucco buildings, depositing us at the hospital doors beneath eighteen floors of polished windows, sparkling into the blue with a new kind of optimism. We all felt it, infectious, and even though we knew the risks, we were believers back then. We could feel it. This time. *This time.*

I never even had a chance. We were unpacking my sketchpads into the slim bedside dresser when the surgeons came and broke the news. The trials had been cancelled, permission pulled by the powers-that-be. They'd had a string of fatalities before me that week; the new drugs were flawed somehow, and they had to stop, and start their formulation over again. They didn't know when they would resume: months, a year from then. They didn't say the rest, but I knew it from the looks on their faces.

By then, it would be too late for me.

"I won't do it again," I said softly to my father, even though we'd both been betrayed by that failed trial. "I can't get my hopes up, and you shouldn't let Mom, either. And compared to Stanford, this is a shot in the dark. At least they'd had success, the chances would have been good for me. And what does Benson have now? Dead bodies on the operating table. I won't do it, Dad. I can't."

He nodded, slowly, reality sinking in again. "I know, sweetheart. I know."

He looked so forlorn; I ached to see him like this. All my childhood, I worshipped him. There was no problem he couldn't solve, no frown that wouldn't be turned upside down by a penny plucked from behind my ear, or an afternoon wobbling on my bright-green bicycle as he jogged, cheering alongside.

But now, of course, my problems were beyond fixing.

"How much longer are you staying in town?" I asked, as gently as I could.

"I'm not sure. Your mother thought that maybe we could go to church together tomorrow for a service."

He looked so hopeful, I had to accept. "I have plans for lunch with Theo, but we could find a morning one. I don't know about the churches here, but there should be one close by."

"That would be nice. It's been a while since we all went together. I know it would mean a lot to her."

"But you'll talk to her?" I checked again. "I don't want another fight, Dad. There isn't enough time."

"I know, sweetheart." He opened his arms to me, and I went, sitting beside him on the bed with my head against his chest as he held me. I took a breath and pulled back, a familiar acrid scent stinging lightly in the back of my throat.

"You're smoking again?"

Dad looked guilty. "Just a couple, now and then."

"But you tried so hard to quit!"

"I know. I'll give up soon. Next year," he promised.

"You better." I settled in close, strangely comforted by the routine of it all—his hugs and the old quitting conversation. We'd done this a hundred times over nineteen years, and now, again, I felt the well-worn grooves of our back-and-forth. "Or I'll tell Mom."

"Don't. I'll never hear the end of it."

"And whose fault is that?"

"My daughter, the taskmaster."

"It's only because I love you."

"You too, Claire-bear."

The snow was falling again, light as clouds outside the frosted windowpanes. Next door, I could hear someone moving around, muffled voices coming from down the hall. He held me, and I tried to remember everything in that moment: the steady weight of his arm around me, and the scratch of his raw wool sweater on my wet cheeks.

Somehow, I knew it would be the last time.

TESSA WAS RIGHT: the city became a snow-swept ghost town, and Christmas morning we walked to church on hushed, silent streets that had been teeming with tourists and last-minute shoppers, frantically hunting down the last, perfect gift. Now, slush-trimmed footprints were the only proof of life; the morning skies were clouded and winds slipped icily under our bundles of coats and scarves as we passed the storefronts filled with ornate decorations, already out of date.

"It's a shame Theo couldn't join us," my mom said, leading the way in her polished black boots. "It would be nice to spend more time with him before we leave. You said you're meeting his family today?"

"His dad. And it's not a big deal," I added, in case she had visions of us all crowded around a kitchen table somewhere, toasting the year ahead. "They don't really do the holidays. I'm just going to support him."

"Let Claire have her plans," Dad spoke up, his hands in his pockets, and his cheeks red against the plaid scarf I'd given as a makeshift holiday gift. "It's better we get back home, anyway. Travel after the holidays is always a madhouse. The airport should be nice and quiet today; you hate the crowds."

Mom strode on, and he gave me a wink. Dad had kept his promise. There had been no talk of surgery or drug trials, but I could see the unspoken words in Mom's eyes, and felt the weight of her anxiety every time she opened her mouth to speak and then bit the words back, remarking instead on the old Boston architecture or twinkling lights. By the time we reached the church, I was ready for sanctuary, for the cool, sweet hum of carols to drown out the rest of all our fraught conversations. The old Trinity Church stood timeless on the edge of Copley

Square, its stone steeples reaching up amongst a grey, gleaming clutter of modern office buildings and department stores, as if the centuries had marched onwards, but it somehow existed in a solemn bubble all of its own. I felt a tremor, intimidated by the grandeur, but the moment we stepped through those ornate wooden doors, there was warmth and brightness, the wooden pews packed and pale sun scattering through vast stained-glass friezes to dance in a kaleidoscope on the worn stone floors.

In a flash, I remembered Theo, the first day we met, the sugar canisters, and those rainbows that had danced in his eyes. It felt like a lifetime ago, and brand new all at once.

"Claire." My mom's voice was hushed but impatient, and I quickly followed them to a pew, shuffling apologetically past morning worshippers to a place by the edge of the great room. I was still awestruck by the building: carved and ornate, the ceilings soared higher, and everywhere, there were statues and frieze scenes, the altar rising up at the head of the room. It was a work of art in itself, every inch constructed with love, a world away from the sparse, modern space of our church back home, with its simple community rooms and the prayer spaces where I had tried, and failed, to find some kind of peace.

The service began, my parents following on the crinkled Xerox handouts as the priest began his homily about the Christmas miracle, about welcoming strangers from afar, and about the world breaking apart outside these stained glass windows, but my mind wouldn't still. I felt the same itch that always stroked softly in my veins in places like this, that bittersweet ache of guilt and regret.

How much easier would this all be if I could just believe?

My mom did. Her conversion was heralded by those first grey smudges on my MRI scans, and as many hours as she spent doing battle with hospital administrators and insurance red tape, she must have passed just as many at the Oak Hills church with the pastor there, talking and praying and talking some more. She'd wanted to take me, too, and over the years, she wasn't the only one: hospital chaplains and therapists all tried to nudge me gently towards faith, the way so many terminal patients managed to make sense of their fate. And I tried. I prayed with my mom in the back of Sunday services, I read the prescribed passages, and I tried to grasp the higher purpose some deity might have for me, how my death might just be the beginning, but the words on the page lay empty to me, and no matter how hard I tried to pour some meaning into them, I still came up blank.

Hope didn't even try. God was dead to her, and even if they'd ever had a relationship, cancer was a deal-breaker, she'd say with a smirk. The end was the end was the end, so what difference would any of it make?

I still didn't know what to believe. In sacred places like

this, with the sweet carols circling up around me, I could almost convince myself that there would be something more, after that end. A part of me wondered, and quietly dreamed, but over the years it had never grasped me with conviction, and that, itself, was an answer, I guess. But no matter how much I wrestled with it, trying to find that thread of faith, I couldn't escape the one certainty I kept arriving back on, the rip-tide current that wouldn't let my mind go.

If there was a God, like they believed, then He'd planned this for me, or worse still, was standing idly by.

I couldn't reconcile that great betrayal, couldn't even come close. Infinite love and power were nothing compared to the cancerous cells slowly multiplying in my brain, and my years of grief and fear and pain—there was no good way to justify them, and even though Mom did her best, her faith was for her own broken heart, not mine. My life now was the only thing that was sacred, and pinning my desperate hopes on a tomorrow beyond death wouldn't change how vital each moment was, right now.

But I sat there with them that Christmas morning, and let the music wash over me, felt the stillness of those soaring skies, and for a moment, at least, the rest of the world—and my own decaying body—seemed far away. There was a purity in those sweet, restful notes, songs that soothed and brought all our hearts together, singing in unison for a few precious bars.

It was Christmastime, and we prayed for joy, for all mankind.

AFTER THE SERVICE, we walked back to their hotel and my parents loitered, awkward on the wet pavement. My father tried to slip an envelope into my hand.

"Dad."

"Humor your old man." He gave me a crooked smile. "Take your friends out, or have a nice dinner with Theo. You deserve it."

I relented. "Thank you." I hugged him tight and swift, pressed my lips to his cheek. "Merry Christmas."

My mom hung back. She looked tight and pinched, those bit-back words still all rippling beneath the surface of her brisk smile. "Mom?" My voice cracked, just a little, as I reached for her. She hugged me hard, almost like it was too much to bear, then stepped back, quickly smoothing my hair down as she looked away, eyes wet. "Remember to call us every day."

"Or a text," Dad interrupted. They exchanged looks. Mom slowly exhaled.

"Or a text," she agreed. "But you need to let us know you're OK, or if there have been any changes. New symptoms. I know you don't want to," she added, "but we need to be realistic now. We need to know how things are progressing."

Things.

I nodded my surrender. "I'll text."

"And you won't pretend things are alright when they're not," she continued, as if she knew how I would try to hide it from them. "If you can't tell us, at least keep up appointments with Doctor Benson." Her brisk mask slipped for a moment, and pure, aching desperation shone through. "And maybe you'll think about the trial some more? I know you don't want to but—"

"Susan." My dad put a gentle hand on her arm, warning.

"I know we agreed, but I can't just watch her . . ." Mom's voice twisted, and she looked away. "There are still things left to try, this doesn't have to be the end."

"It already is, Mom." I took her hands in mine, beseeching. "I promise, I'll call you guys, I'll check in with the doctor, I'll take all my meds. But you have to let me do this. I have time now, a couple of good months, maybe. Please don't try and make me give that up, because I won't do it. I can't. Not even for you."

She pulled away and wiped her eyes, but there was a faint nod before she hitched her purse and looked around, raising her arm to flag down a cab. "You should get going then. You don't want to be late meeting Theo."

"Travel safe," I told them softly. "See you soon."

I knew tears were coming, but I held them back long enough to slide into the backseat of the car and wave brightly out of the window as we pulled away. I watched them recede, small figures on the snow-drenched sidewalk, until we turned the corner and were gone. The next time I saw them, I knew, I would be in a hospital bed, but I couldn't think of that now. The cab driver turned up the radio, and Frank Sinatra crooned softly as we wound our way through the empty city streets. I rolled the window down, and breathed it in, the crisp, clear scent of winter, snow clouds still hanging grey in the sky. I loved how this city turned over between the seasons. Only two months ago, these trees had blazed with burning color, and the skies shone a vivid blue; now the city blocks were dressed in monochrome, a smudged palette of sophistication, greys against charcoal, pale white lights splashed against midnight black. I remembered the envelope in my pocket, and imagined the art supplies it would buy, the studio that sat waiting for me and my canvas, just across the steel-tipped river.

My parents couldn't understand, but if I could have chosen any way to see out the last days of my life, it was right there, with paint smudging my fingertips, and Theo —*Theo*—greeting me with a kiss. This was all I wanted, for better or for worse.

THE PROMISE

CHAPTER TWENTY-FOUR

I FOUND HIM ON the corner in a part of the city I hadn't been before, where the old row houses were crammed together, and the snow was already melted into grey rivers of slush that wound around potholes and trash as I clambered out of the cab.

"Welcome to my neighborhood," he said, a wry note in his voice hiding the tension I could already see in his jaw.

"Merry Christmas," I answered, leaning up to kiss him. I took my time about it, feeling the same rush of gladness that always sparked at his touch, to exist there in the circle of his embrace, to be a part of the world that had him in it. His mouth as delicate as the snow still resting on the telephone wires above, but we finally came up for air; Theo's tension seemed to have eased. He gave a rueful smile.

"It's not too late," he said. "We could still bail."

I shook my head, and tucked my arm through his. "You said, it's tradition."

"A tradition of dysfunction."

We began to walk, slow on the wet street. I could feel Theo's reluctance with every step, and I wondered how many years he'd been traipsing back here for a holiday that was anything but merry. "How about this," I suggested, wanting this year to be different for him. "How about we have a safe word?"

His lips curled in a smirk. "Oh, really?"

I laughed. "Not like that! I just mean, if things get too weird or difficult, you say the word, and I'll come up with an excuse to leave. We'll be out of there in ten seconds flat. I'll fake a migraine, or something. Women's troubles."

He managed a smile. "You don't have to."

"I know, but think about it. Get out of jail free, if it gets too bad."

"What word would it be?" he asked.

"Cranberry. Serendipity. Geronimo."

Theo was laughing for real now. "Geronimo?"

"That's the one then. Code-word, escape."

Theo paused on the sidewalk, bringing his cold hands to my face. He smiled at me with gratitude in his eyes. "You're something else," he murmured, leaning in to kiss me again, and I went to him like gravity, leaning into the sun.

"Something like an ice cube," I said, finally pulling away. "C'mon, the sooner we get started, the sooner we can Geronimo out of there!"

Whatever I'd been expecting, Theo's father was nowhere near close: a spry, dark-haired man in a button-down shirt and faded leather jacket, Liam greeted us the minute we stepped through the steam-coated door of the faded diner down the block.

"Merry Christmas, get in here out of the cold. Theo, my son, and you must be the lovely Claire. Charmed, absolutely charmed." He kissed my hand, beaming. He had a faint Irish accent buried against the Boston burr. "Georgia, honey, let's get some drinks in! Not like that," he added, to Theo. "I'm off the sauce. Fifty-two days, I've got the chips and everything, but we don't want to talk about that, not with this gorgeous creature. Claire, look at you, come sit down and tell me what you're doing with a loser like my son. Just kidding!" Liam let out a hearty laugh and ruffled Theo's hair, then headed for a table.

I took a breath. The diner was almost empty, just an older couple in a table by the windows, slowly spooning soup. A few crumpled paper decorations hung around the register, and a radio played Mariah Carey somewhere in back. The woman behind the counter greeted Theo by name, and he paused to wish her a happy holidays and ask about her kids. She had a smoker's laugh, and patted him affectionately on the arm, giving me a brief assessing look before promising to bring us some water.

"Just water," Theo said quietly, and she nodded.

"He's not lying, been over a month now. He comes by after his meetings, he's really trying this time."

We joined Liam at the table set with plastic glasses and paper covers. Up close, I could see that for all his bright enthusiasm, there was hard living etched on his face: thin sunken cheeks, lines around his eyes. He made a show of holding out a chair for me —"Manners, boy. Don't you forget how to treat a lady," he said with a wink—then sat with a satisfied smile. "It's about time you brought a girlfriend around," he said. "I was beginning to wonder about you. No offense," he added glibly. "I guess it takes all sorts these days."

I felt Theo take a measured breath beside me.

"So how did you two meet then? Are you from that college?" he asked, not pausing. "Perks of the job, isn't that right son? All those pretty young coeds running around."

"No," I answered, before Theo could. "I work in a coffee shop nearby."

"Claire's an artist," Theo said shortly.

"Is that right?" Liam grinned. "Good for you. I've had a touch of the old creative spark myself. Used to act, did Theo tell you that? It's where he gets his brains from, his old Pa. Not that I would waste them in that classroom, stuck with all those boring books."

He launched into a story about local theatre and his shot at the big-time as Georgia brought over sodas, and Theo sat, still so tense beside me. "Took myself to New York, too, could have really been someone. Then I met Theo's ma, of course. Should've learned to keep it zipped, you be careful about that, boy."

Theo flushed, and I could see his jaw clenched tight, so I quickly changed the subject. "Where in Ireland are you from?"

Liam brightened. "Town called Killarney, out on the west part of the island. You ever been? No? Beautiful place, just beautiful." He kept talking, about the community, and his wayward youth, and I finally let myself exhale. This, at least, seemed neutral ground.

Lunch was a limp turkey dinner, cranberry jelly still cold in the middle. I ate a polite amount, but Liam only picked at his food, drinking three cups of coffee and talking a mile a minute. His stories were vivid, full of local color, and maybe to an outsider, he could come across as charming, but I couldn't help notice how every other anecdote contained a sly dig in Theo's direction, a barbed remark bookended by a "no offense" or "just kidding." I wondered if this was how he'd grown up, undercut at every turn, and it made me ache to think of it.

No wonder he never went back.

I found Theo's hand under the table and gave a squeeze. He shot me a pale smile, but it didn't reach his eyes. I checked the clock and saw we'd been here barely an hour, but I wasn't sure how much more I could take—for his sake, more than mine.

"Thing is, your generation doesn't understand real work," Liam was saying. "I put in an honest day's work for a paycheck for thirty years, but if you listened to this one here, you'd think I never earned a dime."

"So does this mean you finally found a job?" Theo asked coolly.

Liam scowled. "You know my back won't take it, not after the accident."

"Right."

It was a soft comment, barely audible, but Liam pointed across the table. "Don't you take that tone. I'm still your father, and you owe me some respect."

"Owe you?" Theo echoed, then seemed to catch himself. "Sure. Whatever you say."

Liam's face set. "There you go again, disrespecting me. You see what I have to put up with?" he demanded in my direction.

Theo froze. "Leave Claire out of this."

"Why, so you can go cry to her later about your

deadbeat dad giving you a hard time?" Liam snorted. "In my day, we showed some fucking backbone."

I was on my feet before I could think twice. "Geronimo," I murmured quietly to Theo, and the relief on his face was a gift.

"We're leaving now," I told Liam, fighting to keep my tone pleasant. There were a hundred things I wanted to say to him, about the man in front of him he just couldn't see, but being right didn't matter; getting Theo away from this poison did. "It was nice to meet you, have a happy holidays."

Theo shoved back his chair, and Liam's face changed in an instant. "Now don't go taking offense! I was just messing around, you shouldn't listen to an old man like me." He smiled widely. "We're not even done with dinner. Theo doesn't mind my jokes, do you, boy? You can't leave now, I promise, I'll be on my best behavior. Promise." He mimed crossing his heart, gave me a wink, too, for good measure, but they were empty words, and we didn't need them.

"Thank you for lunch," I said firmly, and reached for my coat. "But we have to go."

Theo helped me into it, then pulled out his wallet.

"Put that away, son." Liam shook his head, but Theo resolutely pulled a twenty and tossed it down on the table. Liam's smile slipped away, and something bitter took its place. "So that's how it's going to be, huh? My money's no good to you? After everything I've done for you, I'm some fucking charity case now?"

Theo guided me to the exit, Liam's surly voice following us until we were outside and the doors finally swung shut. The wind braced us, sharp and biting, and it was almost a relief after the cloying heat and all that resentment seething inside. I reached for Theo, but he was already striding out in front, head down, and it was as much as I could do to keep pace, fast on the slippery iced sidewalks until we were down the block and around the corner, and his footsteps finally slowed to a halt.

"Hey." I touched his back gently.

"I'm sorry." His voice was tight, and when he lifted his head, there was heartbreak in his eyes.

"What for?"

"For that," Theo laughed, bitter. "All that bullshit. I should have known, God, you'd think after all this time, I would have known what we were walking into. That he couldn't even try and behave himself for one fucking afternoon—"

He spun around and slammed his fist into the wall, so hard I flinched back in shock. He was wearing gloves, but still, I heard the pain in his voice as he swore under his breath. "Sorry. Fuck, I'm sorry."

"There's nothing to be sorry about," I said softly. "You don't have to apologize for him. That man in there has nothing to do with you."

Theo shook his head. "God, I wish it was that easy."

"Let me look at that." I held out my hand. Theo paused, then reluctantly allowed me to peel off the glove. His knuckles looked bruised, but as I gently touched the swollen skin, there didn't seem to be any breaks. "Ouch. You showed that wall. Feel better now?" I asked, trying to get a smile out of him.

"No."

"Weird," I teased. "Because violence is always the answer."

Theo gave a rueful smile. "Clearly."

I lifted his hand to my lips and kissed it lightly. "You'll live. I, on the other hand, will hulk out if I don't get something to eat."

"Hulk, huh?" Theo's smile finally melted into something real, that dazzling warmth that cut through the winter clouds with the power of a hundred suns. "Impossible."

"Oh no, I go crazy, green muscles and all," I laughed, relieved. "You don't want to see me when I'm hangry." I slipped my arm through his, and we started walking again, but this time, I could feel his tension ease, our steps falling in unison all the way down the street.

The Promise

W E FOUND A SMALL Ethiopian café open near the bridge, and spent an hour tucked away in the back, blocking out the ugliness of the lunchtime scene with as much laughter and teasing as we could bring. But Theo's laughter faded, and I could tell, he wanted to talk.

"Has he always been like this?"

Theo tore strips off the bread, a flat loaf studded with cloves and spices. "Not always. He has phases, good years and bad. Even growing up, he could keep it together sometimes for months at a time. Mom would threaten to leave if he didn't get his shit together, so, he'd try. Hold down a job, go to meetings, stay sober. Always just enough to keep me hoping, that this time, it was for real, you know? But then, something would set him off, and we'd be right back where we started. And then once Mom left . . ." Theo let the words trail away. "After that, he just stopped trying."

"How old were you when she went?"

"Thirteen," Theo said quietly.

"And you haven't heard from her since?" I couldn't believe it.

He shrugged. "She sent birthday cards, the first few years. Letters, full of apologies, some money sometimes, too. I didn't write back, and eventually . . . she just gave up. She remarried; last I heard she was down in Raleigh, new kids. A new life."

"And now you have one, too. One you built from scratch." I held his hand, so full of admiration, but Theo just gave me that self-deprecating smile.

"Sure. Because a glorified tutoring job and a room in that house with four other guys is really success."

"Hey." I frowned. "Don't let him get inside your head like that. You made this, all on your own. You worked your way up, you support yourself, you have people in your life who care about you. That's something. It matters."

Theo sighed. "I know. I hate that he still gets to me. Every time I think I'm done, something drags me back in."

I paused. "Do you ever think you'll reach your limit?"

I didn't want to judge him. I knew the invisible strings that tangled around the heart, keeping us pinned to the past, choking for air. I couldn't judge him for trying, for doing his best to be a good son even to a man who didn't deserve the privilege of Theo's love.

"I hope so." He kept toying with his food, a nervous edge. "It's tough, being so close to him, just across the river. It made sense to stay, with the financial aid package Harvard was offering, but part of me still wishes I could have left. Packed my bags and gone, New York, or California, Chicago . . ." Theo shook his head, the possibilities already gone. "But I'm stuck here, and still feel like I could do something, help somehow."

"Not forever," I reminded him, and he nodded.

"You're right. One day."

I wished it for him with everything I had. He should be free and know the love he deserved, not the guilty half-measures doled out by a parent too selfish to see the damage done.

"You're lucky," he added. "I know your parents are overprotective, but it's only because they care. Believe me, it's worse when they don't."

Guilt stung, hard. My own problems seemed a world away, but he was right. My family was probably on a flight right now, heading west, because I'd given them no choice. I was pushing them away, and it was the only way I knew how.

"I'm sorry." My expression must have shown my grief, because Theo immediately took my hand. "I didn't mean it like that."

"I know." I managed a smile. "And you're right."

His lips curved in a wry smile. "There's a poem, by Phillip Larkin," he said. "He was an English writer. About how your parents fuck you up, even if they don't mean it."

I laughed. "Really?"

He nodded, smiling. "It goes on. About how they inherited their parents' issues, and we, in turn, will pass on our own. The only alternative is not having kids at all." He paused, taking a sip of water. "You ever think about it?"

"Children?"

"Kids, family." Theo looked almost shy, but it was like a sucker-punch, straight through my ribcage.

I fought to keep my voice even and carefree. "Not really. It seems a long way off." I swallowed. "You?"

He glanced away. "I know I want them, one day. I just wonder . . . if I can be a good father, or if I'll screw them up like he did."

"You'll be an amazing father." I had to swallow back the tears that were already rising. "You're nothing like him."

We were interrupted by the server then, and I used the moment to slip away to the bathroom. I tried not to cry, weaving back past the coat closet and clatter of the kitchens. I didn't want him to see it, my eyes all puffy and red, but I couldn't stop: I shut the door behind me and stood there, silently shaking in the small dark cubicle, listening to the whir of the fan, my cheeks wet with the future I wouldn't get to see.

These were the things I forbid myself to think about, those long, bitter, aching nights in the faded neon of the hospital ward. Fat-cheeked toddlers and a home of my own, singing in the kitchen with a husband, a family playing safe in the yard. I wasn't lying to Theo, it would have still felt so far away even without my end in sight. I was nineteen, I wasn't anywhere near ready to begin that chapter, but that didn't mean I couldn't grieve, knowing those pages would be ripped out for good.

And Theo . . . it shook me, how easy it was to imagine that future with him. I may have lived a sheltered life, cushioned by the whisper of a hundred hospital gowns, but I still knew enough to recognize that this, between us —how my heart unfurled and took flight from just a glance of those blue eyes—was something precious and rare. Enough to build a future on? I would never get to know. But still, in that moment, sobbing silently as my fingernails bit half-moon imprints into my palms and the sounds of foreign chatter swung through the opening door, I yearned for it with every beat of my aching heart.

CHAPTER TWENTY-FIVE

THE CLOUDS WERE fading to a crisp blue sky when we emerged, so we walked back over the bridge, huddling close against the Atlantic winds. "I think my place might be empty," Theo said, his hands slipping under my coat for warmth.

I shivered, not from the cool of his touch, but the heat that it sparked in me. "I can't, my shift, remember?"

He groaned. "I still can't believe you're open today."

"Mika says it's a public service. All those people needing to escape their family fun."

He chuckled. "Sounds about right. Why don't I meet you after?"

"Perfect. I can give you my gift," I added, feeling shy.

"You didn't have to get me anything," Theo protested, but I shrugged it off.

"It's just something small. You'll see."

"OK, then." He kissed me again. "I'll see you at your place at eight."

We parted on the corner, and I walked on, the streets busier now, and all the earlier pristine snow fading to grey, gritted slush under our heels. The white swathes of yesterday were memories now, and I wondered if I'd see more snow this winter.

If I'd ever see snow like that again.

My heart caught. It was creeping in now, the reality of the end. The prescription drugs rattling in my bag, the now-familiar burst of pressure blooming above my left temple. I thought I could live in denial for just a few more days, but the dark thoughts were already slipping past all my festive plans until everything was a reminder about how little time I really had left. I fought them with everything I had. I would cling on to this, just a few more days before the confetti greeted next year and I would come clean to him, about everything. A few more days to savor this life, memorize the sweetness as it faded out towards the end. So I stuck my hands deep in my pockets and strode on down the street to the café, enjoying the rush of warmth that enveloped me as I stepped through the entrance.

"Close the door!" Mika yelled cheerfully from behind the counter. "Do you want us all to catch a damn chill?"

The café was packed, just like he'd predicted, and there was an extra breath of festive cheer in the air alongside cinnamon and old Bing Crosby songs. "Everyone's just relieved it's nearly over," JJ confided after I'd traded my jacket for an apron and joined him up front. He was swirling an expert holly leaf into the latte foam, wearing one of those novelty Christmas sweaters, with reindeers galloping across the front.

"No holiday haters allowed," Mika interrupted, swopping between us to man the register. "One day a year, we get to spread a little cheer."

"One day?" JJ repeated, teasing. "Say that again on Valentines, or Easter, or—"

"OK, I get the message." Mika gave him an affectionate nudge. "I'll just return your gift then."

"Take my sweater?" JJ grinned, crossing his arms protectively over his chest. "You'll have to peel it from my cold, dead body."

I wanted to hold onto it—that afternoon. Every smiling, relieved face in the crowd, every joke and teasing skit that spun around me with Mika and JJ. Now, some other girl will have taken my place, and slipped effortlessly into their ballet to whirl and spin amongst the dirty tables and bakery case, but that day, it was all my own: the customers blurring into a line of motion, the hours slipping past fine as confectioner's sugar in the air. It was dark before I realized my shift was over; the lights of the city softened around the edges through our breath-fogged windows, jewels winking from the dark street beyond.

I peeled off my apron and grabbed my bag. "Happy holidays," I said to Mika and JJ, slipping out from behind the counter.

"You too, darling."

I stepped outside, ducking through the sidewalk traffic as life threaded through the winter streets again. I walked fast through the bustle and hum, people wrapped in their brand-new holiday scarves, arms as full of shopping bags as the night before Christmas. Hope always smirked about the holidays, how it was all just a ruse to sell perfume gift sets and socks that nobody wanted, but even with the ad campaigns blaring from every magazine and TV, I still thought there was something sweet about it: trying to show someone what they meant to you with just a small, gift-wrapped token, your heart wrapped up in ribbons and bows. My present for Theo was waiting at home, a small painting I'd secretly worked on during stolen moments away from him all week. It wasn't much, but I knew Theo wasn't the kind of guy to care about anything fancy, and I couldn't wait to see his face when he peeled back the paper.

I found him waiting on my front steps, pacing back and forth with his collar high against the evening wind.

"Sorry, I got caught up at work." I smiled, reaching him. "You must be freezing. Come on, let's get inside." I leaned up to kiss him, but Theo flinched away.

My heart stuttered in my chest, a half-beat hesitation that turned to dread when he stepped back into the pool of streetlight glow, and I saw the expression on his face. Guarded and wary, like the way he'd looked on that city-scape rooftop back in the fall, before he'd walked out of my life for what I'd thought was forever.

"What's wrong?" I whispered, remembering the call last time. "Is it your dad? Did something happen?"

Theo looked confused. "My dad? No. He's fine."

"Then what . . .?"

I knew before he said it. I could see it in his eyes, somehow. The betrayal there, it wasn't from some other thing whirling out there in the world, it was because of me.

He knew.

The silence shivered there between us on the grey sidewalk.

"Why didn't you tell me you were sick?"

It was an accusation and a heartbroken plea, all bound up in the crack of his voice, the man I loved looking at me like I had torn something sacred apart. And I had. God, if I could take any of it back, it would be this moment, this wretched unraveling on a dark, cold street corner with my blood pounding hot, shame and guilt rising up to drown me from the inside out.

It all fell away, our castles in the snowdrift sky. The world we'd built together, two heartbeats in the night, melting in an instant to leave nothing but flint-harsh anger on his gorgeous face, barely contained, barely held back from the edge.

"Theo . . ." I took a half-step towards him, and he took a half-step back, automatic, like there was a force field around me he couldn't bring himself to ever breach again. My mind spun over the possibilities, but it couldn't find a grip. "How . . ." My voice was barely a whisper, all the breath had been sucked from my lungs, but still I forced the words out. "How did you know?"

"Your mom told me everything." His words were clipped, but they struck me like ice. "She came by, today, while you were at work. She said I deserved to know the truth."

"I thought they'd gone." My head spun with the betrayal. "I can't believe she would do that. She had no right."

"And you did?"

His reply came, whip-sharp, a slap across my heart. Of course he was right. I shouldn't have been keeping this from him, and no matter how my ugly secrets had been dragged into the light, I couldn't be angry. I had no right at all, no matter how my heart ached with guilt and grief.

"I was going to tell you," I swore, wishing it could make a difference now. "I just . . . I just needed more time. Please, Theo . . ." I begged. "I didn't want to lie to you, you have to believe me."

Theo glanced away, as if he couldn't stand to look at me. "Are you OK?"

I wasn't prepared for the gentleness of his voice. This was even worse. Even in the midst of his betrayal, Theo's first instinct was to care for me. His heart was true, and I'd wasted it on lies.

I nodded, trying to keep it together despite the cracks splintering out through my body, marble veins of pain threading out from my core. "I have meds, to keep the pain under control," I explained softly. "But I'm getting tremors now, in my hand. Headaches."

"When you collapsed . . ." He stopped. "You knew?"

I closed my eyes a moment, forcing myself to nod. "I knew it was getting worse. I thought . . . I thought I had more time."

"Until what?" His voice made me look again, and I saw the anger cracking through the hollow shell of his shock. "Until you fell down and didn't get up again? God, Claire, do you know how worried I've been? I nearly went out of my mind that night, I thought you might be hiding something, and all along, you knew!"

307

Theo caught his breath, ragged, and I saw his hands clench at his sides, two angry fists balled, gripping his anger tightly. "And even now—fuck," he swore. "What am I supposed to do? I can't be mad at you. I'm not allowed!"

"You can hate me," I said, silently weeping now. "I know I deserve it."

"I'm sorry. I can't . . ." I saw him pull himself back together, saw the effort it took to corral his angry words behind that stony expression again. "I can't talk to you right now. I need to think."

"Please, let me explain—" I started desperately, but Theo had already jammed his fists deep in his coat pockets, shoulders tight as he backed away.

"No, Claire. Don't. I need some space," he said, not looking at me. "I need to figure this out."

And just like that, he was walking away, a tense back turned on me, that navy coat lifting in the breeze behind him as he was swallowed up by the dark. The world spun sideways, and I grabbed the railing before I fell, gasping for air as the drums pounded in my brain. I tasted panic, bitter copper fear. Not for the pain blossoming in my head, but my heart wrenching open, tearing apart in my chest to follow him into the night. He was leaving, he was already half a memory, and although I deserved it, I'd lost too much in my nineteen years to let him slip into the shadows and be gone.

Maybe it was the most selfish thing of all, going after him the way I did. I could have let him disappear that night and become nothing more than a memory, something to hold onto as my cancer took its slow victory lap in the months ahead, and the morphine pulled me from this world into the next, but I couldn't help it; even now, I can't explain. Something propelled my feet down that street and after him, a desperate, wild staccato on the icy streets as I raced for my life—for all I wanted from what was left of my life, at least. Because when the end is so close you can taste the bitterness of the drugs that keep you hanging on, some things become simple.

Love, only love, matters in the end.

I sprinted down that street, and the next, his dark silhouette moving fast ahead of me into the park. I had no words, I barely had enough breath in my lungs to keep moving, but I didn't stop until he was in arm's reach from me, silhouetted against the faded white and winter's grey, the bare trees above us stretching into the black night, strung with stars.

"Theo!"

My voice echoed, plaintive and raw, and maybe that was what made him turn. He stood there, his expression still closed off, a stranger. How many nights had I lain awake, tracing the contours of that miraculous face? How many days had I skimmed pencil to page, trying time and again to capture the light that radiated from his kind, true heart?

"Theo, please," I begged him, tears already wet on my cheeks. There was an ache inside me gasping, a darkness ready to obliterate the pale light of the moon overhead. "Let me just explain. I didn't want to lie to you. I'm so, so sorry. I never planned for this, I swear."

"What am I supposed to say to you?" Theo demanded. His voice struck me hard, but I could see him breaking apart underneath it all. "She said you were dying, Claire. That you only have months to live! I thought . . . all this time I thought the two of us could be . . ." He stopped, swallowing back the words, the late-night whispers, all those *what ifs* and *one days* I'd fooled myself into ignoring as I held onto *right now* so tight.

"I know," I said, broken. "I'm sorry."

"You came after *me*." Theo was accusing, wheels spinning in his mind. "I walked away because I thought you were better off without me. I was trying to protect you! And when you showed up at my office I thought . . . that we could be together. That you were in, all in."

"I am! Theo, you don't understand—"

"You lied to me," he yelled, echoing in the dark, snowy park. "The one person I thought I knew better than

310

anyone. Why?" His voice turned pleading. "Tell me, why did you hide this from me? Why didn't you let me in?"

"Because I love you!"

My words seemed to ricochet around us, bouncing off every cold, frozen tree trunk and empty black iron bench. "I love you, Theo," I sobbed. "And I couldn't . . . I couldn't admit that this was all going to end."

There was silence. Hushed by the snowfall, swallowed up into the distant city roar. A terrible, endless silence that my bruised body felt with every desperate breath.

Theo looked away. "I . . . I don't know what to tell you, Claire. I don't know what you want me to say."

Say you love me. Say I'm yours. Say you'll be mine until the end.

But I couldn't. I'd laid my heart, still beating, at his feet, and it still wasn't enough to close the distance between us, or strip the betrayal from those blue eyes.

"I'll tell you anything, Theo. But please, don't push me away."

"I'm sorry." When his answer came, it sounded heavy and final. "I want to talk, but this is a lot to deal with. Please, just give me some time."

Time.

He didn't realize just how cruel that word was, dangling a future as if I had any chance of grasping it, but I'd already hurt him too much. I nodded, even though my body was screaming not to. Every instinct I had was to hold him tightly, and kiss him until this space between us was full again. Full, and right, and the way it used to be.

"Will you be OK getting home?" he asked, and I could already see it, that kid-glove concern I'd fought to keep at bay. I wasn't just Claire to him anymore, I was Claire with cancer, and there was no taking it back.

I nodded, my voice failing me now.

This time, when he walked away from me, I didn't try to follow. I watched him go, a shadow slipping into the darkness, until I couldn't tell him from the night.

Then he was gone.

CHAPTER TWENTY-SIX

HOPE DIED IN the springtime, when the world was supposed to be cherry-blossom fresh and only just beginning. We buried her on a blue-skied day so bright it hurt my heart to look, and marked the headstone with a dozen yellow daffodils, dancing in the breeze. I thought I knew what it was to love and lose, to feel that wretched agony split your world apart, the jagged edged of an empty forever taunting with every raw, ragged breath. I thought I'd seen the worst of it, mourning for her, for me, for the lives we'd never get to lead. And then I lost Theo, too, and discovered that heartbreak comes in a thousand shades of blue.

I don't know how I made it home. Looking back even now, there's nothing but glimpses; my brain snapped tight against the grief. The crunch the snow made under my stumbling boots, the glint of headlights blurring neon in the night. I swam, dizzy through the rush of blood pounding in my ears, barely breathing all the way back. I must have found the footsteps somehow, because I woke up in darkness, still dressed on my bed. My head ached, my lungs burned, and my heart . . . my heart was broken clean apart.

It was over. He was gone. And with him, with Theo's fast-departing stride, he'd taken with him the only thing I had left to cling on to, my sweet and distant daydream of a love that could somehow even make the rage of my tumor fade away.

It was over. It was all my fault.

It was over, and I had nothing left now until the end.

MY MOM FOUND ME that way, curled on top of the covers with my snow-damp boots staining the sheets, weeping so hard my body convulsed to chase the anguish out of me. Every ragged sob sent a sledgehammer splintering through my brain but I couldn't stop, couldn't breathe, couldn't do anything but gasp for air and grip tight to the mattress to keep from falling off the edge of the world.

"Honey . . ." Her voice came slipping through my hysteria, but I was too far gone to pull myself back. "Claire, sweetheart, you need to breathe. Claire!"

Breathe? I could barely feel my own body. I was lost to it, anchorless, pitched wild on the tempest of grief. My sobs shuddered over and my head cracked in pain, and even though she'd done this, broken my life apart, I couldn't resist when Mom pulled me to her and rocked me in her lap like she'd done so many countless times before.

"Breathe, baby," she murmured, her voice cracking with fear. "Please, just breathe."

But he was still gone, and I was still cut in two, and nothing would change that. Nothing would be so perfect ever again. The truth grabbed hold of me, sent me tumbling into its bleak depths, and still I cried. I cried for everything I'd lost, and everything I would never get to lose again. The boy who'd made me believe in forever, even if forever was measured out in minutes, not months and years. I'd been fooling myself, ignoring the fact that every morning I woke up in his arms brought me one day closer to the grave but oh, how sweet that denial had been. A week, a month—I'd sworn that every moment with him would be enough to last me a lifetime, but I'd lied. I could live to a hundred, spend decades in his arms, and I could never have enough.

There was never enough time.

"Shhh, that's right." Mom held me. "It's OK, Claire. It's all going to be alright."

My grief didn't waver, but the body can only take so much. Soon enough, my sobs subsided and my limbs stilled, leaving nothing but an empty ache and a bullet wound through my skull. Mom sat there, gently stroking my hair, until I finally lifted my head and she reached wordlessly for one of the bottles, passed me two pills and the glass of water, and watched as I obediently swallowed them down. "I thought you caught a flight home."

"I couldn't leave you."

I felt bloody, split open, and sanded raw. "He's gone, Mommy." I crumpled at the words. "You told him, and now he's gone."

"I'm sorry, sweetheart." Her voice was soft and she held me tight, rocking back and forth, back and forth. "I was trying to help. I thought maybe, if he knew, he could help you. Look out for you."

I didn't want to believe her, but I didn't have it in me left to fight. She was all I had left now, wasn't she? Her, and Dad, counting down to the end. Could I really hold it against her to try and steal me back, snatch the last few moments of her baby's life alone? I was too sick to even think about it, it all seemed drifting and far away, so I just shrugged my jacket off and fumbled, trying to unlace my boots.

"I've got it."

She knelt on the floor by the bed and un-looped the stays, peeling off my boots and gently undressing me piece by layered piece. I let her, like all those days I was wheeled home from chemo treatments too sick to even

316

stand, until I was wrapped in a soft cocoon of machine-fresh flannel, slipping deep beneath the covers.

"You'll feel better in the morning," she said, leaning in to press a gentle kiss to my forehead, like always. But this wasn't poison racing in my veins, or the sluggish distance of recovery, scars lacing tic-tac-toe across the back of my skull. This was my heart torn open, not my body, and for that, I knew, there was no repair.

Mom closed the door quietly behind her, but sleep didn't come, not just yet. I curled tight, and waited for the pills to work their magic, seeping softly through my pain, threading my body with numb delirium until finally, I couldn't feel it anymore. I couldn't feel a thing. I was empty and floating and free, with nothing but an echo of the ache that had gripped me and the thunder in my skull. But they were waiting, I knew. The wolves were at my door, and tomorrow, it would all be back again: the pain and the loneliness and the bitter slow-burn countdown that ruled my days. The only thing that wouldn't return sure as clockwork with the rising sun was the one thing I wanted more than anything.

Theo.

A slow tear slipped down my cheek. I stared at the shadows on the ceiling and wondered, what was left now for me until the end?

How easy would it be to just slip away right now?

MAYBE YOU THINK it's unspeakable, to crave life and contemplate death in the same desperate heartbeat, but it's the truth. Even as I fought my hardest, pining for another lifetime, another hundred years, those dark, dangerous thoughts still found a way to snake in the back of my mind, when the nights were longest and I felt so alone. The low whisper tempting me with some semblance of control; a way to rule my destiny even as the cancer took me over, one final act to say that this body, this life, was all my own. It sat there on my nightstand, after all: one little bottle. Two dozen tiny pills. Hope kept hers hidden in a tiny glass jar at the back of her dresser drawer. A boy I met in chemo—bald and brazen and barely skin stretched across brittle bones— told me to start hoarding soon, early, and often. *They pay attention later*, he said with a hollow smile. *You need to stock up now, before they dole them out in singles, and never leave you with the lot.*

A way out, before even that effort was beyond you.

A way out, before the toxic end dismantled you piece by gasping piece.

She begged me once, in the hospital, three weeks before the end. I pretended like I hadn't heard her, got up and went to get us sodas from the machine down the hall, my heart racing, sick inside. It would have been easy, that's what she told me, and it was true. I knew where she kept her pills and how to slip past the night nurses who turned a blind eye to visiting hours, how to leave the bottle open there on the table, or even worse, feed them to her one by one, washed down with a sickly-sweet cherry coke, the taste that would linger to the end.

I stared at that neon machine with my hands shaking, knowing that if she meant it, if this was her plan, then nothing would stand in Hope's way. Whether it was me or her or someone else, she would make it come true, the way she did with everything else in the world. An unstoppable force. Unstoppable—until the end.

I don't know how long I stood there, terrified of the choice ahead, but when I finally went back to her room with two cans and a bag of M&Ms, she was watching old *Friends* reruns on the tiny TV screen as if nothing had happened. I scooted up on the bed with her, still wound tight with fear, and we watched the sitcom audience laugh until she felt asleep beside me, breath stuttering as the ventilator whirred on slow.

She never asked again, and maybe that was her gift to me. She went slowly, fearfully, painfully, but she went alone, fighting until the end.

Just like I would, too.

THE PROMISE

CHAPTER TWENTY-SEVEN

WHEN I WOKE AGAIN the next morning, sunlight burned the edges of the heavy drapes, and my heart ached fresh, the safe wisps of chemical denial dissolving fast in the early light to leave me raw and bruised again. I slowly lifted myself out of bed and sat there, staring at the floor. For the first time in months, the day ahead stretched not like a gift, but an enemy, filled with an empty accusation I couldn't bear to face.

You lied. You lied. He's gone.

I forced myself to take a breath and padded slowly to the bedroom door, the frigid floorboards a shock against my bare feet. I could hear voices outside murmured low, and when I pushed it open, my parents looked up from the breakfast table with matching expressions of anxious concern.

"You're awake." My mom leapt up. "I fixed some eggs, but I can make you some toast if your stomach isn't up to it. Your father picked up some bagels, too."

"Better than the ones we get back home," he said, trying to smile. "They were baking them fresh right there in the back of the shop. I'll have to stock up."

They were trying so hard it hurt to even see. All they had to do these days was worry about me. God, how exhausting must that be?

"A bagel sounds good," I said quietly, and I went to join them at the table. "Sesame?"

"Is there any other kind?" My father's smile was cut through with clear relief, so I let him toast me one, while Mom poured juice and nudged some cut apple onto my plate, and we sat there together, the radio playing somewhere down the hall, and the pages of my father's newspaper crinkling with every turn. It was so normal I could almost pretend that this was real. That I was a student at the art school here, and they really had just stopped by for a holiday visit, and would be back again in the springtime maybe, or I would pile some boxes in a car and hit the endless highway back home for the summer vacation.

"You'll need to book another flight," I finally said, pressing my fingertip to catch the last seeds scattered on my plate.

Mom gave him a look. "We were thinking," Dad began cautiously. "If you're happier here, we could stay too. Rent an apartment nearby."

"The hospital here is excellent," Mom added. "Doctor Benson is up to date now with your case, so we can call or go in if . . . if you need anything."

"But only if that's what you want," my dad said firmly, placing a restraining hand on Mom's. "It's up to you, Claire. Whatever you want from these next few months, we're here for you."

What did I want? The question shivered in the air. Even with Theo gone now, I couldn't imagine taking that westbound flight to Texas. Returning to my childhood bedroom and that old familiar cancer ward would feel like a failure, turning on my tail and sloping home. Turning my back on everything I'd fought so hard to build.

And still, I hoped for him. Time, he'd asked for. How much time would it take?

"I'd like to stay," I said softly, knowing I was asking the world of them, but still needing it, God, I needed it so badly.

"Then we'll stay." Dad nodded.

"But what about work?" I asked, twisting inside.

He gave me a faint smile. "Don't worry about that. I've taken a leave of absence. We'd always planned it; they can spare me for a little while." His words landed softly, but I heard my mom's rushed intake of breath. His face changed. "Or a long while," he added quickly. "What matters is that we're here for you."

"Thank you," I whispered, to keep from breaking down. Yet again, they'd rearranged their life to fit the space my cancer had left for them, without question. Without complaint.

Mom forced a bright smile. "Won't this be fun? I'll start making calls about an apartment. A college town like this, it should be simple. We'll get a two bedroom, so you have a place to move when . . . when you decide you want to." She got up and began clearing our plates, bustling with a busy, tight energy. "The city is nice, but I think we should be this side of the river, closer to you. Something with character, there's so much history here, it's a nice change, don't you think?" She ran the water in the kitchen sink, clattering dishes and squirting soap. I leaned against the counter and watched her. I knew her too well; she would sweep us onwards without a backwards glance, not a word about what she'd done to get us here.

"Mom." I stopped her. "It isn't OK. What you did. You had no right."

She stopped breathing, and I saw her jaw tremble as she stared down into the sink, the dish suds billowing up, over her hands. "I know, sweetheart. I just couldn't bear it. It felt like . . . it felt like you chose him. Over me."

"Mom . . ." I slipped my arms around and hugged her from behind. "It was never like that. I thought you'd understand."

"I'm trying." I felt her voice catch, the flinch in her determined spine. "I just can't lose you yet, sweetheart. I'm sorry, it's selfish, but I won't let you go a moment too soon."

I exhaled slow, feeling the desperate tension that gripped her body, holding on: holding on to me for as long as she could. We were all just clinging to the rock face, taking whatever handholds we could find. I couldn't blame her for this, not after everything she'd given up to get me this far.

"I know," I said softly. "It's alright. I know."

THE WEEK PASSED, that winter limbo between Christmas and New Year. Around me, the city came to life again, the streets bright and busy with tourists and shoppers, store lights gleaming in the early-afternoon dusk. My parents found a rental three blocks from the edge of Harvard Square: a second-floor walk-up with wide plank floors and an antique range, with windows that overlooked the tips of the bare park trees. It was fully furnished, and they moved in with nothing but the bags they'd brought from home, but within days my mom had filled the place with the scent of cocoa brewing on the stove and the sound of country classics on the radio playing through the day. They made sure not to smother me—that was Dad's doing, I knew—but we fell into a routine: arriving at my apartment for a breakfast of fresh bagels in the morning before my shift at work, and ending the day with a family meal around their table, curling up in front of the TV until I was almost too tired to make the walk back home. But I did, every night, with Mom's gift of a rape alarm pressed in my pocket and the streetlights shining, all the way back. Somehow, I was still clinging on to some semblance of freedom, and I would keep holding tight for as long as I could.

Six days, and Theo hadn't called.

I turned my phone over in my hands, sat on the floor in the back locker room at Wired after my shift. My legs were stretched out in front of me, tipped with red knit socks, blurring in the background as I focused on the small screen in my hands. Round and round I spun it, a pinwheel of possibility that every day kept coming up short.

Should I call him? The question taunted. Should I be the first one reach out? He'd asked for time, but time was running short. I didn't want to crowd him, but every day that passed without him was a day that tugged him further away.

And again, my heart splintered open. Maybe he was already gone.

The door opened, and Kelsey trudged in, weighed down with a backpack and duffel coat and a long, skinny black scarf trailing in her wake.

"You're back." I looked up. "How was your holiday?"

She tossed her bag down with a thump and then herself after it, sprawled beside me on the smudged, dusty floor. "I got food poisoning off bad turkey, fought with every person in the state of Connecticut, and almost got arrested trying to drive back here as fast as I could," she said. "You?"

I took a breath and confessed. "Theo broke it off. I don't think he's coming back."

Kelsey peeled off a strip of red licorice and chewed. "You win."

I couldn't help but laugh, bleak. "Do I get a prize?"

She offered me the candy. I took a piece, too sweet on my tongue. "What are you doing tonight?" she asked.

Tonight . . . "New Year's," I realized. "Oh."

"I know," she said with a sigh. "Peace and goodwill to all mankind." Kelsey paused and gave me a sideways look. "We should go party."

I smiled again. "Sure."

"No, I mean it." There was a determined glint in her eye now, something sharp and almost dangerous. "You need to forget all this bullshit, just for a night. Start the year as you mean to go on. Don't let *him* make you waste it."

She said it like a challenge, and despite everything, I felt a spark. A lone flame of something burning through my numb, broken heart. "OK," I told her suddenly. "I'm in. What's the plan?"

"You'll see." She stood and pulled me up by my hands. "Pick you up at nine. And wear something slutty." I rolled my eyes, but she laughed. "I believe in you, Claire-bear. Be the change you want to see in the world!"

SURE ENOUGH, SHE was on my doorstep at nine, wearing torn fishnet tights under her coat and her no-shit boots laced all the way to her knees. She looked me over with a critical eye, my plain black dress and boots about as wild an outfit as I could dig from my closet. "You're missing something," she decided, and pulled her eyeliner out of her purse right there at the top of my steps, holding my chin steady with one hand as the other smudged a dark, steely glare over the crease of my eyelids. I stood patiently, the way I had that Halloween, waiting until her handiwork was complete. Kelsey gave me a satisfied nod. "Now you're ready."

"Ready for what?" I asked, skipping down the steps after her.

"You'll see," she said mysteriously, and stuck two fingers in her lips to sound a whistle that stopped traffic, literally—a cab pulling up beside us like it had been waiting for the chance. "Your parents gave you cash, right?" she asked when we had already tumbled inside, but I was already too full of anticipation for the night ahead to even care.

"How did you guess?"

"They have that look in their eyes, like they need to wrap you up safe against the dark streets and dangerous strangers." She grinned, and I laughed with her, the neon city gliding past.

"Something like that."

I'd lied to them about tonight, or at least, told only half the truth. I was celebrating with friends, I'd said, no big plans. I could see more questions burning on the tip of my mother's tongue, but she let it go. It was hard for the both of us now—adjusting to my new independence with them back in my life, close enough to just drop by. For months I'd treasured the freedom of being alone: no curfew, no concern, an adult life for the first time. But to them, I was still their baby. All week, they'd been clutching me closer, but tonight, I was on my own terms again. I cranked the window down to breathe in the night, knife-sharp in my lungs. Kelsey wasn't done with her own makeup, and as we sped across the bridge downtown, she painted on a perfect scarlet smile without even a glance in the rearview mirror. "Did you hear from Guy over the holidays?" I asked.

"Nope." She blotted carefully.

"Are we meeting him tonight?" Something in my chest

caught, that tell-tale flight of hope. *If Guy was there . . . If Theo came along . . .* But Kelsey shot that bird from the sky with another simple, "Nope."

"OK." I tried to get into the party spirit. "Just you and me then."

"Not quite . . ." Kelsey grinned. I must have looked tremulous, because she laughed. "Relax, you think too much." She pulled a slim silver flask from her coat pocket and offered it to me. I paused, but the rush of lights in the dark night had already ignited that spark in me again, and I took a sip, something sweet and strong burning down the back of my throat and pooling like fire in the base of my belly. "Atta girl," she cheered, and took another, longer pull. "It's time to leave this shitty year in the dust. To new beginnings." She passed it back to toast, but I couldn't cheer for the glimpse of the year ahead of me, not when I still needed to let go of everything I was leaving behind.

"To the end," I said at last, and drank, fire burning in my veins as the icy wind slipped through the windows. Then Kelsey checked her phone and lunged forwards, between the front seats.

"Take a right here," she demanded, and the poor driver tried to argue.

"There's nothing here, look." He pointed to the GPS screen.

"Trust me, take the right!"

I looked outside the window. We were slowing, crawling through an industrial area, half-hidden under the bridge. The streets were deserted, shadowed warehouse lots looming large with no comforting lights to point the way. I shivered. "Why do I get a bad feeling about this?" She fixed me with a look. "Oh ye of little faith." Kelsey checked her phone again. "Here! You can drop us right here."

The cab stopped, idling alone on an empty street. "Umm, Kelsey?"

"C'mon, pay the man." She was already scrambling out, wrapping her coat tightly, and even though I half-wanted to stay right there and direct the driver back home, I couldn't leave her either. I quickly passed some cash and followed, hurrying after her down the dark alley. "Wait, Kelsey. Where are we?"

She turned, still backing away. "No more questions," she ordered me. "This is an adventure, OK? Wherever the night leads." I looked at her, tempting with that reckless smile, and was hit by a déjà vu so strong it knocked my breath away.

That was Hope's smile. God, I hadn't seen it in so long.

"Tick tock," Kelsey called, spinning on her heel again and plunging on into the dark. And even though we were stranded God knows where amongst shipping containers and empty stacked boxes, that glimpse of Hope was all I needed to find solid ground again. I didn't just see her there in the lines of Kelsey's face, I *felt* her, too. Felt her presences as strong as if she was right there with us, bickering with Kelsey and pushing my hair back in place, scooping us onward towards adventure and the unknown.

My fears slipped away. This was right where I was supposed to be: on the edge of something, out reckless in the night. Right now, my heartbreak didn't matter, or the empty days waiting to count down on the other side of dawn. I had tonight, that was something. My last New Year's Eve. I had to make it count.

I strode after Kelsey, rounding the corner to find her checking her phone again, lost in the maze. "Do you have directions?" I asked, taking her phone, and control. There was a message on her screen, co-ordinates it looked like, and Kelsey looked around, frustrated.

"Whatever happened to 'be here at this address,' none of this treasure hunt bullshit?"

"Wait, listen." I caught her arm. Down here, there was noise from the city, but something else too, a steady beat. A deep bass that rippled through the still of the night. I looked around, trying to pinpoint the location. "This way," I decided, and we hurried on, breaking into a laughing run as our footsteps pounded, and we slipped down the alleyways following the ever-closer beat. Louder, louder, we skidded around a final corner, and then we arrived: a massive warehouse looming out of the shadows, spilling thunderous music and laughter and party-goers out into the dark. Kelsey pulled me on to join them, bathed in the pulses of neon green and diamond yellow that pulsed from inside. We cut through the lot, already crammed with cars and trucks parked haphazardly like their passengers had abandoned them at will, and then we were up the front steps and inside, the music so loud it hit like a weapon, chasing the last thoughts from my brain and blissfully swallowing me whole.

This was a party.

The cavernous room was crammed with a wild mass of bodies, lights swooping overhead in a glittering constellation as the crowd dipped and thrummed. It smelled of smoke and dampness and beer and sweat, like promise and possibility, a thousand strangers strung out on the edge of infinity, lost in the magic of their own design. Kelsey shed her coat in a heap in the corner, and I followed suit, ducking through the throngs, until she found us a spot in the middle of the room amongst the sweat-damp revelry. The music was slipping from hip-hop beats to dance and back again, but whatever skittered over the treble line, the beat remained the same. The beat was all that mattered. It demanded surrender, and seized our heartbeats without remorse. It left no room for doubt or rejection, or the hundred other self-loathing disappointments still lingering in my broken mind. It was simple and intoxicating.

And finally, I let go.

WE DANCED FOR HOURS, until my lungs burned and my heartbeat crashed louder than even the deep, smoky bassline. Breaks for water, gulped ice-cold from a bottle; breaks to gasp the cold night air, to fix our sweat-drenched makeup and squeeze tight in the snaking line to a dirty bathroom stall—and then back to the music, every time. Kelsey kept her magic flask full all night, of what, I'll never know, but I drank all the same, fire burning through my body, a giddy high, and by the time midnight ticked closer, I was ready for it, ready to put this year behind me and fall, reckless, into the next.

"Water!" I called to her, hoarse over the music, then mimed a drink, a nod to the edge of the dance floor. Kelsey shook her head.

"You go!" she yelled, leaning closer. Her eyes slid to the guy dancing nearby, his gaze on us. Tall and lanky, with a smile I would have thought too sweet for Kelsey, but midnight was coming and she was assessing her prey, so I left her there spinning into his embrace and fought my way to the edge of the chaos. A guy was selling drinks

just outside in the chill of the parking lot, overpriced
sodas and beer from a long-melted cooler, and I peeled
off five bucks to claim a lukewarm bottle.

"Mystery girl."

The voice from behind made me startle, choking. I
spun around, spluttering water and coughing for air.
"Clara, right?"

It was the boy from the party, a lifetime ago, that first
night out with Tessa and her friends. The dark-haired one
who'd wielded words like offensive weapons, trying to
argue and cajole. Now, he was watching me, amused, his
pale skin sweaty from the heat. "Claire," I said,
recovering.

"That's right, the waitress."

"Barista," I corrected him, sharper.

"Relax." He grinned. "I didn't mean anything by it."
Jamie was his name, I remembered now. He'd
disappeared into the background the moment I'd seen
Theo at the party, and even now, that memory—*Theo and
I on the back porch, trading junk food and swear words*—
danced brighter and more vivid than the guy standing
close, a couple of feet away. My heart ached to think of it,
but I pushed the hurt down, determined. Fresh start.
Blank slate. My heart was still pounding, and my blood
still sweet with adrenaline and alcohol, and I focused on
that instead, and the cold night around me, right here.

There was no going back.

"How's it going then, *Claire*?" Jaime asked. "I wondered if I'd see you again."

"Really?" I arched an eyebrow. "You knew where to find me."

"True. I guess I've just been busy, with school."

"Good for you."

My tone was light, and anyone else might have been deterred by the edge of steel just beneath the surface, but Jamie's lips curled in a slow grin. He moved closer, and took the water from my hands; drinking a long gulp. "Happy New Year," he said, like a challenge.

I took the bottle back from him. "Not yet. We've got another . . . four minutes to go." I checked my phone.

"It's already tomorrow in Papua New Guinea," he replied. "And for all we know, that countdown is wrong."

"Way to take the fun out of it." I gave him a pointed look. "Let me guess, you don't celebrate the holidays either, because they're just a testament to crass commercialism."

Jamie laughed. "They are. You seem too smart to buy into that bullshit."

"Lucky me."

Jamie was even closer now, leaning against the wall, my body half-shielded from the party by his lean frame. I could smell him, feel the heat of his skin and the focus of

his attention. I glanced up and caught his gaze, full-tilt.
Dark eyes, laughing at the edge. "You look different," he
said, still watching me. He reached out, and touched the
edge of my hair. "Something's changed."

"You like doing that, don't you?" I didn't flinch from
his stare. "Trying to make me guess what you think about
me."

Jamie's smile cracked into a laugh. "Someone's on
edge tonight. I thought I told you to relax."

"And you're going to help with that?" I asked.

He grinned. "Maybe. Maybe not."

I opened my mouth for another quick retort, until the
truth cut through me like ice. This was what I'd judged
Kelsey for, wasn't it? The game-playing, the arch replies.
Using words as weapons, not offering them like
revelations, trading people's hearts as conquests, not
precious, treasured gold. It was a way to pass the time,
sure. A mouth on mine as the final moments of the year
slipped past. But I knew what it was to taste real love,
and I didn't have time to waste.

I didn't have the luxury of a cheap, empty mistake.

I turned away from him, just as the countdown started
inside. *Ten! Nine! Eight!*

"Claire?" Jamie sounded confused, but I was already
walking fast away from him, and I didn't look back. I
needed to get away, somewhere to take a breath and hold

the sadness flooding through me, the cold empty truth of
the end.

Seven! Six! Five!

I saw a fire escape just ahead, a rickety iron frame
barely bolted to the wall, but I lunged for it, my boots
clattering as I hurled myself up, gripping the railings
tight. I cleared the top and emerged on the rooftop,
gasping, a flat plane overlooking the dark river, and the
humming neon skyline beyond.

Three! Two! One!

Liftoff.

And just like that, it was midnight. I was alone on top
of the world as the celebrations exploded in the party
below, cheers and whoops and sirens, *Happy New Year*s
drifting out into the night. I sank down on the low wall by
the edge and hugged my knees to my chest, breathing it
all in as my pulse raced to catch up. The sky was dark and
clear, and down on the water, a lazy barge drifted by.
Across the river, somewhere, a distant burst of starlight
suddenly dazzled in the sky: fireworks swooping up, then
shimmering as they dissolved back to earth.

Should old acquaintance be forgot . . .

The old song slipped into my mind, and just like that,
she was there beside me. Hope. Hair falling out of a
messy braid, in a sweatshirt and jeans and that bright pink
lip gloss. Scooching in close, her arm linked through

mine, head on my shoulder the way she'd curled up so many nights.

"This is it then," I whispered, tears stinging my eyes.

"This is it," she agreed.

We sat there together, watching the fireworks pulse and fade. They were beautiful: blazing for an instant, too bright to last for long. Maybe that was all we could hope for in the end. A moment of brilliance. A chance to burn, wild in the night. I loved Theo with everything I had, but nothing lasts forever, no matter how hard we try: the earth kept spinning its slow, lazy arc as we lived and loved and felt our hearts swell and bloom and break.

This was all we had. This was our beautiful world.

And I was finally ready for the end.

I wiped my tears away and took another breath, fogging the crystal night air. Then I slowly climbed back down to earth again. I called a cab, drove back across the midnight river, and climbed out onto the dark sidewalk in front of a door with peeling blue paint. I climbed the dark staircase past stacks of junk mail and old flyers, until I opened the door on the third floor and stepped into the studio.

My studio.

I looked around, just feeling the peace there, the possibility. I'd moved my canvases in that week, my paints too, and cleared aside the previous owner's things into neat boxes in the corner. Now the walls were clear, the tall windows shining from the streetlights outside, and my easel waited, brushes lined up on the table.

I slipped my coat off and let my mind open.

It was the new year, and there was still so much to do.

CHAPTER TWENTY-EIGHT

AFTER WEEKS OF being held hostage by limbo and sluggish grief, I was suddenly a whirlwind. I cut my hours at the café, telling Mika I was taking some classes and could only cover a couple of shifts a week. I couldn't bring myself to give it up completely, but my body was rebelling, faster than my prescriptions could keep pace. The headaches were raging, deeper and sharper every time, and the painkillers that numbed the chaos left me drained and sleeping, curled through the afternoon in my parents' apartment with a cold compress numbing the fire. After that afternoon with Kelsey, trembling on the bathroom floor, I knew I couldn't hide it for much longer, but I couldn't bear to give them the truth, so I faded out, instead: turning down invitations to drinks and movies, and politely blowing off Tessa's suggestions for a group trip out of town. I hated the duplicity, but I was sparing them and me both. I didn't want their sympathy and sadness, not when I had so much work to do.

I spent my time at the studio, instead: every stolen minute, hours I snatched fiercely, forgetting food and plans and even sleep to pour my heart out on the waiting canvas, the kind of frenzy of creation I couldn't even put into words. My work consumed me, pounded through me in a heartbeat drum, claiming every moment of my imagination as my brush moved and my soul poured out onto the waiting page: over and over, and still it wasn't enough. My mom didn't understand, but Dad did. I heard them arguing one night after I showed up on their doorstep, half-delirious with a migraine attack I'd ignored for too long, caught up in a half-finished canvas that was so tantalizingly close to being done. I lay there, soft in the folds of those sweet hydrocodone clouds, and heard their voices slip under the door, dancing lightly on the outskirts of my pain.

I don't understand why she's hiding herself away, not now.

It's not hiding. Don't you see? This is what she needs to be doing. She wants to make a mark, somehow. She knows she's running out of time.

He was right. My art sustained me now, it was the only thing that mattered. The only thing I'd get to leave behind. The studio became cluttered with sketches and oils and torn canvases daubed with my midnight fever dreams, so I started giving them away. I left them at

Goodwills and thrift stores and even street garage sales, slipping them unseen onto the shelves for some stranger to discover and take home. They were pieces of me, every last one, and I sent them into the world with a prayer. I wanted my work to travel, to be hauled into shiny new apartments and old dorm rooms. I wanted to sit, propped on the mantle to watch over the moments of someone else's life, bearing witness to the days I wouldn't have to come.

I wanted to last another decade, a century, if only through the smears of paint trickling over a foreign page.

"SURE YOU CAN'T stay another couple of hours?" Mika looked harried, brushing back his copper curls as he fought with the temperamental espresso machine. The line at the counter was six deep, and every table taken. School was back in session again and everyone was working hard with bright resolution. "All my covers are out sick, and just look at this place."

"I'm sorry." I ignored the pang of guilt. After all, it was already buried under a nausea and dizziness that wouldn't take another shift on my feet. "Can't. You'll be fine."

I ducked away to grab my things before he could protest again. The walk wasn't far from the café to the studio, but these days, it felt like a marathon. I wasn't supposed to be walking far any more, my parents gave me plenty of money for an Uber or cab, but I trudged determinedly along the busy midday sidewalks, tracking the new failure of my body by how soon my lungs burned and my chest ached. Two blocks. One. Soon, I wouldn't be able to make it out so often at all. Already, my parents were murmuring about moving me into their place, and I was crashing out there more often than not. An afternoon painting may have freed my spirit, but it left me with a weary debt to pay at night. I kept my head down against the wind and battled onwards, trying to hold onto that peace I'd felt on the rooftop, trying not to rage and retreat from the end.

This was it, Hope and I both knew. And I could either hold the truth gently, with grace and resolve, or waste these days to fury and wretched despair. I didn't want to go like that, not after everything, so despite the echo of heartbreak lingering in my chest, I focused on the brittle chill against my cheeks and the sweetness of my coffee, still hot in my mittened hands. I clambered those last stairs to the studio, already thinking of the canvas waiting—a new year's skyline, fireworks tumbling into the night—when I saw the door was open.

I stopped. "Hello?" My parents had come by a couple of times to check on me before, but they knew I didn't want to be disturbed. "Who's there?" I asked on the threshold, my voice catching. For a moment I wondered if the original owner was back to reclaim his territory, then the door swung wider and he was standing there: flooded with pale sunlight through the windows, burning up in the middle of the paint-splattered floor.

Theo.

My Theo.

My heart caught, wildfire in my chest. I'd made myself forget just what he did to me, but I felt it all rush back in a pure, sweet blaze. Honey racing in my veins, stardust bursting in every pore. His presence washed over me, everything I'd been ignoring since that night he walked away. I was dormant. I was empty. And then . . . then I was simply alive.

"Hey," he said, and I took a quick step towards him like gravity, before I saw his body was still guarded, hands in his pockets, unsure. I forced myself to stop, suspended just a few feet away from him.

"Hey," I echoed, a thousand questions racing in my mind. "What are you . . .? How did you get in?"

Theo held up a key. "I kept one, in case you lost yours."

"Oh." I gave thanks I never knew—that I hadn't spent the past weeks waiting for the sound of it turning in the lock. I wouldn't have gotten a thing done but sit in nervous, empty expectation, day after day after endless day.

I forced myself to put my coffee cup down and close the door behind me. I slowly shed my coat and scarf and mittens, while my head spun and my heart raced fast enough to skip right out of my chest. I tried to think clearly, but God, you don't know what it was like, just being in the same room as him again. His body, right there, draped in worn corduroy and a soft knit sweater beneath his coat, blue enough to make his eyes sing a summer's sky song. I ached to hold him, with a kind of sharp-edged desire I'd never felt before, something urgent. Necessary as air.

I curled my fingertips into my palms. "How are you?" I asked softly.

Theo gave me a smile that was ragged and weary at the edges. "Not great. You?"

"Not great."

Sunlight spilled over us, the dim snow clouds gone for good this week. Everything was bright and crisp outside the windows, and Theo seemed to shimmer in the studio's warm, dusty air. He looked at me, gaze searching, and it took everything I had not to reach for him and never let go. "How are you feeling?" he asked slowly.

I looked away. "It changes, day to day. It's catching

up with me now," I admitted. "I always knew it would, I guess I just thought . . . I could hold it off a little longer, that's all."

"I did some reading," he ventured, and I looked back. "They say the pain . . . the symptoms . . ." He struggled to find the words, and I knew why.

"It isn't pretty," I agreed.

"Is that why you didn't tell me?" Theo asked, looking wounded. "Because you thought I couldn't handle it? Or that I wouldn't stick around?"

"No!" My cry slipped from my lips, horrified. "God, no. It wasn't like that. I didn't tell anyone," I swore to him. "I wanted . . . I just wanted to pretend I had more time, as long as I could. I know it was selfish of me, and I never should have lied. But . . ." I tried to find the words to tell him, a way to fit the vast expanse of my life into one small neat explanation that would help it all make sense. "The cancer, it's been my whole life for years now. The only thing that mattered, every single day. No matter what I did, it was always there. It was always going to win. I couldn't bear to go like that, so I came here to have something else. I wanted something all my own, before it took everything from me. Can you understand?"

Theo didn't answer for a long moment, and when he did finally speak, his voice was tinted with a desperate plea. "I want to, Claire. God . . . these past weeks have been agony. I have so many questions, I don't know where to start."

"I'll tell you anything," I said, meeting his eyes. "I swear, I won't ever lie to you again."

He nodded slowly. "OK. OK." Theo took a breath, bracing himself for battle. "Start at the beginning, and leave nothing out."

So I DIDN'T. We sat there, cross-legged on the splintered floor, and I gave him everything, holding nothing back. Hope, chemo, the trials and more, I walked him through the footprints my cancer had imprinted on my life, year by year, day by dwindling day. He listened the way only Theo could: absorbing every breath into the depths of those gentle eyes, and when I finally reached the present day—my parents' arrival, the quickening symptoms, my last-ditch race to reach New Years—I slowly stumbled to a halt. "I knew it couldn't last," I said, steady in the truth of my guilt and shame. "I knew I had to tell you, that you deserved to know the truth, but . . . I wanted it to be different, so badly. And when I'm with you . . ." My breath shivered, and my heart ached. "I could almost believe I'd live forever."

There was nothing else to say. I fell silent, waiting on the tightrope of his silence again, wondering which way I would fall this time.

Theo looked down, tracing old paint stains on the floorboard, turning my confession over in his mind. "How can you even stand it?" he finally asked, his eyes searching mine. "How can you go work a shift serving coffee, and have dinner, and carry on like normal when all along . . . you're going to be gone?"

That was the question. From the outside, it was unthinkable, how life could ever go on with a death sentence like this, but the first thing I found out, the very first thing after those words were set neatly on the hospital desk, is that it does. The AC in the car on the ride home was busted, and my favorite show still somehow danced on the TV screen; my body asked for food and relief. And so it goes. The sun rises in the morning and sets at night, and in between, the hours stretch, ordinary life stumbling on outside the windows with such reassuring regularity that in the end, despite the shock and grief and limitless anger, you find yourself slipping back into old routines as if nothing ever changed.

What other choice is there? Let the cancer kill me twice over: rip the present tense from me as well as my future? All I could do was fight for every moment of life, chase whatever sweetness I could claw bare-handed from the world.

Love, for the very last time.

"You think you can't go on, but you do," I answered simply. "And all those things that seem so normal—the café, my art—it all matters so much more. That's why I

349

came here, because I couldn't bear to let it all slip away without even trying. I just wanted to know what felt like, even just a taste. I never thought I'd find a life like this," I added, my heart shivering with loss. "I never imagined I would meet you, or fall in love . . ." I swallowed back the words, the second time I'd let them fall in front of him, but Theo didn't flinch. His eyes were hot on mine, still fighting this, I could tell.

"Your mom said there was a surgery . . ."

My head snapped up, and suddenly I realized, crystal clear as the dazzling sunshine outside the windows. This was why she'd done it. This was the real reason why she'd told. To use him against me, corral my love into her last-ditch try.

"No," I said shortly. "It's just a trial, they haven't figured it out yet."

"But she said, there was a chance—"

"It's not real, Theo. She's desperate now, she'll do anything to try and keep me. She doesn't understand, it's no use."

"And you're OK with that?" Theo was trying to understand; I could see it in the agony of his face. And even though I'd spent the past week trying to feel it, accept my fate however fast it came, it caught in my throat, a bitter protest I couldn't swallow down.

"No. Not yet. But I have to be."

He took another breath, and I longed to touch him. To feel that steady rise and fall pressed against me, nestled safely in the crook of his arm. But our hands both slid flat against the floor, our bodies mirrored, the line between us still marked.

"How much time do you have left?"

"A little while." I closed my eyes then, I had to. It hurt too much to look at him and tell him my final calendar, red crosses marking down the days. "A few weeks like this, until the symptoms get too much for me. Then I'll be in bed, the hospital maybe, on painkillers, a ventilator to help me breathe." I was matter of fact, but my voice cracked to think of it. "Sometimes you go fast, the body just shuts down, but sometimes . . . you can drag it out a few more weeks after that."

"Claire . . ."

His voice came, closer, and the whisper of his breath warmed my cheeks. When I opened my eyes, he was in front of me, so close I could see the grey flecks shivering in his eyes. So close, I felt his next words more than heard them.

"I'm sorry," he whispered, his features crumpling with despair. He cradled my face, forehead resting against mine. "I'm so, so sorry."

"Don't be." I split open, chest wide with the ache and the glory of it. "You're the best thing that ever happened to me, Theo. You're all I ever wanted in the world."

He kissed me, soft and searching, and I melted into him without a sound. We were weightless there for a moment, an infinity, strung on the sweet caress of his fingertips and the taste of his lips against mine, and then we fell. Hot mouths and reaching hands, and an intensity that burned me from the inside out. I pressed myself to him, imprinting this moment into the darkness of my mind, spelled out in glittering sensation, every breath, every beat.

This was what I'd lived for. This was all that mattered in the world.

When we finally surfaced again, I was raw and trembling, and I saw it in Theo's eyes: he felt it just the same.

"How many things do you have left on the list?" he asked, and I was so lost in the feel of his hands stroking over mine that my brain stuttered, one step behind. I looked at him, blank, and he smiled. "Hope's list. That's why you brought it, isn't it? To finish every entry, before . . . the end."

The list. I nodded. "A few things left, I didn't know how to try them. Skinny dipping at dawn, see the top of the world," I remembered sadly. "She got more abstract in the end. She wanted to taste it all."

"So we'll find a way." Theo lifted my hand and

brushed a kiss on my knuckles—quietly determined. "We'll make it count."

We . . .

"Together?" I asked, my heart catching, snagged on the hook of that one precious word. It was more than I could ever ask, but he offered it all the same, like it was the most natural thing in the world.

"Together," he whispered, his eyes true, and I knew we were bound in this forever now.

I'd love him until the day I died.

THE PROMISE

CHAPTER TWENTY-NINE

THEO WALKED ME home, and arranged to meet me later with a mysterious text, just an address:

800 Boylston, 6pm.

"Dress up," he'd told me with a wink, so I spent an hour tearing through my wardrobe and wrestling with hair and makeup, anticipation sparkling sweetly in my veins. Mom found me with Tessa, deep in her closet, searching for a dress of hers that would fit my taller frame.

"You're going out?" Her voice was disapproving. "You said you couldn't make dinner; I wanted to check you were feeling OK."

"I'm fine." I turned. "Just a little tired, but I took a nap, I won't be out long. Just dinner with Theo," I added, already looking back to check my reflection. "What do you think? It's not too short?"

"It's perfect," Tessa declared. Simple navy chiffon spilled over my body from a strapless bodice. "I wore it to department cocktails last month, it's super-comfortable. And I think I have some shoes somewhere . . ." She began rooting through some boxes in the back of the closet, while I twisted this way and that, trying to settle into the sophisticated swirl of fabric against my skin.

"What do you think, Mom?"

Her frown melted, just a little. "You look beautiful, honey. Where is he taking you? I didn't know you two were . . . talking again."

"He didn't say, he wants it to be a surprise."

Tessa bobbed her head up with a diplomatic smile. "Here are the shoes. Hi Mrs. Fortune," she added.

"Hello, Tessa. Back in classes?"

"Yup," she sighed. "It's twenty-four seven, barely a moment to rest. In fact . . . I'm already late for study group." She passed me the pumps and gave a wink. "You look incredible, go knock him dead."

I heard her clatter out of the apartment as I set about twisting my hair up and slipping on the strappy shoes. Mom stayed in the doorway, watching me.

"Don't," I said without looking.

"Don't what?"

"Please don't try and take this away from me." I glanced up. "I have my prescriptions, and your number, and Doctor Benson's too. I'll take a cab and walk slowly and not stay out too late."

"I'm just worried, sweetheart. You're pushing so hard."

"What else am I supposed to do?" I countered. "Just sit around, waiting to die?"

It was a low blow, and we both winced to feel it.

"I'll be careful, Mom, I promise." I softened. "Theo will take care of me, you don't need to worry."

"I'll always worry, it's my job." But she let me be as I fixed my makeup and slipped into my coat, and even waited on the frozen corner with me for a car. "Be good," she warned me, holding the door for me to slide inside.

"I'll try not to elope to Vegas and get another tattoo," I teased, just before I slammed the door behind me. Still, I heard her voice echo after us with shock as we drove away.

"*Another* tattoo?"

T HEO MET ME IN the lobby of a sleek, fancy building downtown. He was clean-shaven and pink-cheeked from the cold, glowing under the shimmering chandeliers.

"So what's the big surprise?" I greeted him with a kiss, feeling effervescent, already walking on air.

"You'll see." Theo offered me his arm, an old-fashioned gentleman, and I slipped my hand through it, nestled in the crook. "You look beautiful," he added, leaning close to whisper in my ear, and I flushed, my heartbeat racing, my blood running hot in my veins. It felt like our first date all over again, just as giddy and quick, and I had to focus on putting one foot in front of the other, unsteady on my borrowed heels as he led me across the lobby. "Hungry?" he asked.

"A little," I said, but it wasn't the kind dinner would sate. My stomach was tangled, and it took every last measure of self-control not to take his hand right now and tug him closer for a reckless kiss. We stepped into the elevator, and Theo hit the button for the top floor. "Fifty-two?" I read off the dashboard, but another couple crowded in beside us before he could answer, and I stepped back, into Theo's embrace. His body was flush against mind, his hands resting softly on my waist as he traced slow circles just inside the thick flannel edging of my coat. I could feel him through the thin silk, the burning path against my skin, and it was agony to stand so close, so strangely intimate, and all the while these strangers beside us murmured about a party next week, and who was going to tell Doug about the new promotion. The threads of heat snaked through me, radiating out from that single tiny touch, and by the time the elevator arrived at the top with a cheerful *ding!*, I was trembling, so aware of Theo's body against me, it felt like my desire was splashed scarlet across my face for anyone to see.

"What do you think?" Theo's voice came, and I

blinked, the world around me rushing in again, bright with the warm glow of lights, the ring of china, and gentle conversation. And the view, my God, the view.

I went to the windows, drawn without a word. Boston lay spread before me, glittering in the dark: golden grids twisting out to the bright highway, and the dark shadows of the country beyond. Miles and miles of it, the black landscape shot through with white and red and neon green, so far below us, it seemed like a dream.

"The top of the world," I realized, turning to him with amazement. "How did you . . . ?"

"I thought of it as soon as you said." Theo joined me, triumphant. "It's not Mount Everest, but it's something."

"Are you kidding? It's incredible." I threw my arms around him then, not caring if we drew stares for my hot, quick kiss. "Thank you."

"I booked us a table. The whole restaurant revolves," he added. "But slowly, so you can get every view."

I hadn't noticed until he said it, but he was right: there was a strange movement to the whole room, barely fast enough to grasp. Theo gave his name to the hostess, and we followed her to our table, crisp with white linens and silverware on the edge of the glass-enclosed room. The menus were bound in thick, cobalt leather, and our water sat in heavy cut glass. I paused, waiting until the server had whisked away, before leaning in. "Theo, this is too much," I whispered, not wanting to offend him, but painfully aware of the people around us, all dressed up with elegant clutch purses holding slim credit cards and crisp folded notes.

"Don't worry about it."

"Theo . . ."

He smiled at me across the table, looking so damn perfect it almost hurt to stare. His skin gleamed gold against the white of his button-down shirt, a world away from his usual sweaters and bundled coats. "You only live once," he said, and it was too true to think about, so I smiled instead.

"Well, in that case . . . let's just cut straight to dessert."

"Dessert?" he echoed, surprised.

"Cake. Ice cream. Pie. A perfect balanced meal." I grinned, and he laughed.

"Sounds like a plan to me." He beckoned our waiter back, and traded the heavy menus for the slim dessert page instead, and soon the table in front of us was covered with so much sugar, my teeth itched. Gooey chocolate torte and whipped fruit sorbets, lighter than air, and frozen hot chocolate piled with marshmallows and cream. We tasted everything, feasting on sweetness as the room slowly spun, and the city pulsed below us like a living thing, lightning running through its veins.

"How are classes?" I asked, skittering my spoon at the

bottom of the ice-cream glass, reaching for one more bite. Theo shrugged. "Fine. My thesis chapters are due, but I'm behind."

"Why? You were so excited in the fall."

"It doesn't seem so important anymore."

"Of course it is," I insisted. "You've worked too hard for this to just let it slip away. Think of all the work you've put in even to get this far. The hours, the papers. The loans," I added with a wry grin.

He laughed at that. "I guess. It's just . . . I've been thinking, what does it matter? Getting the degree or not, it won't make a difference." His voice faded. "It won't change things, for you."

"Nothing will," I said firmly. "But this is you we're talking about, and the rest of your life. I won't let you throw that away."

"It doesn't feel right." He looked away, gazing out at that distant dark horizon, and when he finally met my eyes again, I could see the sadness there, the bittersweet regret. "I had all these plans, dreams for us together. I thought . . . I thought you'd be here. That we'd have a future, a real one."

My heart split open, and I held his hand tightly. "I want that too, more than you'll ever know. But you can't waste everything you've worked for, not now, or . . . after. I can't stand that. I won't let you."

"Is that an order?" he teased lightly.

"Worse, a dying wish," I shot back. "So don't even think about breaking it."

"Low blow," he told me, and even though his words were still light, I could see the pain in his eyes.

"I know. But there have to be some perks to this, right?" I took another taste of torte, determined not to let tonight slip into sadness. "I learned the hard way from Hope—it's impossible to argue with a dead girl. So, now it's my turn. And I won't let you use me as an excuse for anything, Theo. I'll haunt you until the end of time if you do."

W E STAYED IN the restaurant until the spire had made another full rotation, the full breadth of the glittering world. Then we paid the check, and Theo ushered me back to the elevator, and it was empty, the doors sliding shut on us alone. We looked at each other for a long moment, the air between us suddenly electric. I saw it shimmer in his eyes, that pulse, that undeniable hunger, and then he came to me: hands on the wall on either side of my head, his body arched, barely touching as he finally kissed me the way I'd been needing all my life.

I lost myself to him that night. Not a blind surrender, but a gift—to feel that kind of love, in every heartbeat, every breath. We stumbled from the lobby to a cab, and back to his place, barely coming up for air. There was something frantic in our kisses that night, as if the clock was already ticking just above us, and we were stealing every moment, running out of precious time. Through the door and down the hall, we shed coats and scarves and clothing until the door slammed shut behind us and Theo paused, gripping me tight. "Wait," he whispered to me. "Just wait."

My blood boiled for him, curling deep inside, but he touched me so gently, it was like time stilled, and we were suspended in the golden hum. Lips on my bare neck, fingertips sliding softly down my spine. He peeled my dress from me an inch at a time, covering my skin with a hundred kisses until I was gasping and molten in his arms. I didn't know if it would be the last time, so I held nothing back. No shame, no doubt. Just a love that seemed to make everything right, steady as the pulse ticking under the pale skin of his collarbone, the flinch of his stomach, the way our bodies fused together, searching in the dark for answers that would be gone by morning.

"YOU SHOULD DO IT."

After, we lay on his bedroom floor, cocooned in a fort of blankets and pillows. My body still hummed, a live-wire, too hot to touch, so we were side by side, faces tilted together, his eyes dark pools in the night. "Do what?" I asked, drowsy and half-delirious still.

"Haunt me. I could get used to having you hanging around."

I laughed. "A friendly ghost."

"Very friendly . . ." Theo's fingertips skimmed my bare stomach and I shuddered. "But seriously," he said, his voice sleepy. "Do you ever think about it? If there's anything . . . after."

"Sometimes . . ." I sighed. "But it doesn't make a difference to right now, so who knows?"

"You don't wonder?"

"I did. I do," I admitted. "Maybe I'll move on, somehow, or maybe it really is the end. Hope put it on her list, you know," I added softly. "The final entry says, *Begin again*."

"That's nice."

I smiled. "She used to say it couldn't all just be for nothing. She didn't believe much in anything, but she believed in that." I trailed off. "But I won't ever know until it's too late, so . . . you can go crazy thinking like that. You just need to focus on today. Tonight."

Theo fell silent again. I pressed my palm to his heart, feeling it beat.

"Tell me about this surgery."

I sat up so fast the world tilted. "Don't."

"Come on, Claire, I just want to know." Theo sat as

well, and our fort came tumbling down around us. "Tell me why you don't want to do it. Your mom said it might be the answer. I just need to understand."

I wanted to bolt. Just like that, something had slammed between us—the distance between his eager curiosity and my long years of disappointment. But he didn't know; how could he unless I spelled it out for him?

There were no miracles in these Hail Mary prayers, only desperate, dangerous hope.

"It's a clinical trial," I said, twisting to face him. "Do you know what that means?"

"They're testing it."

"It means we're guinea pigs," I told him, heavy in my chest. "Someone, somewhere in a lab came up with a theory. They ran the simulations, tested all the chemicals in a tube, maybe even fed it to a few hundred rats to see if it killed them right away or not. And enough of those little critters survived long enough that they're trying it on humans now, too. Pumping us full of whatever drugs they think are fierce enough to destroy the cancer, and just praying they don't kill us instead."

"But they work sometimes, don't they?" There was naked hope on his face, so bright it seemed to fill the room. "I mean that's how medicine evolves. Something doesn't work, and then it does."

"In a dozen years, maybe. But we're not there yet. I

would die on the table, Theo," I told him, trying to make him see. "It's not even fifty-fifty, the odds of this thing yet. It's still so early, and you can never tell . . ." I bit back my frustrations. "I have a little time left, on my terms, not another shot in the dark that could put me in the grave. I've made my choice now."

Theo looked stubborn. "So you'd rather die for sure in a few months than take the risk to have years, maybe more?"

I scrambled up. "You don't get to judge me. This isn't your life on the line."

"I'm not judging, Claire. I'm just trying to understand."

"Understand that I've spent the last five years wrestling with this, OK?" I had to reach for the chair to steady myself as the room dipped and spun. I tried to pull my dress back on, but it was twisted and tangled in a clump of silk. I tugged at it, frustrated. "I've been through this too many times. Coming so close, and getting my hopes up, then having it all pulled away. I can't do it again. I just can't. I don't have the time!"

"Shh, Claire, it's OK. I'm sorry." Theo was on his feet, pulling me close. "I'm sorry."

I let him hold me, the wild fury in my chest clawing and raw. I had to fight so hard to keep it at bay, but there it was, rearing up in an instant. The unfairness of it all. He was asking the impossible. He wanted the best for me, I knew, but this was torture of a different kind. It brought those whispers back, taunting in my mind with their tempting hum. *What if, what if?*

"Let's go back to sleep," he said, trying to tug me towards the bed, but I shook my head. I was too wide-awake to dream tonight, and I knew there was worse to come.

"I need to get back. I'll be passed out all day tomorrow, and I'd rather be in my own bed." I dressed quickly, feeling his eyes on me, and trying to stay steady despite the giddy spin. I didn't have long until the nausea gripped me completely, and I couldn't let him see me like that: broken and clinging to cracked porcelain.

"I'll walk you."

"It's OK, I need to take a cab."

"So I'll ride with you," Theo said stubbornly.

"No, Theo, it's OK."

I ordered a car and bundled up tightly, arming myself against the cold, and the look of disappointment in his eyes. Coat and scarf, shoes and mittens, but it still wasn't enough to stop my stomach swimming, and the pain roaring, a muffled thunder in my brain. My phone buzzed with a text. The car was already downstairs. He followed me down the hall, and stood there in the doorway, watching as I braced myself for the outside world.

"Thank you for dinner," I said, looking away. I didn't want to hurt him, but he couldn't understand. "I'll call you tomorrow."

"Claire, wait." His fingertips caught mine, tugging me back, and I had no choice but to look at him again— the perfect face that still ripped me open, even now. "I know you've made your mind up," he said, imploring. "But if there's even a chance . . ." Theo caught his breath, looking down to where his fingers intertwined with mine. "I know it's selfish, but just think about it, please. For me."

"Don't ask me that." I pulled away. "You don't understand. Ask me anything but that."

I took the stairs too fast, in heels too high. The world was still off-kilter, and when I stepped out, there was nothing but air.

"Claire!"

I didn't fall far, a few steps maybe, crumpling painfully into the concrete as I grabbed for the rail, but my head hit hard, and my knees stung, and the world dipped again, turned on its end as the pain ricocheted through me, hot shards slicing through my skull.

"Claire, are you OK?" I fought for balance. Theo was holding me now, cradling my face, stricken.

"Claire? Say something!"

The nausea rose up and it was all I could do to hold it back, gasping on the dirty ground. I shook with rage and sickness and fear, God, that ice-cold terror stuttering through my limbs. I didn't want him to see me like this, but it was no use. I was losing this battle, I could feel it, helpless now against my traitorous body, no matter how hard I tried.

My tumor was done waiting. It was claiming me as conquest, already marching to a victory drum.

"I'm calling an ambulance," Theo said, and I gripped his arm tightly.

"No, please," I managed to beg through the tremors. "I'll be OK. I just need a minute."

"It wasn't a question."

"No!" My sob ripped the hallway apart. "There's a car outside," I gasped, steadying now. "It can take me home. I'll be fine, this happens all the time."

But Theo just set his jaw in a determined stare. "Wait here, don't move an inch." He took the stairs two at a time back up to the apartment, and it was barely ten seconds before he bound back down, half in his coat, with keys in his hand. "Put your arms around my neck," he ordered, and I didn't have the energy left to protest. He lifted me like nothing, carrying me carefully down the rest of the staircase. Outside, a car was idling on the curb, and he deposited me gently in the backseat before climbing in beside me. I sank against him, drained. I heard his voice from far away, talking to the driver, but the words didn't sink in, and it wasn't until the lights flashed outside and a siren wailed, too close, that I realized: he wasn't taking me home.

CHAPTER THIRTY

ANOTHER NIGHT IN the emergency room. Another narrow hospital bed. My parents met us there and we all waited for another round of tests that wouldn't tell us anything we didn't already know. Doctor Benson was off that night; a nurse was trying to reach him, so we sat, together, in a tense silence broken only by distant sirens and the wail of a drunk, fighting just outside.

"I'll go get some coffee," my dad said at last, rising. "Sue?"

Mom nodded. "It'll probably be a long night. You don't need to stay," she told Theo gently. "These things can take a while."

"Thank you," he said, so polite. "But I'm not going anywhere."

They went in search of the cafeteria, and Theo climbed up onto the bed with me, holding me to him as the drugs slipped through my veins. I felt lifeless, a faded carbon copy of myself, but I was past shame now. That had gone the way of dinner, wretching violently into the bathroom stall as he held back my hair and murmured soothingly until I was crumpled and utterly used up. He'd helped clean me with damp paper towels, dressed me in a paper-thin robe, and by the time my parents burst anxiously through the doors, I was already hooked up to an IV machine with a blissful cocktail snaking into my soul.

"You shouldn't be here," I whispered into his chest. I was holding onto him for dear life, and hating myself for it with every breath. "I didn't want you to see me like this."

"Shh." He stroked my hair gently. "What's a little vomit between friends?"

I tried to laugh, but it stuck in my throat. This is what I'd become: the invalid, the needy, wretched girl. It seemed like only yesterday I'd cycled the autumn-blaze city for hours: my limbs strong and burning, my lungs gulping in a bracing chill. I'd been invincible, and I hadn't even realized.

I'd tasted the best of it, and now there was nothing but the slow crawl to the end.

"Please," I said again, tears stinging. "You can't stay. You don't know how bad it'll get."

"Then I'll find out." Theo didn't hesitate, but why would he? He hadn't seen it up close the way I did with Hope, how even watching from the sidelines ripped you apart, tearing tiny pieces from your heart with every desperate breath. All that was ahead of us now, and I couldn't save him from it, even if I tried.

THEY SAY THAT DESPAIR is a deadly, treacherous thing. Patients who give up in their hearts see their bodies fail long before the fighters; the ones resolved to endure somehow make it out, through sheer force of will alone. Every specialist told us the mind-body link is a curious thing, and sometimes there were no explanations for the way determination makes all the difference in the world. But sometimes I wondered if hope was more dangerous by far. Hope that slipped unbidden into the back of my mind, tempting me with possibilities I knew were out of reach. Ever-decreasing odds, and wild-card draws. *If one in five make it, maybe I could be that one . . .*

Lying there in Theo's arms as the city slowly woke from its slumber outside the windows, I felt hope start whispering again, that desperate, reckless plea. Maybe I didn't have to go like this. Maybe, against all odds, there was another way.

What if? What if? What if?

DOCTOR BENSON ARRIVED with the dawn, his shirt buttoned up wrong and his white coat crumpled. "I'm sorry to drag you in," I said quietly, wondering about the family he'd left behind to rush here this icy morning, but he just smiled and polished his glasses before perching them back on his nose to check my charts.

"It's fine. Now, what happened here?"

"She fell and hit her head," Theo answered for me.

"Barely," I added quickly. "Just a tap."

The doctor gave me a look, unconvinced, and checked through the tiny printed numbers and digital films. "It looks like there's no contusions or bruising. But I thought we talked about taking it easy," he said. "At this stage, you need to be reducing all stress from your daily routine. Any exertion is only going to push your body to breaking point. Which is clearly what happened tonight."

"Claire." My mother's voice was full of reproach.

"I'm being careful," I insisted, my jaw set. "I've cut my hours, I sleep half the day, I barely walk anywhere anymore. You can't expect me to just give up. Not yet."

Benson softened. "I'm not saying that. I just want you to understand your limitations are changing. Things that were manageable even a week ago may no longer be wise, given the rate of your tumor's growth. You need to take this seriously, Claire."

"Because I've been acting like dying is such a joke."

Silence hissed through the room, and I felt even Theo flinch beside me. I caught my breath. "I'm sorry,"

I said, to him, and my parents, and even the doctor too: all of them looking at me with such concern on their tired faces. All of them here with me, despite the costs. "I'm trying, I really am. It's just hard, carving my life down into a smaller and smaller box."

"I know, sweetheart," my mom said, moving to take my free hand. "But we've talked about this. You always knew this day would come."

But there was a world of difference between words and this—the reality of my failing body, the too-quick decay of my poisoned mind. It was coming, the car crash in the distance, too fast to swerve away. I could only watch it rear up in front of me, and brace for impact as best I could.

Unless . . .

"What about the trial?"

My voice slipped out before I could think. I felt every head in the room snap towards me, but I kept my gaze fixed on Doctor Benson, there at the foot of the bed. He looked back at me, measured. "I thought you'd decided against any more treatment."

"I have. I did. But . . ." I swallowed. "Are you still running it?"

He dipped his head slightly. "We're still active, yes."

"So you haven't killed everyone yet."

Benson allowed a smile. "No. In fact, we're seeing

some improvements. The last test group went remarkably well."

"How well?" My mom couldn't keep her questions back; she leaned forward, her face so naked in the early fluorescent lights. "If you're seeing improvements already, that's good, right?"

"As I said, this is a very small test group. It's almost impossible to draw conclusions yet." Doctor Benson cut her off. "We have seen another three recent cases that showed a significant reduction in their masses. Still, the risks haven't changed," he added, warning. "This is an incredibly experimental treatment."

"But you're hopeful about the results?" she pressed.

"We're learning a lot," he answered, still so measured. "I thought Claire was clear about her wishes."

"I am," I answered in a small voice, but I didn't feel so clear anymore. "But if, *if*," I emphasized, looking to mom, "I wanted to be a part of the trial, am I still a candidate?"

He paused, reluctant. "You're on the outer limits of our test profile. And given the rapid rate of acceleration, we would need to move ahead immediately."

My heart clenched. "Now?"

"Within days." He nodded. "Otherwise your tumor will be too advanced to even try. But as I said, the risks involved are significant. I can't in good conscience enroll you, not unless you're completely committed to this course of action."

There was silence again, weighing in the tiny room.

"Thank you." My father moved forward then, and shook his hand. "We appreciate you coming out."

"Take care," Benson told me. "And remember, no stressors of any kind. Environmental or emotional," he added, as if he could see the tension that was shimmering between me and Theo.

"I know," I exhaled in defeat. "I'll do my best."

WE TOOK A CAB to their apartment through the early-morning city, and I collapsed, exhausted, into bed without protest. I could hear the low murmurs from outside my bedroom door, my parents' voices and Theo's too, until I drifted to sleep and woke in the later-afternoon twilight, the day already gone.

One more day down.

I shivered, even wrapped up in feather-soft pajamas and a robe. It was all slipping away too fast; I couldn't keep my icy panic at bay. I'd barely even gotten started living, and although I knew I'd had more of a chance than most, it still felt like a cruel joke to rip this world away from me so soon.

How could I leave Theo now?

A sob slipped from my throat as I lay there, holding

my pillows tight. I wanted so much more than this, wanted it with a fierce rage that gripped me from the inside out. I thought I would be ready by now, but I didn't bet on him, and God, it hurt too much to bear. The loss rolled through me, and the tears came again, stinging with futility, but still I cried. I cried for the years I'd spent not knowing him, and the years he'd spend without me, long after I was gone. I cried for the empty space I'd leave at my mother's table, and my father's stoic tears. I cried for Hope, and Lucy, too, and every passing face on those endless cancer wards: too-short lives fading now in photographs in sad, gilded frames. The space in the world they used to be, God, such a waste of every breaking heart.

This was the side of life we never mentioned; these were the silent griefs we kept hidden, to keep from falling apart. Because I loved him, and it made no difference. Death would take everything, strip me bare of every moment, just like the others, until I was only a memory to them all, a dying flower on a long-buried grave.

The bedroom door creaked open behind me, but I couldn't stop my sobs. Weight pressed into the mattress, and then familiar arms came around me, strong and safe. I didn't have to look to see. My body knew him by heart.

He'd stayed.

Theo didn't say a word that evening, he just held me

through the storm. And soon enough, my body tired of weeping, my breath steadied, the grief slipped away. We lay there together as the skies darkened, velvet pricked with stars. "I'm sorry," I whispered, turning to face him at last. His eyes were shadowed in the darkness, but we were so close, my lips moved against his.

"Don't be."

We breathed together, a shivering thread between us, suspended in the night.

"If I could take it back . . ." My heart ached. Not for me, though. No, I would trade every gorgeous moment with him in a second if it could save him the pain ahead. But Theo cradled my face softly, and when his lips found mine, it was as much as a confession as a kiss.

"I wouldn't. Not for anything. I love you, Claire, and I wouldn't change that for the world."

Love.

The word whispered around us, a soft tattoo on my heart. I'd waited a lifetime to feel this, and even though it was already slipping away, it still shone bright enough to split the night in two.

This was all I wanted, and it would have to be enough.

I pressed my lips to his, damp with tears, and tasted what was left of our forever.

THE PROMISE

CHAPTER THIRTY-ONE

WHAT WOULD YOU do for love?

It's easy to rattle off the hypotheticals, safe scenarios on a distant page. I'd die for you. I'd kill for you. Run into a burning building. Throw myself in front of a moving car. It seems incredible, but the truth is, people do it every day. For all our capacity for fear and hate and violence, we have goodness in us, too. Self-sacrifice and devotion, without a second thought. My mother, dragging the both of us headlong through trials and testing, surgeries and prayer, never pausing for a moment, never giving up the fight. Kelsey's kindness, that careful watching eye. Theo, crouched there beside me in a bathroom stall, carrying me down the stairs, holding me through the darkness that night as my bitter heart broke in two.

Love made miracles possible every single day, but it would take more than a miracle to save me now.

THE PROMISE

THE NEXT MORNING, I left Theo sleeping, sprawled and peaceful on my unmade bed. Part of me wanted to bind myself tight to him, spend every last moment soaking up the brightness of his sleepy morning smile, but I needed space to think, and whenever I was with him, I couldn't see straight: he was always the only thing in view.

I quietly pulled on a pair of jeans and thick winter socks, found a T-shirt and sweater, and closed the door gently behind me. Dad was drinking coffee by the window. He looked up, surprised, and then concerned.

"It's OK," I said quickly. "I can still get out of bed."

"I know." He relaxed. "Sorry. I guess we're all on edge."

"Is this what it's going to be like now?" I asked sadly. "You guys flinch if I even try to leave the apartment?"

He gave me a rueful look. "We can't help it. Your mother would have bundled you back to Texas weeks ago if she had the choice."

"Wrapped me up in cotton wool and put a bolt on my bedroom door?"

He smiled. "Something like that." He glanced past me, to the bedroom. "Your gentleman friend stayed all night then."

"Dad!" I couldn't help laughing, he looked so

uncomfortable. "Nothing happened. But I'm surprised you let him."

"You and me both. But your mother said he would be a comfort to you."

A comfort, and a prompt.

"I know what she wants," I said softly. "She wants me to do the surgery. She thinks having him here will make me choose."

"And what about you?" he asked, worry lines deep on his face. "What is it you want?"

I used to be sure, but nothing was simple anymore. All those resolutions I made were before Theo, before I knew what it was like to want an eternity so badly it broke my heart to think of the end.

"That's what I need to figure out."

I TOOK A CAB TO the city. Dad didn't want to let me go alone, but I had my cellphone, and I needed the space. Everything they wanted was pressing down on me—him, Mom, Theo, and all their unspoken fears. I needed to step out from under that weight if I was ever going to get some clarity for the dozens of contradictions swirling in my mind. So I went to a place I remembered from the fall, a hidden corner of the city I'd discovered by accident, months ago now. Tucked away behind the old, grand walls of the Boston

Public Library buildings I'd found a small courtyard, a square footprint of calm guarded from the rest of the chaotic city streets. Today, it was almost empty, the visitors preferring the warmth of the café inside, so I was left alone on a wrought iron chair beside the frozen fountain pool, watching the sparrows chase after a stray scatter of pastry crumbs on the ground.

I always liked sparrows best. Hope said I needed a better Patronus—a soaring eagle, or a strong, vicious hawk, but there was something brave about their delicate fluttering: quietly resilient, even for their tiny size. The door from inside suddenly opened, and a toddler came barreling out—spiral-curled, with pink cheeks almost hidden beneath her bright red hat. The birds flew up as she lunged for them, gurgling with laughter, and a split-second later, a woman followed.

"Gentle, Eloise, don't scare them!" She was young, in her thirties, maybe, in boots and a puffed up jacket. "Sorry," she said, noticing me. "They're her new favorite thing. Ducks, too. All she wants to do is go feed them."

"It's OK." I smiled. The woman took a seat, pulling snacks from her bag, and called the girl back over. A trio of teenagers hustled out and sprawled at a table, dangling book bags and coffee cups as they gossiped and huddled around their glowing cellphone screens.

Life went on.

My breath shivered in the cold, icy air and I fought the sting of tears. Life went on. My death would barely make a ripple on the surface of the world. These people here would never even notice. My parents would mourn, and Theo, too, but in months and years, the traces of me would slowly fade away. Tessa would find another roommate, and strike out on the water with her crew every morning, barely thinking of the girl she used to know. Another group would spin behind the counter at Wired, a different crowd of students lining daily for their coffee fix; someone else would fill my studio with their clutter, and even my paintings would gather dust in storage somewhere, fading in the summer afternoon light.

I would be gone.

Unless . . .

I felt it flutter in my chest, that seductive hope, dancing just out of reach. The surgery. The clinical trial. I knew the data and the facts and all the slim, reckless odds, but my heart couldn't help it. It wanted to believe. The same desperate instinct that had driven me here, to this glorious blank slate of a city, craving *more, everything, now,* was awake all over again, grasping for that light in the distance, demanding just a little more time.

Was this how Hope had felt? Clinging to life so hard as her body stuttered and stumbled, watching the wires and tubes multiply to a halo, snaking oxygen around her head. I always wondered why she fought so hard at the end, when they'd exhausted every option, and there was nothing left but pain. Well, now I knew the truth. Pain was living, at least. Pain was one more moment on this endless earth. And pain was all that was left ahead of me now. A slow death, watching my parents try to keep it together, and Theo be brave, for my sake. Feeling my organs fail, and the tumor—that fucking tumor—take a victory lap inside my brain. I already felt it dancing; it had been waiting so long for this day to come, and there was nothing I could do to stop it.

Nothing, except roll the dice.

The choice clawed at me, splitting my chest in two. One bad month, or a chance at a future. You'd think it would be simple, but you don't understand the odds. If I got on that table tomorrow, had the doctor slice me open and pump chemicals into my brain, I might not ever wake up again, and that one bad month I still had left would just be gone.

How much time could I cling to? How much loving was still left for me to do?

I wasn't ready to die, but I knew now, I wouldn't ever be. I'd been running from the truth of it for so long, as if someday, somehow, I would wake up in the morning and be at peace with my end. And maybe I would have—back in Texas, where all I had to lose was safe, and contained, well-worn footsteps I'd been traipsing my entire life. But here? The bright city was alive around me, and somewhere back across the bridge, a boy waited for me in a sunlit bedroom with a love that brought me to my knees. The fire in my heart was raging, and now I knew I wouldn't ever stop wanting more.

But how much did I want it? How much of my life would I trade for a chance at forever with him?

What would you do for love?

I SAT IN THE COURTYARD all afternoon, watching kids melt down in fevered tantrums, old women chat, and harried library staff steal a cigarette break alone. I wanted to stay suspended forever, the world kept at bay outside the old crumbling walls, but my phone buzzed with worried texts, and I knew I couldn't hide there for long. I called a car and headed back to the apartment and found them all waiting there for me: Mom fussing with something in the kitchen, Dad working on his laptop, and Theo spread on the couch with his reading lists and papers, marking with a red pen nibbled between his lips like nothing was wrong.

My heart swelled for them and broke, all at once. This was my family, the love I was lucky enough to find in this world, and leaving them would be agony, either way, in the end.

"Claire." Theo looked up, and a smile spread across his face. Automatic, the way my senses leapt whenever he walked into the room. "Hey, how was your afternoon?"

"Good." I slowly peeled off my scarf, then stopped, the knit stripes hanging in my hand. "I had some time to think."

My mom stopped her clattering in the kitchen. My dad quietly folded his laptop shut. I felt their eyes on me, but Theo was the only one I could look at: the man who had strolled into the café a hundred days ago, and turned what was left of my bitter-sweet world upside down. I wasn't looking for a guy to walk through the door and change my life that day. I thought I wasn't that kind of girl at all. But here I was, forever changed. And love, only love, mattered in the end.

"I thought about the surgery," I said softly. "I want to do it. I can't just give up, not now. I have to try."

For us.

I didn't finish, but he knew. I saw his expression shift —bloom wide open—as he realized the choice I'd made, because of him.

"Claire—"

His voice was lost under my mom's shriek, and then she was hugging me, already gulping with noisy sobs.

"Thank you, sweetheart. Oh God, thank you. I know it's a risk, but you'll make it. I can feel it, this is going to work, it's all going to be OK."

Dad stood there, guarded. "Are you sure? You heard what Doctor Benson said. You need to be committed, a hundred percent." He looked so protective, but I saw it there too: that flicker of longing, so close you could almost touch.

"I'm sure," I nodded, and then he was holding me too, the both of them sandwiching me tight with iron-clad relief. Our last, desperate chance. I knew they'd prayed for it even more than me, but even smothered with their hope, I couldn't stop from glancing over their reaching arms to where Theo still sat, silently watching us.

He didn't speak, he didn't have to. I could see it all in the silent reflection of his stare. I curled a private smile, and he smiled back, bright enough to set the world on fire. I felt it blazing, and I knew I would never take it back. Yes, I'd roll the dice on forever, and risk everything for that smile—not just what we'd shared, but for the chance of a thousand more to come.

I wasn't done loving him, not ever. Not yet.

THE PROMISE

CHAPTER THIRTY-TWO

SO HERE I AM. At the end of my story, or the beginning; I still don't know just yet. It feels like I've had a lifetime waiting to start over again, but the time slips by so fast. I've been lucky, I know. Most tumor patients barely see twelve months, and I've had five stolen years, but those years have passed in a heartbeat, and now they're already gone. One minute I'm a girl, skidding downstairs for an afternoon snack, and the next, I'm barely a woman, waiting in a hospital gown as they hook me up to the monitors and prepare to do battle one last, brave time.

Tick, tick, tick.

The surgeons move fast, just like Doctor Benson said they would. They whisk me through the paperwork and mandatory counseling in the space of a single afternoon and check me into a small, neat room on the third floor of the surgical wing, with windows overlooking a bleak, busy intersection and a square patch of dark, starlit sky.

Mom is fussing as usual now, unpacking my pajamas and sweatpants in the metal dresser, while Dad introduces us to the nurses and brings armfuls of fresh flowers from the gift shop downstairs, "just to brighten the place up." It's sheer blinding optimism, preparing for the weeks I'll spend in recovery here, when the surgery itself still looms, too dangerous to face, but I let them plan and hope for the best while Theo sits, still silent beside me, holding my hand tight.

"All settled in?" Doctor Benson arrives in the doorway, checking one last round of charts before his day is done. "Good, good. We've got you scheduled first thing in the morning, so no more food tonight, I'm afraid, and let's keep liquids to a minimum, too."

I nod. I know the drill.

"Any more questions? Concerns?" he checks again, still watching me warily as if he doesn't believe the dozen forms I've signed of my own free will. "It's not too late for second thoughts."

"Anyone would think you didn't want me here." I try a joke that falls flat through the tension in the room. "Worried my tumor is going to have you beat?"

Benson smiles. "I'd like to think I'm up to the job," he says, and flips my charts closed. "But this is your decision, Claire. I don't want you thinking for a moment that it's not your choice."

Choice. The word seems laughable. As if any of the last

five years have been my call. I've been on the run, forced into a defensive crouch, sent spinning off course by every new symptom until I'm exhausted just trying to keep up. But this surgery, this one last shot, this is finally a choice of my own.

"I'm in," I say, determined, and Theo's hand tightens at my side.

"Alright then." He nods and looks around the room. "I'll see you all bright and early. Try and get some sleep," he adds to me. "It's going to be a long surgery, and you'll need your strength."

"You too," I tell him, and he smiles.

"Good night."

He retreats into the hallway, and my mom plumps my pillow again. "Do you need anything else, sweetheart? I can ask the nurses again about a trundle bed. I'm sure they'll let us stay."

"No, it's fine," I reassure her. "You guys need to rest, too. I'll see you in the morning." Mom looks like she's going to object again, but my dad places a hand on her shoulder, and she swallows back her words.

"Sleep tight," Dad says instead, and then they reluctantly leave us, their heads bent together as they disappear down the hall.

It's just Theo left, and me.

"Do you want the light off?"

I nod, and he hits the switch, unraveling the blinds with a rattle to hide the outside world. "Come here," I say, patting the bed beside me. He climbs up and curls one arm around my shoulders, glancing cautiously to the door.

"I thought they said no visitors after hours."

"They don't mind, not tonight, at least. Besides, what's the worst they can do—take away my ice chips?"

I feel the rumble of his laugh, and I sink deeper into his embrace. His breath is steady, an easy, ebbing tide, and slowly, I forget the orderlies chatting down the hall and the surgery room waiting, instruments soon to be lined up neatly on a gleaming metal tray. I hold him and think of a tomorrow after that: watching movies here together, sneaking jello while my incisions heal. Back at my apartment for the springtime, walking to work under cherry-blossom skies and staying up late to watch the rising moon. The dream is so seductive, it already has a hold on me. Close, so close my mind refuses to think of it any other way.

This can't be the end.

I try to sleep, but my mind ticks over, too loud, and it's almost midnight when Theo turns to kiss my forehead. "Are you scared?" he asks softly.

I nod. "I don't want to leave them. They'll fall apart without me."

"I'll look out for them, if . . ." Theo pauses. Even he can't say it. "I'll make sure they're doing OK."

"You don't have to do that."

"I know."

I take his hand and trace the faint lines of his palm, curl his fingers around mine. "I didn't get to finish the list." I feel a pang. Theo draws back to look at me. "What's left?" "The skinny-dipping one." I reply. "I guess she didn't figure on me dying before the spring." Theo flinches against me. "It's not a dirty word," I say, tired. "It's the truth, remember. Eighty-twenty, it's stacked against us now."

"I know. I just can't bear to think of a world that doesn't have you in it."

I look up then and see the anguish written vivid on his face. Theo's voice catches, and the steady mask slips; he's raw and broken, holding it together by a single breath. "It doesn't make any sense to me," he says through a sad, clenched jaw, "how we could find each other and then already be out of time. It's not fair. None of this is close to being fair."

I press my palm to his cheek, wordless. I know the powerlessness he's fighting, that wretched struggle against fate. But I can't argue with him, not tonight: this is what we have. Ten more hours together, maybe. One last night.

And I'm not finished living just yet.

"What would it take to get a car tonight?"

Theo pauses at my question, but then I see him race ahead, catching up. "Moose has one I could borrow, it's a beat-up wreck but it runs, just about. Won't they miss you?"

"We'll be back before morning."

He looks torn. "You need to rest."

"I've only got one more thing left," I say, half-pleading. "I can't leave it unfinished, not this time."

He hesitates only a moment longer, and then flashes me a grin, my partner in crime to the bitter end. "You get dressed, I'll stand guard."

I laugh and carefully scramble out of bed, pulling on my warm winter clothes while Theo keeps watch by the door. "The nurse just left the desk on break," he whispers, hurrying me. "Quick, before she comes back this way."

Hand in hand, we creep down the hallway, walking fast to the stairwell when we make it clear past the doors. After that, it's easy: two doors and we're on the street again, nobody giving a second glance to the couple in bulky winter coats as we spill onto the midnight sidewalk, giggling like we've just staged a prison break. A quick cab later, and we're back at his apartment, me waiting just inside the doorway—stamping my feet against the cold—while he pleads with his roommates and emerges, victorious, with a stash of blankets over one shoulder and the keys dangling on a leaf-shaped chain.

"You weren't kidding about this thing," I say, as he wrenches the door open. Peeling blue paint and a dent in the passenger door; it looks as if it could barely run a mile, but there are four wheels and a working engine, and that's all we need tonight. "Are you sure it'll go?"

"Fingers crossed."

Huddling inside, Theo sets the heater on full, and cajoles the engine to life; it splutters with protest. "Your chariot awaits," he says with a grin, and I laugh with the thrill of it, snapping the seatbelt on tight. This is our adventure, one last reckless goodbye.

"Where are we going?"

Theo pauses, then spreads in a slow, quiet smile. "I know a place."

So I curl up in the passenger seat, and watch the lights of Boston glide past, snaking outside the steamed-up windows as we fly onto the neon freeway, heading south, out of town. "I never left the city," I say, looking out at the dark shadows looming and the empty highway trail. "All this time, I didn't even take a day trip somewhere, into the country, or down the coast."

"We'll go this summer," Theo says, his arm draped over the console, his right hand steady on my thigh. "I have a couple of months off when school's out. We can go anywhere you choose."

"Even California?" I tease, remembering. "You can teach me how to surf."

Theo smiles into the highway lights. "Even California, someday."

The rhythm of the dark road washes over me, and right then we're perfect, complete in this gold-lit bubble of our own. I want to hold onto it, preserve every moment even as it passes, but the miles slip by in a dream, and I must have fallen asleep, because too soon, Theo is gently shaking me awake. "Claire," he whispers softly. "We're here."

I squint through the sleep and rub my tired eyes. It's still dark out, but the first pale rays of dawn are slipping over the horizon, shadows looming all around. Theo is crouched beside me, the door open, nursing a steaming cup of gas station coffee. "Where's here?" I ask, yawning.

"I'll show you. Come on."

He takes my hand and helps me out of the car. We're the only vehicle in a dark, empty lot, but I can hear the ocean, somewhere close by, and smell the sharp tang of saltwater in the gently whipping winds. Theo hoists the blankets and leads me into the dark, past the lone streetlight flickering on the edge of the asphalt, the ground giving way to softness beneath my boots as the shadows reveal themselves to be sand dunes, tipped with the rustle of swaying grasses and reeds.

"I came here once in summer, back when I was a kid." Theo's voice is hushed, but it still jars against the silence, miles from the hum of city life. He walks beside me, guiding every step. "Mom decided, spur of the moment, and we all drove down for Fourth of July weekend. We stayed in a crappy cheap motel, and ate PB&J sandwiches from the cooler, but it was the best vacation I ever had."

The dunes open up before us, and there it is, the endless midnight sea. Dawn is sneaking over the edge of the horizon, turning the dark waves silver, and streaking the sky with light.

My heart shivers in my chest. "It's beautiful," I whisper, like we're in church. And I guess, in a way, we are. The great world is waiting, magical and vast, too magnificent for words.

Theo drops the blankets. "Are you sure about this?" he asks, still so careful. But I've come too far to turn back now, and the sun is rising. We don't have much time.

"Hope said there's nothing like it." I unpeel my coat, trying not to shiver against the icy ocean breeze. My sweater follows, then I kick off my boots. "Besides," I say, as I strip down to nothing. "You only live once."

I turn and run towards the water, and she was right, there's no feeling like it in the world. Cold and sharp, pure and free, my bare feet pound the wet sand and the water hits me like a slap. I cry out loud at the shock of it, but I keep going, wading out into the foaming waves and then ducking under, my body already numbing against the frigid cold but still feeling so alive, I could weep with joy.

I surface to find Theo beside me, grabbing me close.

"You're crazy!" he yells, trembling with the cold, but his smile is like the sunrise, and I laugh, our naked bodies tangled and twisted, shifting in the waves. We run for the shore again, already shaking uncontrollably, the air now like ice against our wet skin, and then we're huddled under the blankets together, holding on for dear life against the chill.

"If we die of hypothermia, it's all your fault," Theo says, his teeth chattering. I wrap my arms tight around his waist and feel the pale heat of our bodies grow stronger.

"But it was worth it, wasn't it?" I turn to watch sun break the night sky wide open, flooding the world for a brand new day. Theo watches with me, falling silent as the sea turns again from slate to silver to a pale aching grey.

"It was all worth it," he says against me, as our heartbeats dance, together in the dawn.

THE DRIVE BACK is different, the dusty freeway hushed and empty, and the minutes counting down, closer to the end. I hold Theo's hand tightly, and try not to feel afraid, but I can't help it. Fear is blossoming wide open in my chest, thinking of what lies ahead today: the best or last day of my life. I know that the panic is a good thing; it means I have something left to lose. He's right here beside me, his steady hands on the steering wheel and his brilliant mind guiding us home, but still, I wish the road would last forever. I come close to telling him a hundred times: turn the car west, let's just keep driving, away from those sharp surgical tools and the syringes of poison waiting for me, someplace safe, where we can just treasure each other, alone.

But every time, I remember the sunrise. Those first, clear gasps of morning light, peeking over the horizon, the cold water on my bare skin, and how alive I felt to be breathing, blessed to see another day.

I want a lifetime of sunrise, and this is the only way.

I hold onto that memory the entire ride home, and soon we're outside the hospital again. "They probably have a search party out for you," Theo says, finding a spot to park. It's seven a.m. already, and I know my parents are already upstairs somewhere, pacing the floor.

"I should go up alone and take the worst of it. They can't exactly hold it against me." I smile, but Theo shakes his head.

"Together," he says, lifting our hands.

"Together," I echo.

Together until the end.

W E HEAD UPSTAIRS, and I brace myself for the scene to come. But when we hurry off the elevator, and find my parents waiting in the hall, they don't even scold me. "They'll be at your room for pre-op rounds in five minutes," my dad says, hustling me down the hall.

"You didn't eat anything, did you?" Mom demands, anxious. "There isn't time to push it, even one more day."

"No, Mom, I didn't eat. And I slept some, too." I change quickly in the bathroom, and I'm safely back in my robe by the time the medical team arrives to make the final checks. If they notice my hair is still damp, and my skin smells of saltwater, nobody says a thing, they just click the side rails of my bed into place.

"We'll give you a moment," Doctor Benson says, motioning, and the interns melt back a tactful distance into the hallway outside.

There's silence.

"So this is it," Theo says, his voice twisting.

I nod, catching a sob in my throat. "This is it."

I look around the room at my parents' faces—the ragged heartbreak hiding in their eyes. We only have minutes now before they wheel me out, but how could that be even close to enough time?

How can you fit a lifetime of love into just a few short words?

How can you ever find a way to say goodbye?

Mom clutches my hand tightly. "We'll be right here, sweetheart," she says, her voice catching. "I'll be praying for you."

I nod, the tears coming now. It's all happening so fast, there isn't enough time. "Dad?" My voice trembles.

"It's alright, baby girl." He leans over and hugs me, swift and hard. "Whatever happens, we'll be OK. You don't need to worry about your old mom and dad."

"I'm sorry." I frantically wipe my tears away. "I didn't want to cry."

"You and me both." He gives a watery grin, and then we're both laughing together, crying and laughing because there's no other way.

"I'll see you soon," I promise, and he has to turn away before he breaks.

"I'm counting on it, sweetheart."

Now there was only Theo.

"I'll walk you in," he says, holding my hand tightly. The doctors return, and slowly begin wheeling my bed down the hallway, towards those distant swinging doors. I force a smile and wave back to my parents, clutched together in the doorway, holding each other up for air.

Closer, closer.

"It's going to be OK," Theo promises softly, keeping pace with every step. "You're strong, Claire, you're the strongest person I've ever known. You've made it this far, it can't be over—" He can't even finish, and we're at the doors, but it's too fast. This is all slipping away too fast.

"Wait," I beg the doctors. "Please, just give me one more minute."

They stop, and I don't care that they're watching, because this is all I might have left. This one moment. This one last moment of loving him.

I pull him closer, and kiss him with everything I have to give. "It was you," I whisper fiercely. "You were my second chance. These were the best days of my life, and it was all because of you."

"Claire . . ."

"No, there's no time." I cradle his face in my hands. I want to hold onto him forever, every beautiful plane, those lines I've etched into a sketchpad so often that I know him by heart. But the brushstrokes blur with my tears, water seeping over the page. "Just promise me one thing," I beg. "Please, Theo, whatever happens, you have to promise me."

"Anything," he swears.

"Promise me you'll live. Every day, the way I wanted. Don't ever waste it, not one single breath."

He nods, just once.

"I love you," I whisper. "I'll always be right here."

And then we're moving again, and his hand slips away from me, and the last thing I see is his face as we disappear between those swinging doors.

I hold onto it, every memory, down the long hallway, and into that pristine room. The first day I saw him, all the way to this, the last. As they lay me back on the operating table, I fall into his arms; I kiss him a hundred times as they slip the mask over my face, and I watch the dawn break with him, shaking joy from every limb, while the doctor waits, steady above me.

"Are you ready, Claire?" his voice comes, so far away.

The sun is rising, and it's a brand new day.

I close my eyes and say a final prayer.

And I begin again.

THE PROMISE

ONE YEAR LATER

THEO

CLAIRE DIED AT 6:13 p.m. on the twenty-second of January, ten hours into the surgery we hoped would save her life.

Looking back, it's clear she knew it somehow, when she said goodbye to me that one final time. The odds were too high, and her tumor had already ravaged too much of her, but still, we went on believing in miracles, right up until the end. I can still see the look on the doctor's face as he slowly walked towards us; the way her mother crumpled and her father gripped my hand without a word.

The best thing in my world. I'd barely started loving her, and she was already gone.

SPRING PASSED IN a blur of whiskey and pain. I was failing her with every moment, breaking that last whispered promise, but I didn't know any other way. I woke every morning with a bullet wound gaping in my chest, and drank until the wretched ache numbed away. I blew off classes and friends, let my work gather dust, slipped so deep into the darkness I could hardly find the air to breathe.

It was Kelsey, of all people, who finally dragged me out. She kicked my door down one bleak afternoon and yanked the drapes open, flooding sunlight, too bright, in my bloodshot eyes.

"I never took you for your father's son," she said, standing over me, and I couldn't even ask how she knew.

This was what I was becoming. This was how I failed Claire, every single day.

So I clawed my way back to the world, one broken, empty moment at a time. I made up hours and papers, finished out the year, and took a leave of absence, bought that beat-up old car with five hundred bucks in cash, and drove it to the one place I'd been avoiding. The room I knew would break my heart all over again.

Her studio.

Her parents hadn't asked; it was hell enough for them to pack up her old apartment and ship a hundred pieces of her life back home. Now, I stand in that doorway and try not to crumple all over again remembering the look on her face when I showed it to her. The luminous excitement, the pure, bright disbelief.

You got me a studio? I can't believe you got me this! I take a breath and open the door, and it hits me all over again.

She's everywhere.

Every brushstroke, every blazing canvas. Propped on every surface, and piled on every patch of floor. Claire's spirit, as vivid as the day we first met, shimmering there in the dusty sunshine like she's about to step out of the shadows with a paint smudge on her cheek. *It's still wet,* she'll tell me, beaming. *But you can see it, can't you? I think I got the light just right.*

But she'll never look at me like that again, or tug me closer for a sweet, hungry kiss. I'll never unwrap her body inch by yielding inch, and lose myself in the constellation of her smile.

She's gone.

The loss rolls through me, and I can't stop the tears this time. I slip to the floor, and weep for her like it's the first time. All these months hiding, all this time trying so hard to forget.

She's gone, and the world keeps spinning.

She's gone, and it will never be the same.

I remember her talking once about everything she lost when Hope finally slipped away. She said every death left a wound on the surface of the earth. Someone's heart broken, a space in the fabric of existence that could never truly close. We patch it up, and smooth down the ragged edges in time, but those scars always stay there: an indelible mark of the life that was left behind.

"We're not supposed to forget them," she'd whispered to me, tracing circles on my ribcage, a flutter against my beating heart. "We're just supposed to honor them, any way we can."

So I honor her today, carefully rolling each treasured painting up and packing them in the backseat of the car beside my jumbled duffel bags. It takes me hours to disassemble the world she built, but finally, the walls are clean, and there's only one thing left: a small gift-wrapped square I find buried in the back of all her canvas rolls. My name is lettered neatly on the sea-blue tissue, and it punches a jagged hole through my heart when I realize: this is her Christmas gift to me, the one I walked away from when I first learned the truth.

I could lose another lifetime hating myself for those lost, empty weeks. The time I wasted running from her, those months in fall I tried pushing her away. If I could stop the world and spin it back on its axis I would, a hundred times. I would kiss her the very first day I saw her. Hold her tightly, and never come up for air.

But those are seconds long since gone. I peel off the ribbons and slip the last painting out into the light. A small square canvas, stretched across a delicate frame; lines in oil and bright, sharp colors. The criss-cross of rooftops, rolling down to a river blue.

I know this scene. It's the view from the rooftop, that Halloween, when it all began. Every moment, every slant of sunset light, captured here by memory. A first, gorgeous chapter in our story, a gift for me to remember, because she knew one day she'd be gone.

I finally lock up the studio, and get back behind the wheel of my car. But for the first time since I felt her hand slip out of mine in that surgical hallway, I feel Claire with me again. Every painting, every last sketch, it's all right here around me. She made herself immortal, the only way she knew how. The glimpses we shared with each other, the best and worst scenes of all. Our love is all around us, and it will be, as long as I'm here to tell our story.

I made her a promise, and I won't fail her yet.

So I DRIVE WEST.

Choked, snaking freeways, and wide-open country roads. Mile by mile, state by state, the country opens up in front of me, swallowing up my limitless grief. I was scared I'd lose her, straying too far from our familiar streets, but the farther I get from Boston, the more I feel her, curled up beside me in the passenger seat. She has sunglasses on and her toes painted red, propped up on the dashboard as she trails a hand out the window in the breeze. She wanted to see the world, and now I'm showing her, in my way. Gas station rest stops, and old, broken down motels. Forests and riverbanks, desert plains, and more. I don't know where I'm going, and some days, I drive just to get lost, and spend another few hours with her, sleepy at my side. The weeks bleed past, summer blazing on every street, until I cross the border into Texas, and realize there's been a destination to this escape all along.

Her parents meet me on the front steps and help me carry everything inside. "Are you sure?" her father asks me, looking older than I remember, battle lines on his face, and that sagging, empty gaze I recognize every time I look in the mirror. "You should keep something, whatever you want."

"I have a few things," I say with a nod. That rooftop painting is in the front seat, and her sketchbooks, too—a hundred idle scenes that drifted through her mind, a journal of those weeks and months in Massachusetts, from the very first day until the last. "But she'd want you to have them. And maybe Hope's parents, too."

Her mom hugs me tightly and tries to make me stay, but I'm itching for the road again, and the solitude with Claire beside me. "Thank you, though," I say. "I'll call when I get to California, and maybe I'll stop by on my way back in the fall."

Susan trails me outside, and pauses on the sidewalk. "I found something of hers in one of the boxes. I think she'd like for you to have it."

A small red notebook, too ordinary for words, but I know the minute she passes it to me that it's the most important thing Claire left behind.

I shake my head. "I can't."

"It's yours," she insists, pressing it into my hands. "They're just words to me, but you know the story. She'd want you to remember."

SO I DRIVE WEST again. And somewhere outside El Paso, in a faded old Mexican diner booth, I pull my laptop out of my bag and start a new page.

And I write.

I write for days, through New Mexico and Arizona, through the desert and into the golden California plains. I write because she's fading now, with every passing mile, and I need to capture her, freeze it quick, before she disappears forever. I write the story she drew, in a hundred fleeting frames, the secrets she told to me, and the days I can only dream. She whispers in my ear with each new chapter, and curls up in my arms every night, and even though it breaks my heart to think of ever finishing, I can't stop. It's bigger than me now. I drive and write and dream of her until I reach the ocean, and then I lock myself in a beach motel for days, living off black coffee and late-night donuts until one night I type the final words, and rest my laptop closed, and just like that, it's over.

Our story.

This story, right here.

THE SUN IS RISING as I stumble out into the motel parking lot, blinking and bloodshot from too long in the dark. The beach is just across the street, ocean stretching in a midnight band. Once, a girl ran naked into the water, and I watched her go, and swore I'd love her forever. But the beach is empty today, and nobody turns a head as I keep walking, down the shore and out into the waves.

The water swells up over me, cold and crystal clear. I'm crazy, dressed and wet and empty with grief, but as I stand there, I know it's time to let her go.

I look to the waves, and I feel Claire here beside me as the dawn breaks and the world comes alive. She found a way to begin again, and somehow so will I.

I made her a promise, a long time ago, and I'm going to keep it, with every day of my life.

Promise me you'll live.

THE END

ACKNOWLEDGEMENTS:

This book has been a labor of love, stretching over several years, and I want to thank everyone who played their part. To the friends who have given me such love and support in challenging times – to Elisabeth Donnelly, and Elizabeth Little; Corinne M, and the rest of the Squad. Thank you to Anthony C., Cheryl A., and Yuval R. for priceless counsel, Melissa Saneholtz for appearing in my life exactly when I needed her, and as always, my mother, Ann, for everything.

ALSO BY MELODY GRACE:

The Beachwood Bay Series

1. Untouched
2. Unbroken
3. Untamed Hearts
4. Unafraid
5. Unwrapped
6. Unconditional
7. Unrequited
8. Uninhibited
9. Unstoppable
10. Unexpectedly Yours
11. Unwritten
12. Unmasked
13. Unforgettable

The Oak Harbor Series

1. Heartbeats
2. Heartbreaker
3. Reckless Hearts
4. Just One Night

Made in the USA
San Bernardino,
CA